D0777165

1/95

NURSE DAWES IS DEAD

NURSE DAWES IS DEAD

Stella Shepherd

St. Martin's Press
New York

Library of Congress Cataloging-in-Publication Data

Shepherd, Stella
Nurse Dawes is dead / Stella Shepherd.
p.   cm.
ISBN 0-312-11867-8
1. Montgomery, Richard (Fictitious character)—Fiction.
2. Police—England—Fiction.   I. Title.
PR6069.H454N87   1995
823'.014—dc20   94-35468   CIP

First published in Great Britain
by Constable & Company Ltd.

First U.S. Edition: January 1995
10 9 8 7 6 5 4 3 2 1

For Tom and Sylvia

Author's note

The Victoria Hospital and its staff, as described in these pages, are fictitious. Residents of Nottingham past and present will nevertheless detect a more than passing physical resemblance between this hospital and the old General in the city centre. The General, actually founded in 1781 and funded by benefactors, was Nottingham's major hospital for almost two centuries, growing apace with the decades in order to serve the burgeoning local population. Those of us who were lucky enough to study and work there during its hey-day in the 1970s remember it as cramped and architecturally piecemeal, yet imbued with a sense of team spirit and purpose.

The advent of the Medical School, however, had harbingered the slow death of the General. Today, the excellent Queen's Medical Centre, built opposite the University campus in a rationalization of facilities, fulfils the needs of modern Nottingham, ably complemented by the clinical services at the existing *City Hospital to the north. The corridors of the General no longer echo with the sound of running feet – but it lives on in our affections.

S.S., September, 1993

* aka the District Hospital in *Murderous remedy*

NURSE DAWES IS DEAD

1

Cynthia Masters needed a drink. Just a small one, before lunch; after a morning of strained concentration she felt she had earned it.

Packing her book away into a smart black leather organizer bag, she left the centre quickly to avoid conversation with the others, and followed the curving street which led towards the bustling heart of Nottingham. She would treat herself to a meal today: that would fill in one of the featureless hours stretching ahead of her – two, if she made the drink last. As she emerged from Sheriff's Crescent traffic noises, muffled and distorted, began to impinge on her consciousness. Where should she go? Flappers on Cross Street had nice little alcoves where one could sit alone, undisturbed. Cynthia wanted privacy: with late August sun on her face and the subtle taste of dust and exhaust fumes in her mouth, she negotiated her way through the streets leading towards the restaurant, and tried to deny the tug of anticipation she felt.

It was cool inside. The barman nodded to her as he carefully secured a tiny paper umbrella at the summit of an unlikely-looking blue cocktail and slid it towards a hovering waitress. 'Yes, madam?' he said.

'Vodka, please.'

Did she detect the minutest *frisson* of surprise on that neutral, composed face? 'Coming up,' he said. 'Would you like tonic, or lime . . . ?'

'Er – lime. Yes, lime.' That's what a lady of her appearance would ask for. Immediately she regretted it. She didn't want lime: she wanted the drink neat. Her fingers began to fumble with the gilt fastener on her bag.

'Slice of lemon? Ice?'

'No, thank you.' She paid him and looked around for somewhere to sit. The stools alongside the bar were too exposed: anyone perching up on those was a potential target for prying eyes from all quarters of the room. The seats and tables opposite – of a white wrought-iron design placed randomly beneath the trellises and climbing plants of a mock pergola – were only marginally better. Best of all was the dining area where a handful of diners sat, some almost completely hidden in the cunningly-fashioned panelled alcoves which lined the right-hand side of the restaurant. 'I shall be eating,' she announced. 'May I take this to my table?'

Cynthia didn't catch his reply, but she saw him signal to a different waitress, who unleashed a wide professional smile in her direction and led the way to a polished wooden table.

'For one, madam,' she said.

Disappointingly, this table was not adjacent to the wall. Cynthia paused in confusion, realized that all the prime tables were set for two or more people, debated whether to ask for one anyway, quailed, then acquiesced: the critical moment had passed.

'Thank you,' she murmured, sitting down blankly. The drink was still in her hand: she took a grateful gulp and shivered, hating the sweet cordial but craving the power of the spirit base to relax and soothe, lift her away from the day's ever-lurking anxieties. Vodka was reputed to leave no tell-tale traces on the breath . . . Cynthia had two years of reason to believe that this might be true.

Slowly the tension left her shoulders and she began to take more notice of her surroundings. The restaurant was actually quite small, but judiciously sited gilt-rimmed mirrors gave an impression of space, while prints of vintage Rolls Royces and languid, monocled young men wearing spats projected the requisite twenties ambience. Faint strains of saxophone music reached her ears, and her foot tapped lightly to the Charleston; she was sitting right in front of the speaker.

She sipped a second vodka and lime as she studied the menu. The dishes were cosmopolitan, with no bias in favour of any particular country. Prices were medium to steep; hopefully the quality of the food would provide a justification. Wines, too, were well marked up. Money wasn't a problem, but guilt dictated her choice of mushroom omelette and a glass of Chardonnay.

As she waited to order, Cynthia glanced furtively at the diners nearby who had already started their meals. They were mainly young work colleagues, the men sporting dark suits and the ladies still 'power-dressing' in contravention of the supposedly gentler image of the nineties. Yuppies, she thought with a shudder; they made her feel inadequate, old. She drained her glass, and her eyes continued their survey under lowered lids. Two men together, talking earnestly with much waving of hands . . . another couple, callow-looking, the girl lumpish, the boy trying desperately to impress with the wine list . . .

At the nearest alcove table sat someone Cynthia knew. This revelation alone was enough to give her an unpleasant start, but as she looked away with a flush of shame preparatory to the inevitable second glance, the name at first eluded her.

The girl was young, and very beautiful. The tumble of dark curls around her face invested her with an exotic style, yet the pale blue eyes and the pure magnolia sheen of her cheek made the temperate climes of England her most likely origin. Her make-up was minimal but immaculate, only the vermilion flare of her shapely mouth overstating its case. As she leaned forward, totally intent on a companion as yet invisible behind a tall potted plant, her lower leg emerged from beneath the table. Gold glinted from the slender ankle: suddenly Cynthia made her identification.

This was Loretta Dawes – Nurse Dawes, who worked at the Victoria Hospital with Leo. Cynthia had been introduced to her at Easter, when Leo's senior registrar had hosted a dinner party for colleagues at his flat; that handsome young rogue Peter Verity had been another of the guests. But Loretta had first come to prominence on a different occasion: the hospital's Christmas Review. Wisely eschewing the slapstick roles, she had appeared in a series of skin-tight costumes, raising the lust of virtually every male present to fever pitch.

Only five feet separated their tables, yet Loretta was oblivious to Cynthia's presence. She was deep in a confidential conversation – girl-talk, it seemed, because abruptly Cynthia found her ears attuned to the voice diagonally opposite, rendering her an unwilling eavesdropper.

'I wanted to tell you about my lover. He's very special to me . . .' A rattle of crockery overlay the next few words, then Cynthia clearly heard: 'Leo Masters.' There was no doubt. She strained to catch more, but just at that moment the waitress appeared, ushering three newcomers to an adjacent table. They carried drinks; there were whoops of laughter and much scraping of chairs; Loretta was still speaking, and Cynthia could hear none of it.

Putting a hand up to her face to shield herself from possible recognition, Cynthia stared intently at those moving crimson lips. Her lip-reading skills were poorly developed as yet, but Loretta enunciated well, and to her growing horror Cynthia found that interpretation came easily.

'. . . those wives who won't let go', she read, 'when their marriage has been dead for years. They've got no self-respect . . .'

She remembered the episode of the unanswered phone, and the mysterious button in Leo's car. Suspicion had been growing for weeks. Cynthia gripped her glass with terrified fingers and lifted it to drink, but it was empty. The diners at the next table had quietened down now as they studied their menus. The sound of Loretta's words began to reach her again.

'I love him and he loves me. That's the bottom line, really – the only thing that counts.'

Oh, the confidence of youth! The arrogant certainty of a stunning young woman that whatever she wants is hers for the taking! Feeling sick, Cynthia stumbled to her feet, turning away from Loretta as she did so.

'Are you ready to order now, madam?'

She stared stupidly at the waitress with the Colgate smile, who had materialised from nowhere.

'I – no. I've changed my mind. I'm sorry.' Head down, she scuttled past the simulated alfresco cocktail area and out into the hot street.

*

10

Robin Winterley, Fellow of the Royal College of Surgeons, and his wife Frances lay in their comfortable double bed, no part of their bodies touching. His eyes were closed, but she knew he was awake: his jaw had not relaxed. She stared at him longingly for a few seconds, then slowly raised herself up on to her right elbow and whispered, 'Robin?'

There was no reply.

'Robin?' She leaned over and gently kissed his shoulder. A fleeting grimace crossed his face before he rolled away from her and curled into a tight ball.

'Not now, Fran. Go to sleep.'

'Can't we just talk for a few minutes? We hardly ever seem to get the chance.'

'Fran, I'm not in the mood for another two-hour psycho-analysis session. Especially at midnight. Believe it or not, I'm tired.'

'You're always tired.'

'So would you be, if you did my bloody job.' He paused. 'Go on, then. What is it this time? Let's see if you can actually compress it into a five-minute summary of the problem.'

His tone made her hesitate. 'It's nothing new . . .' she began.

'You amaze me,' said Robin. He turned on to his back with a resigned sigh and gazed up at the ceiling, hands behind his head, the elbows keeping Fran at a distance. Despite the obvious lack of encouragement, she saw no alternative but to plough on.

'Robin . . . Now that your consultant job in Southampton is all fixed up – indeed, imminent – can't we . . . can't we have a baby?'

'Oh, Lord, is it that all over again?'

'But what's *wrong* with wanting a baby?' Fran heard her voice quaver, near to tears, and felt the tightness in her throat. 'You make it sound like a crime. We've been married eight years, and apart from poor little James you've made sure that we didn't have a child to complicate your precious hospital life!'

'James was the result of your wilful disobedience. How many times do we have to go through this? You chose to marry a doctor. You agreed to share the difficulties. You know perfectly well how I've had to spend my time: late theatre lists, on call, exams, writing papers. I haven't been sitting around with knitting and magazines.'

'Neither have I!' she retorted fiercely. 'Who types all your papers? I'm in the middle of transcribing an MD thesis for Alan right now. That isn't the point, though. Of course you're busy, but *I* would be looking after the baby, not you.'

'Look, Fran.' His voice softened. 'I think we've done things the right way round. Medicine's very nomadic in the early years – a job here, a job there, a hospital room, a hospital flat. Remember the trouble I had getting on to a decent registrar rotation? Everything's so uncertain. It's no way to bring up a child.'

'That's past history, Robin. I'm talking about now. You're a senior registrar, and in five weeks you'll be a consultant. The top of the ladder. *Why* do we have to wait any longer? Barry and Sue have got two lovely children, and he's only a senior house officer.'

'Barry and Sue. I might have known they'd crop up. Where's Barry's next job going to be? He doesn't know. Would you have wanted me to put you in Sue's present position? All that worry?'

'Yes, I would! We'd have been a *family*, and faced up to the problems together.'

'It's easy to talk that way when your future's secure. Barry's not particularly clever. He may not make it. If you want my humble opinion, I think you spend too much time over there with Sue, and it's bad for you. You come back all broody. Listen, Medical Records have a vacancy for a secretary: the pay isn't great and they're having difficulty filling the post. Do you want to apply for it on a temporary basis, until the flat's sold? Then you wouldn't be lonely when I leave for Southampton.'

'I've no intention of being lonely, or bored. I've got my freelance work, and I'll be busy packing up all our things.' Frances rolled away from him. 'By the way,' she added, 'don't kid yourself that your opinion's ever humble.' She buried her face in the pillow, and lay stiffly, in total silence.

After five minutes he gave another heavy sigh, turned in the bed and began to stroke the soft blonde hair at the back of her neck. 'Let's talk about something we can both agree on. We

12

haven't celebrated my new appointment yet. Where would you like to go for a special dinner?'

She stirred slightly, then spoke in a quiet, muffled voice. 'Wouldn't you rather have a party, so all your friends from the hospital can join in? We've room enough here.'

'But I thought you didn't like my friends. You spend all your time resenting the fact that they see more of me than you do.'

'Don't be silly. I get on very well with Leo, and Kevin, and Peter, not to mention Sister Brocklebank. They've been here to dinner before. We'd invite Barry and Sue, of course, and John. It would be a sort of "goodbye" party, if you think about it.'

Robin considered. 'Yes, it's a good idea. We'll have a buffet, or one of your hot dishes if the weather changes, and everyone can bring a bottle. Are you sure you'll be able to cope?'

'Oh, easily. Sue's bound to offer to help.'

'So I should imagine,' he said drily, 'considering the time you spend coddling her infants. Well, that's settled, then. We'll decide on a date and I'll spread the word. And Fran – '

She looked up suspiciously.

'We'll have a meal out anyway. Just the two of us.'

'I'd like that,' she said. 'Goodnight.'

'Goodnight.' He wriggled for a few minutes, finding the optimal position for his long limbs, then commenced a deep steady breathing.

Fran continued to lie still, like a corpse, except that tears were pouring silently from her eyes and soaking into the pillow: bitter, stinging tears for little baby James, who had died before he was an hour old.

2

Nottingham's Victoria Hospital, a sprawling structure built piecemeal over the years on the same rocky eminence as the castle, dominated both the city to the east and the leafy residential crescents to the west. Many departments within the building shared the same spectacular view on the west side: the escarpment fell away abruptly beneath their windows; down below, the substantial Victorian houses with their trees and walled gardens seemed to stretch like a scaled-down model all the way to the misty sage hills on the far horizon.

Standing on the narrow paved terrace overlooking the drop were two student nurses. The taller one, a devastatingly attractive brunette, closed her eyes, tilted them up towards the sun and breathed deeply. 'Ah,' she sighed. 'Pity this isn't the Med. I've half a mind to call in sick this afternoon and start working on a late tan.'

Alison Blake, her companion, gave a reflex frown. 'You can't do that, Lorrie,' she stated. 'There's nothing wrong with you.'

'*I* know that, you know that . . . they don't. The wards are so stuffy at present, there's probably some industrial law we can invoke anyway . . .' She threw back her head with a toss of raven curls, and emitted a peal of laughter. 'You should see your *face*, Alison,' she chuckled. 'You take everything so seriously. I was only joking. Of course I wouldn't leave the patients.'

Alison crossed her plump arms. 'One can't always tell,' she said huffily. Mingled annoyance and envy assailed her as Loretta once more surrendered her creamy cheeks to the warmth pouring from the heavens. Her friend was in high spirits at present: she had passed her nursing finals with minimal effort and virtually no curtailment of her hectic social life, and was now scanning the journals for a suitable staff nurse position. Alison, by contrast, had worked very hard and just scraped through. She knew herself to be a plodder – kinder, perhaps, and more painstaking than Loretta, but less intellectually gifted. If the State Roll hadn't been withdrawn, that would have been her preferred niche: basic nursing, direct patient care. Let those who sought extra qualifications forge ahead! But the profession was changing rapidly. Too late to be an enrolled nurse, afraid that health care assistant might prove too limiting, Alison had opted for RGN training with some trepidation. Now that she had actually passed, new decisions loomed. She wished she had a quarter of Loretta's confidence. She wished, though she tried to curb the sin of envy, that her figure was lithe and slim, not pinkly porcine, ballooned with comfort eating. 'You'll get a melanoma,' she warned.

Loretta merely gave a tolerant smile and strolled to the edge of the parapet where the updraught stirred the skirt around her long slender legs. 'I wonder how many people will be at Robin's party on Friday?' she mused. 'Radiology have got something on, as well. Some fancy dress do.'

'I thought I'd go to Mr Winterley's,' said Alison diffidently, 'if other nurses are going. I'd like to see him receive his leaving present.' It was also highly likely that Peter would be there. 'Will you be taking Gordon?'

'Gordon?' For a moment Loretta looked abstracted.

'Yes, Gordon.'

'No way.' She shook her head in amused dismissal.

'Why not?'

'Why should I?'

'Well . . . because it's a weekend and he's your boyfriend.'

'Phooey. He's just someone I go out with from time to time.'

'Oh. We all thought . . .'

'You shouldn't think, Alison. It's bad for you.' Loretta swung her gaze once more towards the horizon, but a faint flush now stained her cheekbones, and merriment played around her mouth. When she turned back, the aquamarine eyes were dancing.

'There's someone else!' gasped Alison intuitively.

'Could be.'

'There is! Oh, do tell me, Lorrie. Is it one of the doctors?'

Loretta waved an admonishing finger. 'Naughty Alison,' she said. 'Wants to spoil the surprise. Everyone will know soon enough, and I guarantee it'll cause a stir.'

'Why does it have to be a secret?'

'You can't guess?'

'No.'

Loretta paused, delighted complacency at war with discretion. She flicked Alison an assessing glance. 'He's married,' she said.

An ice-coated rock dropped to the bottom of Alison's stomach. 'Lorrie, *no*. You can't do that.'

'I can do anything I want.' The triumphant animation faded,

15

and Loretta's beautiful face grew sober. 'What is the point,' she went on, 'of getting bogged down with someone who's got to dedicate the next fifteen years to their career before they've achieved anything to speak of? Or someone like Gordon with no prospects? Life is too short. I've seen too many of my old schoolfriends turn into whining drudges for the lack of a bit of cash. That's not going to happen to me.'

'But . . .' Alison was deeply shocked.

'I won't be a girlfriend of convenience for some junior doctor, always waiting, always being let down. You have to define what you want in life, then go for it.'

'But doesn't he have responsibilities? Children?'

'Don't start one of your lectures, Alison, or I'll regret having told you. You'll understand when you know. I love him, and he loves me; that's all that counts.'

'I . . .'

'Shh. Now, what about that party? Shall we go together?'

Alison wrestled with her puritan distaste for the confidence she had just received. Part of her was flattered that Loretta wanted her company, was still her friend despite defecting to brash Paula Thompkins for so many months. They had gone through their training together, shared many of its woes and rewards, and without Loretta's guidance Alison's social life would have been very meagre indeed. Only those three special outings with Peter had been hers and hers alone . . .

'What about Paula?' she hedged.

'We've had a disagreement,' said Loretta succinctly.

'Oh. Then . . . yes, let's go together.'

Loretta flashed her a wide, careless smile, then consulted her watch, gave a little cluck of surprise, and began to make her way back to the ward.

John Dyson's digital watch bleeped sharply as he peered down the microscope at the last histopathology slide he intended to report that evening. A feeling of pressure was building up behind his eyes, and he knew that an unpleasant headache was inevitable if he carried on. The urgent material had all been dealt with. He could manage the workload, but would still be glad to see his consultant back from holiday the following week.

He reached out for the dictaphone and began to dictate in steady, measured tones, describing the appearance and staining properties of the cells that he could see. This particular specimen was of borderline malignancy; he was unable to offer a more definite conclusion. The surgeons in general, and Robin in particular, would be disappointed.

The trouble with Robin was that he saw everything in black and white. Medicine, of course, was anything but black and white, and the grey areas needed especial care. The entire management of a patient could hinge on one pathological report: the decision to carry out major surgery, or a course of radiotherapy, or the administration of powerful drugs. There was unspoken pressure for each report to be definitive. John always resisted the temptation to guess, however, or make dogmatic statements, or over-extrapolate. His credo was simple: if the sample was from his father, how would he want the pathologist to report the slide?

Fingering his short beard thoughtfully, he decided on a pre-emptive strike. Once again he thumbed the 'record' button and added, 'No further useful comments can be made on this inadequate tissue sample.' For a moment he smiled: Robin had done the biopsy himself, and it *was* on the small side. Then he repented. Running back the tape, he substituted the less contentious word 'scanty' for 'inadequate'. It was no good gratuitously insulting Robin, and then expecting to go to his party.

Stretching his arms luxuriously over his head, John climbed off the stool and placed the dust cover over his microscope. It was ten past seven. Perhaps he would call in at the Mess bar for a pint and a bit of company. Some of the other doctors were bound to be there relaxing.

First, he needed to lock away the dictaphone. Without thinking, he pulled open the desk drawer, and there was Jackie's photograph smiling up at him. Carefully he took it out and propped it on the shining surface, studying every detail. God, he thought. She was so beautiful and so alive. Why did she have to die?

17

Amazing that four years did so little to blunt the agony and profound sense of loss. Sometimes it didn't even seem very real. If he closed his eyes he could hear her delightful bubbling giggle, and see her long legs running across the sand, brown hair flying behind her like a flag. Would things have been any different if they had known what was going to happen? He doubted it. At least they had had three marvellous years together, years of loving and being loved. No one could take that away.

He returned the photograph to the drawer, and locked it in with the dictaphone. Gradually, Jackie's laughing face blurred in his mind, and took on the sharper features and pale complexion of Frances Winterley. She was one of the few people who had understood his devastation, who hadn't avoided him or trotted out meaningless platitudes. Her own experience with baby James, bare months before Jackie's death, had left its imprint, and equipped her as the only comforter he could relate to. She had been his lifeline, and he had slowly grown to love her.

Ah, Jackie! he thought. Am I disloyal to you? I still miss you. You can't imagine how much. Yet . . .

Yet what? Frances was Robin's wife, heart and soul. Despite his neglect and the endless humiliations, she was entirely faithful to him, and John would never dream of trying to persuade her to act otherwise. Only once had his self-control snapped, and he bitterly regretted the incident. She had smiled, and told him not to worry: they were still friends. Now all he could do was hover on the sidelines like Sir Galahad, and be ready to offer his help and protection when she needed them.

His thoughts returned to the subject of Robin himself. He really didn't deserve any wife, let alone one like Frances. Over the years, the less attractive side of his character had revealed itself to those who knew him well. He was immature, with an over-inflated ego, and one day, John decided grimly, he would trip himself up.

The bleep in his pocket went off suddenly, a piercing series of signals. Feeling weary now, he rang the switchboard operator.

'Putting you through,' he heard, then a different voice said, 'Peter Verity here.'

'Pete! How are things with you?'

'Busy, I'm afraid, but I rang the squash club during a hiatus and I've got a court for Friday. Are you interested?'

'What time?'

'Six. We can go on to the party directly afterwards.'

'Count me in.'

'Good. Must go now. See you!'

John replaced the receiver and shrugged on his jacket, lighter of heart at the prospect of sport. He would beat Peter; he always did.

'With your permission, I'll have my drink now.'

'What?' Cynthia's mind had been on vodka; the housekeeper's utterance was startling.

'My cup of coffee.' Mavis Beecham made a great play of peeling off her rubber gloves, sighing and straightening her back. She had been employed by the Masters family for fourteen years now, two days a week for two hours at a time, and a very comfortable situation it was. Leo paid over the odds, and added frequent one-off bonuses whenever he was told of the workshy Mr Beecham's latest mythical ailment. When in company, Mavis took care to appear brisk and vigorous, but her solitary work was slipshod.

'Go ahead,' said Cynthia, skirting round the housekeeper's stocky frame and scanning her well-thumbed collection of cookery books. She reached for *Special Dinners* and began to scrutinize the index.

'Are you having guests tonight?' came a loud voice at her elbow.

'No; I'm just looking for something nice for Leo.' As soon as she had answered, Cynthia felt angry with herself. She didn't owe Mrs Beecham any explanations. All those years ago she had foolishly allowed the housekeeper to start on an over-familiar footing, and it had never been possible to retract. Her own eagerness to please had been as much to blame as Mavis Beecham's thick-skinned, prying nature.

19

'A drink for you, Mrs Masters?'

'No, thank you.'

'I can't manage without my coffee. That's *my* poison, I always say. Still, each to her own . . .'

Cynthia flicked her eyes upwards to find the housekeeper regarding her slyly. Taken aback, she looked down again. Surely Mrs Beecham hadn't guessed? How could she? She only came in the mornings . . . No, this was pure paranoia. The woman was just making conversation.

She heard a faint background noise as she studied the ingredients for Apricot Strudel.

'Postman's here,' boomed Mrs Beecham. 'I'll get the letters for you.' Cynthia stood by the table as she bustled out, bitterly recalling that only four years earlier she would have heard the sharp clank of the letter-flap herself, and identified it immediately.

'Oxford postmark,' read Mrs Beecham shamelessly on her return. 'Looks like Laurel's writing – is she still enjoying university? This one here looks like a bank statement: I suppose that's Mr Masters's province. These others are just circulars.'

'*Thank* you, Mrs Beecham,' said Cynthia as firmly as she could, holding out her hand. She felt obscurely stung by the remark about the bank statement, even though it was true: Leo did handle all their finances. Carried away by the emotion she seized a nearby vegetable knife, slitted the top of the envelope and drew out the printed sheets.

'Mm,' she said in feigned concurrence, running her eye down the list of entries. One withdrawal gave her pause: a cheque for five hundred pounds had been drawn three weeks earlier. Five hundred pounds? She couldn't think of any recent item which might correspond to such a capital sum.

Aware that Mrs Beecham was staring at her, Cynthia tucked the statement back in the envelope, glided into the next room and placed it on top of the bureau.

'You might like to do the dining-room next,' she said pleasantly as she returned to the kitchen. She wanted to bake Strudel for Leo without any distractions.

'Oh, I thought I'd finish here, do the sink and the front of those cupboards,' replied the housekeeper, draining her coffee mug. She pulled on her gloves before Cynthia could object, and began to whisk a grey dishcloth busily behind the taps.

At twelve o'clock on the dot Mrs Beecham departed, leaving Cynthia feeling resentful, frustrated at her inability to be firm. It was ridiculous to be under siege in her own kitchen, enduring patronizing comments on her culinary skills from the hired help! How had she allowed the housekeeper to formulate inflexible rules, decree where and when she would work? Was it because the woman feigned offence so determinedly when crossed?

I don't like her, thought Cynthia. I don't like her, and I don't want her here. With the children away, there's no need anyway. But Leo will think I've gone mad if I suggest we do without a housekeeper. He sees our role as providing employment for someone less fortunate.

Familiar sensations of vague anxiety caused her stomach to churn. Cynthia had her own rules . . . twelve o'clock meant that she could pour her first drink. In controlled haste, she checked the front of the house for the milkman, the postman, any prospective visitors, then took a tumbler from the glass-fronted cabinet in the dining-room and flitted up to the large spare bedroom. There, in the walk-in closet where all the children's old games were piled, her fingers closed gratefully on the neck of a vodka bottle.

By three o'clock, Cynthia was uneasily aware that she had drunk more than her usual quota. She knew why: the figure 'five hundred pounds' kept recurring in her mind. Was it anything to do with that button in the car? Had the money been spent on some grasping young nurse like Loretta Dawes? Cynthia regretted her ignorance where the family finances were concerned. She didn't even know Leo's salary – and besides, any putative figure would be complicated by his variable earnings from private practice. She had tried to gain access to the file of previous bank statements, in order to make an intelligent comparison, but they were locked away in the bureau and she couldn't find the key. Suddenly even that seemed suspicious . . .

In an effort to shake off the miasma of incipient paranoia, Cynthia took a magazine from the rack and leafed through its glossy pages. Cookery, gardening hints, an article on Lindisfarne . . . a questionnaire. One of those worthy self-testers where you answered 'honestly' then had your character, motivation or whatever, analysed.

This one was about alcohol consumption. 'Do you plan your day around the availability of alcohol?' asked one question. 'Do you have a drink before going to a social event: never/seldom/ sometimes/usually/always.' 'Do you ever feel guilty about your drinking? . . .' Hurriedly she turned the page. She didn't need a magazine preaching at her, suggesting that she had a problem: alcohol was her only crutch.

The door bell, especially amplified, vibrated in the background. Cynthia rose from her chair in agitation, thrust the glass underneath it and scuttled to the nearest mirror. Her pale face swung into view, looking drawn and nervy, the eyes not exactly bloodshot, but dimmed. She tugged a wayward strand of hair into place, began to walk towards the door, then paused: she didn't *have* to answer.

Another ring sent her to the window. Cautiously, she peeped round the heavy green velvet curtain and saw a thin young woman, a gamine with close-cropped hair, a baggy purple jersey and black leggings. It was her niece Paula Thompkins.

'Hi, Auntie Cynth, I thought you must be out,' said the girl as Cynthia admitted her.

'I only just heard the bell,' she lied. 'How are you? Is it your afternoon off?'

'Yes. I've come to ask a favour. On Friday the radiologists are holding a fancy dress party, and I haven't a thing to wear. I was going to try and cobble something together, then I remembered that you made a terrific Georgian ball-gown for Laurel a few years ago, so I rang her this lunchtime and asked if I could borrow it. She said I could.'

'Well, of course, Paula, you're welcome. It's upstairs, but – she *was* fifteen when I made it, so I can't guarantee the fit. Still, you look as slender as ever.'

'Size eight, going on ten,' supplied the girl.

Cynthia remembered with trepidation that the costume was hanging with various old evening gowns in the same closet where the games and her bottles were stashed. 'I'll bring it down to you,' she said, but Paula bounded up the stairs regardless and hovered close by as Cynthia slid hangers from one end of the closet rail to the other.

'Oh, look, Monopoly!' she squeaked, darting to the floor of the cupboard. 'It's *years* since I've played. Laurel and I used to enter into pacts against poor Edwin, so we ended up with all the hotels and he went bankrupt. I'm surprised he continued to play with us. And there's Cluedo! We used to fight over who would be Miss Scarlett . . .'

'Here,' said Cynthia, whisking out a garment of rustling lemon taffeta. She stripped off the protective polythene and held it out to Paula. 'Let's go into the front bedroom,' she said. 'There's a long mirror there.'

'I copied the design from a picture of an early Hanoverian lady,' she continued minutes later, guiding the petticoat over Paula's small dark head. 'There's a fan to go with it somewhere, and you might need a curly wig to look properly authentic . . . goodness, I think this could be too large for you.' She straightened the lemon silk over-skirt and released the folds of the Pagoda sleeves, then stood back while Paula scrutinized her reflection thoughtfully.

'Laurel always was better endowed than I was,' said the girl. 'I've got no bustline to speak of, so this *décolletage* is wasted on me. Why couldn't the Hanoverians have gone in for high necks?'

'I could make you a fichu, if you like, or add another layer of frills to the neckline itself. And it would be easy enough to alter the bodice and waistline to fit . . .' Cynthia was concentrating with all her energy, as the numbing effect of the alcohol threatened to slur her speech. Miraculously, Paula seemed to have noticed neither the bottles in the closet nor any fumes in the vicinity of her aunt.

Together they debated the pros and cons of the outfit. 'I don't want to cause a lot of work, Auntie Cynth,' said Paula, frowning over her shoulder at the elaborate figure in the mirror.

23

'It's no trouble.'

Still Paula demurred. 'This is beautiful,' she said at last, 'but it's too *feminine* for me. That's the real problem. Perhaps I should just wear a cloak with some breeches and boots, and go as a cavalier.'

'An outfit like that would suit you, certainly,' smiled Cynthia. 'Why not think it over for a day or two, then let me know what you decide? You said the party's not till Friday.'

'Thanks; that'd be great.' Paula held up her arms like a doll as the froth of taffeta and silk was pulled over her head then stood, skinny but unembarrassed, in her skimpy underwear as Cynthia returned the gown to its polythene cover. Suddenly, she chuckled. 'It's as well Uncle Leo's going to the other party,' she said, 'or you'd have to kit him out in something splendid. I can imagine him as some character from a Rider Haggard story, an explorer in Africa armed with a great elephant gun . . .'

Cynthia's fingers tightened round the hook of the coat-hanger. Paula glanced at her face, and flushed. 'I'm sorry,' she said immediately. 'I didn't think . . .'

Africa . . . Leo had done some latter-day surgical pioneering in the Gambia four years earlier; while he was saving lives by the score, a viral infection had deafened his wife virtually overnight. This was not, however, why Cynthia had stiffened. She had heard nothing of Leo going to a party, a hospital party where pushy young nurses would be making themselves oh-so-available . . .

'I'd forgotten about Friday,' she murmured.

'Uncle Leo said you wouldn't be interested,' nodded Paula. 'The noise, and all that . . . He's probably only going himself because he's Robin's boss, and somebody has to make the speech. If I were you, I'd rent a video and have a bottle of wine.'

Cynthia gave a distracted smile and turned towards the closet before her new discomfiture became blazingly apparent. It was ridiculous, she told herself, to read sly gibes in every innocent remark: why shouldn't Paula speak of wine? But Leo's reported comment was less easy to ignore. He hadn't even mentioned the party to her, let alone allow her to make up her own mind about attending! Was he afraid that she would be a burden, fail to cope, show him up . . . or was he planning an uninterrupted evening in the company of Loretta Dawes?

Leo came home at six forty-five and 'unwound' as was his custom, with a whisky and the *Guardian*. After a suitable time had elapsed, Cynthia nervously approached his chair.

'Paula was here this afternoon,' she said, her voice sounding anything but light and conversational.

'Oh yes?'

Did she imagine it, or was there a wary look in his eyes? 'Yes. She wanted to try on an old fancy dress costume of Laurel's, for a party on Friday. I gather you've an engagement for Friday as well.'

'That's right.' He turned a page and appeared to scan an article. 'Robin's leaving do. He's off to Southampton in three weeks' time, and we've got a presentation for him.'

'I didn't know . . . You hadn't said anything.'

'Sorry.' He murmured something else, but the words were lost in the newspaper.

'I can't hear you.'

'I said, things have been very busy recently.'

'I see.' She twisted her hands together, gripped by an impulse to seize his whisky and empty it down her own throat. 'Am I invited?' she asked.

Now he turned his face towards her. 'I didn't think you'd want to come,' he said, looking surprised. 'It's not a quiet little cocktail party: there'll be heavy background music and a see-thing crush of people. You can come if you want, of course . . .'

If it was a bluff, Cynthia hated herself for being unable to call it. For he was quite right: she would never cope in conditions like that. Even a small gathering could be full of hazards if people didn't make due allowance for her disability. But nevertheless, he should have asked her. 'I'll think about it,' she said, and he nodded non-committally. They both knew she wouldn't go.

'A letter from Laurel came today,' she went on, picking up the small pile of mail from the table. 'Oh, and there was this bank statement. I'm afraid I opened it by mistake.' She passed him the slit envelope but he made no effort to remove its contents. 'I, er, was curious about one entry,' she went on. 'A debit of five hundred pounds. I couldn't think what we'd spent it on.'

'A standing order?' Now he was unfolding the sheet, looking anywhere except at her, his shoulders rigid.

'No, a cheque.'

'Can't imagine . . . oh, wait. It'll be the school fees. That's right, there was a one-off supplementary payment. Edwin's cello lessons, and the tennis coaching.'

Did he really expect her to believe that? Cynthia opened her mouth to challenge him, then closed it again. She didn't want to force him into a corner; she was afraid of what might be revealed. Better to accept his explanation for now. She wanted it to be true; let that be enough.

She sat down opposite him and picked up the magazine she had earlier discarded. It fell open at the alcohol quiz, and she found herself staring once more at the questions. 'Has your drinking ever caused an argument between you and your partner?' Only once, she thought, and Leo was disgusted with me, even while believing it was an isolated occasion; if it ever happens again, I'll lose him for sure.

A panicky feeling twisted her insides. Leo had definitely been edgy recently. Supposing it was already too late? Supposing he was deeply involved with Loretta Dawes, and was just waiting for the right time to break the bad news? Cynthia couldn't bear it. She loved her liberal, hard-working, popular husband, loved and needed him. Without him she would be alone, helpless and unqualified in a cold world of strange, distorted sounds.

'There's something I've been meaning to ask you,' she said, fighting against a growing obstruction in her throat. 'You know when I vacuumed all the car mats the other weekend? Well, I found a button in your front passenger area. It's a carved brass button, good quality, probably from the jacket of a lady's suit. It's upstairs; I can bring it down if you like. I wondered if you'd given one of your colleagues a lift, or that lady from Schroder Pharmaceuticals, or someone . . .' Cynthia was rambling, she knew. She made herself stop, and waited, willing him to proffer the kind of explanation she wanted to hear.

Leo turned another page, then raised his amber eyes to hers. Cynthia stood, lungs immobile, the breath in them stilled.

'I really don't remember,' he said.

3

Barry Pritchard let out a yelp as the screwdriver he was wielding skidded from the head of the screw and lightly gouged his finger. Below the ladder where he perched, his blonde wife Sue appeared in the doorway, but sympathy was not forthcoming. Instead, she giggled.

'What are you *doing* up there, Barry?' she asked. 'Wrecking the joint? I thought you were meant to be *helping* Robin.'

'Yes, thank you, my finger will survive and my tetanus jabs are up to date,' he replied.

'Come on, you're not really hurt, are you?'

'I dare say I might struggle through the evening with suitable quantities of a liquid anaesthetic.'

'Not too much, I hope. Mother would notice, and never let us hear the end of it.' She turned to Fran Winterley, who was quietly placing glasses on a nearby table. 'She's staying with us for the weekend, so we didn't need to engage a babysitter for Tommy and Christine.'

'Good,' smiled Fran. 'That means you won't have to rush off just as the party gets going.'

'Will one of you kind ladies pass the speaker up to me, please? Mind the coil of wire at the back . . . thanks, Fran.' Barry swayed precariously on the ladder as he fixed the dark rectangular box to his crudely fashioned bracket, then climbed down and beat imaginary dust off his hands in a gesture of satisfaction. 'There!' he said. 'Pritchard Stereo Systems Inc. Music guaranteed to reach all corners of the flat – not to mention the building. Have you got accommodating neighbours, Fran?'

'We invited them, just to be on the safe side, but I don't think they'll come. Mrs Raymond is about ninety, and the Farthing family are out a lot anyway . . . Do you want to test the circuitry with a cassette? Here's one . . .'

'This is where we find that Robin's electronics and Barry's are incompatible,' snickered Sue. 'Or there'll be one of those deafening feedback whines like you get at pop concerts.'

'Rubbish.' Barry took the cassette from Fran. 'What's on it?'

'Oh, it's a composite that Robin's been recording. Golden Oldies plus a few more modern tracks . . .' A door thumped in the distance. '. . . The Stones are on it, the Doors, Dire Straits, Eurhythmics, even Duran Duran.'

'Speaking of Golden Oldies, here's Robin,' grinned Sue as their host staggered into the room with a crate of bottles. 'You'll be pretending all your Doors records are a result of that Oliver Stone film.'

He relinquished his burden with a gasp. 'Ten out of ten, Sue: they're originals. I'm keeping them in a safe place.' He flopped down on the nearby sofa. 'What's the situ, Fran? Are we on schedule?'

She glanced at her watch. 'Quarter to five . . . I suppose so, barring unforeseen mishaps. Sue and I have done all the basic food preparation, and we thought we'd serve it on the kitchen breakfast bar. We opted for risotto in the end, because it's easy to cook in bulk, and the weather's been cooler these last few days. Canapés can be such a fiddle . . . So that leaves you the main table here for your bar. Is that white wine you've got? We must chill some of it.'

'Have a glass now if you like. We deserve a break. Wine, Sue? Barry – lager, beer?' The largesse issued from Robin, but it was Fran who actually prepared the drinks. The four friends stretched out in a circle, and chatted idly.

'Will you miss us when you go to Southampton?' asked Sue of Robin. 'Or will you be too busy involving yourself in the Cowes scene?'

'I'm no sailor,' he said. 'You're thinking of John.'

'You don't have to *sail*! You simply hang around, wearing the right clothes and trying to look rich.'

Robin shook his head. 'I anticipate being very busy,' he said. 'At least until I've got to grips with the new post.'

'Have you found a house yet?' asked Barry.

'No, but estate agents are sending details, and I'll be able to start searching in earnest very soon.'

'In the mean time, you're leaving poor Fran behind to sell the flat.'

'That's right. I've offered to fix her up with a job so she won't be lonely, but she's not having any of it.'

Fran gave an enigmatic smile. 'I have to be on hand night and day to let the madding hordes of prospective buyers over the threshold. Seriously, we mustn't miss a sale. I want to join you as soon as possible.'

Robin took a swig of his lager. 'By the way,' he told her, 'don't be surprised if some people in weird costumes arrive here tonight. Radiology is holding a fancy dress party, and a few of the nurses hope to attend both parties. I've said it's okay.' He drained the glass and stood up with an air of purpose. 'Right, let's sort out this drinks table.'

'I see you've decided against champagne cocktails,' observed Barry.

'That was never a viable idea,' said Robin dismissively. 'The cost would have been prohibitive, and we don't have enough champagne flutes. In any case, guests are bound to bring a variety of drinks with them.'

'What he means is, it isn't viable because it was *my* idea,' said Fran. 'One main type of drink on offer would have greatly simplified matters – like punch at Christmas – and of course we wouldn't have used expensive champagne. A good sparkling wine would have been fine.' She shrugged. 'Now you've got to faff around with different mixers, bits of lemon, ice, cherries, God knows what.'

'I'm sure I'll manage,' said Robin stiffly.

'Music, Maestro,' called Sue to her husband. Barry waved crossed fingers in the air, padded to the cassette deck and inserted the tape. For a few seconds there was silence, then the opening bars of 'Brown Sugar' exploded into the room. He bent to the amplifier and turned up the volume even more before proceeding to gyrate across the room in a grotesque but accurate parody of Mick Jagger.

29

Sue rolled her eyes. 'Husbands can be *so* embarrassing,' she said.

The wardrobe door creaked protestingly as Loretta opened it to its widest extent and began a long, searching survey of her reflection in the mirror she had just revealed. The lighting was poor (typical Nurses' Home economy, she thought) but the creature staring back at her, matching look for look, and parting vibrant crimson lips even as she did, had a shimmer all of its own which transcended the spartan surroundings like a glow-worm in a moorland bog at dusk.

Her features had always held a subtle hint of the exotic, and warmed to the bright colours which could be so disastrous on other girls. Loretta, however, had discovered long ago that for really special occasions, her face and form should be allowed to speak for themselves. Tonight was one such time. The stark black dress she had chosen was cunningly relieved by a slender gold belt, and the twinkle of matching jewellery at her wrists, neck and earlobes. Above spike-heeled suede court shoes was a further muted gleam: her favourite eighteen-carat ankle chain. The figure in the mirror executed a slow and graceful pirouette, then smiled at her in complicity; they both knew that the real radiance came from within.

Loretta was ready early. She contemplated lighting a cigarette, then decided against it: Alison would be able to tell, and out would come the ill-concealed looks of pained disapproval. Not that Loretta was usually overly bothered about other people's feelings, but tonight was not to be tarnished, and there was no point in antagonizing Alison unnecessarily. She sat at the desk, chin in hand, her thoughts straying as ever back to her lover. It was a pity she had given her word to keep quiet for the time being. She was bursting with pride, longing to tell them all, to see their faces. There would be disapproval, of course, but also envy and a grudging respect that *she* had been chosen . . .

After a few minutes of complacent musing, Loretta rose from the chair and picked up her small black clutch bag and keys. She glanced briefly around the room to assess its state of tidiness, then shrugged on a black velvet jacket and tapped out into the corridor with a light, determined tread, locking the door after her. Alison's room, number 23, was just next door on the left. Loretta knocked swiftly, and a muffled 'come in' issued from the depths.

Alison was fastening a pair of ivory patent T-bar shoes. 'Hello, Lorrie,' she said as her friend entered. 'You look super.'

'Thanks. That's a pretty dress you're wearing.'

So much was true at any rate, she thought. The dress would have suited someone else very well, but Alison unerringly chose the wrong sort of clothes for her short, overweight figure. Tonight, it was a cream concoction with a high neck, resplendent with lace, ruffles and flounces. Loretta was vaguely reminded of a Danish pastry. 'I thought we might take a taxi,' she suggested.

Alison was dismayed. 'I can't afford it,' she said with a helpless gesture. 'Surely we can walk; it's barely a mile away from the hospital.'

Her companion sighed, and displayed an elegantly shod foot, rotating it at the ankle where the gold chain reflected the sparse gleam of the overhead light. 'Look at these heels. I can't walk a mile. It'll have to be the bus, then.' She leaned against the lintel while Alison counted the change in her purse. 'Everyone says it's going to be a pretty wild party. I'll definitely need a taxi coming back!'

Loretta gave a little laugh, then noticed that Alison was looking more stricken than ever. 'Oh, come on!' she said, not unkindly. 'Consultants have been invited, so it'll probably be bore of the century.' *Right up your street*, she almost added, but stifled the words. Alison could be such a wet rag at times. It made her wonder: what *was* the basis for their friendship? Perhaps that was a question best ignored . . .

'Drink up, Pete. Time we were going.'

John Dyson rose from the bar table at Westwood Squash Club, picked up his holdall and waited while Peter drained his glass of beer. Together they sauntered out to the car-park and climbed into John's blue Orion.

'I'll beat you yet,' threatened Peter as his friend drove smoothly along the Derby Road towards their next port of call.

'When fish fly.'

'Like salmon, you mean? . . . I shall. I nearly did it tonight, and with a few coaching sessions from Ted . . . I reckon you're sunk. You'd best take up bowls.'

'Whatever you say.'

He turned off the road and negotiated the narrower byways, finally approaching the low, exclusive block of flats where Robin and Fran had lived since their marriage. A more modest block opposite was owned by the hospital, its units rented out to married junior medical staff. All the rest of the hospital accommodation, including the Nurses' Home, was clustered around the Victoria itself.

The cul-de-sac leading to Robin's home was jammed with cars. John reversed into the street they had just left and slotted the Orion in behind a white Rover before climbing out. At eight o'clock on a late summer's evening the light was fading: distant strains of music and laughter floated towards them from a row of open windows in the private block of flats.

'Sounds as if we've come to the right place,' said Peter. They quickened their pace, then suddenly he nudged John in the ribs. 'Is that Leo's wife?' he murmured. 'Over there, in the Peugeot. What's her name: Cynthia?'

John glanced across the road, saw a greyish-haired woman in the driver's seat. 'I'm not sure,' he replied. 'She doesn't normally come to these noisy things because of her hearing difficulty . . .' He peered again as they drew level. 'Actually, you're right. It *is* her. I wonder where Leo is? She doesn't seem to be in any hurry to join the party.' He debated whether to cross the road and say a few words, but the figure in the Peugeot had now bent forward so that she was scarcely visible. 'Probably changing her shoes,' he muttered. 'Let's go.'

They entered the glassed-in foyer, climbed carpeted stairs to the second floor and rang the appropriate bell. The rise and fall of animated conversation on the other side of the door was clearly audible, but not the individual words. They waited. Nothing happened. Peter shrugged, and rapped sharply on the door with his knuckles. It was opened a few seconds later by Robin, who smiled broadly at them.

'John, Peter; glad you could make it. Come in.'

The small lobby was packed with a seething mass of humanity, most people holding glasses aloft, some already developing the characteristic flushed cheek and glazed eye. In one corner, a senior house officer on call was trying in vain to hold a telephone conversation, while two other doctors formed a miniature queue behind him, tapping their feet impatiently. Across the hall, John noticed staid Sister Brocklebank apparently flirting with a medical student. 'Half the hospital seems to be here,' he shouted over his shoulder to Peter, who was pinned not too unhappily between two student nurses.

Robin was leading him to the other end of the hall, where the press of people was less. 'Come through into the kitchen,' he beckoned. 'It's much quieter, and the food's nearly ready.'

John remembered the bottle of Mouton Cadet he was clutching, and decided to hand it over when there was less risk of its being jostled out of his grasp. He gained the kitchen with relief. 'Phew! I thought we were early. It's as well your flat's large, Robin. Have some plonk, with my compliments.'

'Thanks. I'll get you a drink. Wine? Beer?'

'Beer, if you don't mind. I won't mix my drinks.'

As Robin's tall frame moved out of his line of vision, John noticed that there were ladies in the kitchen. Frances and Sue, both wearing silk trouser suits protected by aprons, were busy with the machinery of feeding the five thousand. Sue was stirring something in a wok keeping hot on the cooker, while Frances stood at the breakfast bar, serving food from a second wok on to a row of plates. Delicious aromas wafted across the room.

'Good evening, ladies.' John gave a small bow. 'I was priding myself on being invited to a small gathering of the select tonight. Instead, I find the heathen are *en masse* without.'

'Hello, John. Yes, the heathen are without at present – we haven't fed them yet.' Fran's chuckle was throaty.

'Take a seat,' suggested Sue, waving a wooden spatula airily in the general direction of some kitchen stools. 'They'll be at a premium later.'

John perched behind the door, away from any potential trampling feet.

Fran approached him with a steaming plateful of fish risotto, and a fork. 'Would you like a bib?' she asked.

'No, thank you,' he growled. 'If you can stretch to a serviette, though, I'd be grateful.' He took a mouthful, and assumed the expression of a connoisseur. 'Delicious. Er, what's in it?'

The women looked at each other, and giggled.

'What's not in it would be easier to answer,' said Sue. 'There's white fish, prawns, nuts, raisins . . .'

A serving hatch flew open in the opposite wall, and Barry leaned through. 'We're ready if you are,' he called.

'Now *there*'s an offer,' muttered John, catching Frances' eye. She smiled back at him and began to pass steaming platefuls of food through into the extended living-room beyond.

'Why don't you use the hot-plate, and let people help themselves?' he asked. 'It would save you a lot of work?'

'We did that last time. The greedy devils ate everything in the first half-hour, and the late-comers went hungry. This way we can at least *try* to ration them!' Frances smiled again, but for the first time that evening John noticed the dark circles around her eyes, only partially camouflaged by make-up.

Barry's head appeared again in the hatchway. 'Chatting up our womenfolk, John? You're on a loser with Sue. I gave her a chastity belt for her last birthday. I should settle for a beer instead. Here you are.' He held out a large glass which began to tilt alarmingly, requiring rapid rescue.

'Listen, Barry,' said Frances. 'Now that some of our guests have been fed, let the others come into the kitchen for their meal, then Sue and I have a chance to meet them.'

'Rightho, Fran.' He vanished abruptly, like a jack-in-a-box, and the hatch closed.

Frances turned to John. 'In answer to your observation of five minutes ago – yes, we were just going to have a few people over initially, but then we kept thinking of others with whom Robin has worked at the hospital: you know, the surgical nurses, the Theatre staff, secretaries, medical students . . . It's ended up as a kind of free-for-all. I don't mind. They're all glad he's got the Southampton job. It's nice that they were prepared to come. We can manage, can't we, Sue?'

Sue took a sip of her white wine. 'We certainly can.'

A steady stream of people passed through the kitchen during the next half-hour, each receiving a heaped plate from Frances. John was content to sit in his corner eating, drinking and watching the way she performed even the most mundane taks with grace. Occasionally, he exchanged a few words with the new arrivals, but he was loath to leave his comfortable niche and plunge into the fray next door.

When Loretta and Alison made their entrance around eight forty, he made an effort to be sociable. He had known them by name since the dinner at Easter, but like any other red-blooded male he had noticed Loretta at the infamous review, and at previous hospital parties, where her appearance was invariably striking. His admiration for her was tempered with a mild distates for her reputed prodigality.

Behind Loretta trooped Alison, head down, for all the world like a pet spaniel. She was looking uncomfortable, probably because this party was rowdier than she had anticipated, or perhaps she was miserably aware of the perfect foil she made for Loretta's dark beauty. He felt a fleeting twinge of pity.

'Hello,' he said, sliding off his stool. 'Have you come to break the hearts of all those unfortunate medical students in the hall? Sister Brocklebank appeared to be doing nicely.'

'Hardly,' replied Loretta, amused. 'They were all discussing rugby when we came past.'

'Have you got a drink?' He looked at Alison.

'Er, no, but Mr Winterley suggested that we get our food first and then join him in the living-room.'

'Fair enough. I can recommend this risotto. It's superb.'

Alison's face wore a doubtful expression. She glanced up at Frances, who had just taken a fresh wok from Sue and was stirring its contents. 'Just a small one, please, Mrs Winterley. I'm on a diet.'

'Call me Fran. How about you, Loretta?'

'Oh, a normal helping, thank you. I'm quite hungry.'

'Would you like tabasco sauce – or soy? I can put some on.'

'Yes, thanks: tabasco.'

Frances served up a small portion for Alison, and a substantial amount for Loretta, shaking the sauce bottle briefly over it. She slid the plates back down the breakfast bar towards the girls. 'Cutlery is on that table under the hatch,' she said, pointing. 'Help yourselves to salad.'

Moments later, Peter Verity appeared in the kitchen doorway, carrying his empty plate.

'Come to do your Oliver Twist act?' teased John.

'I have, as a matter of fact. Is there anything for a poor, starving boy, Fran?'

'I see no such person here?'

'Cruel. Don't you realize it's the best of compliments? The seal of approval for your glorious risotto? Go on, you've got plenty.'

'All right. Don't tell them all, though. We're still expecting quite a lot of people to come. Sauce?'

'Yes, please. Some of that soy. Now let me do *my* good deed. You were on white wine, if I remember. May I get you a top-up?'

'Hmm. I think I'd like orange juice, Peter, if you don't mind bringing me one. Better still, ask Robin to pass one through the hatch.'

As Peter left the kitchen with the two nurses, after performing his self-appointed task, John became aware that Frances and Sue were watching him. 'Go and join them,' encouraged Sue. 'You can't stay here all night. You'll miss all the fun!'

'Let me wash up for you . . .' he began.

'No!' Frances clucked in mock exasperation. 'We'll get on much more quickly without men galumphing about the place. Go on, enjoy yourself. Make some nurse's evening. We'll come and circulate when we can.'

'Just a few more minutes,' he said.

4

Alison stood with Loretta near one of the open windows. The atmosphere inside the room was damp and overheated, only partially ameliorated by the faint draught behind them. People stood in groups, talking animatedly, or gyrated to the heavy beat of the music. She blushed to see Sister Brocklebank executing some kind of tarantella in the corner with the charge nurse from Ward 1; somehow it didn't seem at all in keeping with her dignity.

'I didn't know you were on a diet, Alison,' commented Loretta, manipulating her fork with dexterity.

'I'm not,' she muttered. 'It's rather unfortunate, but I don't like fish, and I'm allergic to prawns. They make me feel sick. I came out in a rash once. It seemed ungrateful to say that to Mrs Winterley, so – I told an untruth.'

'Well, don't make it sound like the clap of doom. I'll finish it off for you if you can't manage it. Look, I'd like a quick word with Leo over there, while he's free. Would you keep an eye on this for me? Thanks.' She deposited her plate on the window-sill and strode over to the consultant before Alison could answer. For a moment their heads were visible across the undulating sea of dancers, then a particularly manic specimen leapt into Alison's field of view, and she turned her attention once more to the food. She chewed slowly, trying to separate the flakes of fish and prawns from the rice and other ingredients with her fork, a difficult task in the poor light. The old familiar feeling of embarrassment stole over her, as if everyone was covertly watching, deriding her for having no one to talk to. Parties so often became a painful ordeal; she only felt truly comfortable among small groups of reliable friends, like those from church.

The dancers were really too awful to watch. Alison took another tentative mouthful of rice, then set down her plate next to Loretta's and turned towards the opposite end of the room.

There was Dr Dyson with Barry Pritchard, laughing over some joke. Mr Cox, the younger consultant surgeon, was holding an earnest discussion with one of the orthopaedic juniors and a theatre sister she knew. Alison wondered whether to join them, then decided against it. Cox was a pale, thin, unpleasant man with a petulant mouth and pointed chin, totally devoid of any sense of humour. From the occasional words she could hear, she deduced that he was giving one of his favourite professional hobby-horses an airing.

Feigning nonchalance, she took her last sip of pineapple juice. Now it was finished, despite her careful husbandry. Where was Loretta? Her meal would be cold. Alison craned her neck, then jumped as someone tapped her lightly on the shoulder.

'Your glass is empty, Alison,' smiled Peter. 'Would you like another of whatever it was?'

'In a minute, yes, please. It was pineapple juice.'

'On its own? You're not into those fancy drinks, then, like Pina Colada?'

'No. Oh, please don't add anything. I'm sure I'd be able to tell.'

'Perish the thought.' He spread his hands in a wide, innocent gesture before his facial expression became more serious. 'I hear congratulations are in order,' he said. 'You are now Alison Blake, RGN. Have you applied for any staff nurse posts yet?'

'No. I – I don't feel ready to manage a ward just at present. I'd like to do some form of nursing with the elderly, perhaps get on a training course for the Certificate. I don't feel nervous when I'm with old people. The trouble is, I'm not sure I'm clever enough for more study.'

'You've got this far. I think half the battle is knowing what you want. Good luck to you. Are you having any holiday this year?'

'Yes. A week with Mother in the Lake District: Grasmere.'

'Where the poets come from! That sounds marvellous. I'll just go and get your jungle juice.'

She watched him thread his way expertly through the crowd, her eyes dwelling on his handsome profile as he reached the drinks table. The aquiline nose, the high cheekbones, the jet-black hair – she knew his features off by heart anyway. He had never been out of her mind for long since those three exciting outings almost two years ago, from which she had built such high hopes. She remembered every detail: a thunderous performance of Rachmaninov at the Albert Hall, *Pygmalion* elegant beneath the green and gold of the Theatre Royal, and the splendour of Chatsworth House, with its Emperor Fountain and fine park, regal against a wooded Derbyshire hillside. It had taken her two hours to pack a picnic on that day; everything had to be perfect . . . As soon as Peter had met Loretta, of course, the edifice had come tumbling down. That relationship had barely lasted three months, but to Alison it seemed her own chance had gone for ever.

It was kind of him to come and talk to her tonight, she thought. He must be itching to exercise his charm on the expectant gaggle of pretty young nurses tittering in the far corner of the room. With a sudden hurtful stab of insight, Alison knew herself to be plain, boring and hopelessly out of place at this gathering. She felt ludicrously close to tears.

Minutes later, Loretta appeared, chewing on her lower lip and looking oddly put out. She barely glanced at Alison. 'Hi,' she said shortly. 'I see you didn't manage much of your food.'

'No, I started feeling sick. It's only me. There's nothing wrong with it, I'm sure. Do you still want it?'

'Yes, all right.'

'I'm afraid it's nearly cold.'

'Never mind; mine was pretty lukewarm to start off with. I'll just finish it now, then come on to yours.'

'Thanks, Lorrie. I didn't want to offend Mrs Winterley.'

Alison stood awkwardly while Loretta was eating, then felt a wave of relief as Peter emerged unscathed from the mêlée and presented her with a tall glass of ochreous fluid and pineapple pieces, tinkling with ice-cubes. 'A special drink for a special lady. Don't fret, Alison, it's not a cocktail. One hundred per cent pineapple juice, today's dose of vitamin C.'

'And sugar,' added Loretta in a flat voice. She averted her face, then seemed abruptly to collect herself. 'Shall we have a dance, Pete? Alison – Brock said something about wanting a few words with you. She was in the corridor with Jane.' She held out her hand and Peter took it easily, naturally, steering her among the dancers until they melted into the mass and were lost to view. Alison's eyes ached. A queer, hollow pain twisted her stomach as she walked blindly towards the door.

By ten forty-five the party mood was completely unfettered. Formalities were over; Leo Masters had delivered a stirring speech while Robin had accepted his gift, a cut glass decanter, with a creditable show of modest surprise. A staggered influx of lively, masked revellers from the Radiology party a mile down the road had strained the capacity of the flat, but nobody seemed to mind: wine and laughter were on everyone's lips. This occasion would go down in memory.

John Dyson encountered Peter creeping furtively down the hall – where there was still some oxygen – and grinned at him. 'I can't take all this,' he said. 'I'm not as young as I was.'

'You need worry. I must be over the hill as well. That little dark nurse from Theatre is wearing me out!'

'You mean Nurse Sykes?' John's expression was bland.

'That's the one.'

'Well, she's about fifteen feet behind you, and closing.'

'Hell!' Peter's eyes flickered about him in alarm, seeking an escape route.

'Try the utility cupboard,' whispered John.

'You're kidding.'

'No, I'm not. It's just round the corner, on the left. There's a queue for the bathroom, so it's your only chance.'

'Thanks, pal. I owe you one.' Houdini-like, he vanished, while John laughed inwardly at the girl's thwarted bewilderment as she reached the corner.

Peter was back within five minutes, and together they lounged against the wall making desultory conversation. A click heralded the opening of the kitchen door. Out stepped a buxom young woman with flowing blonde curls and a handspan waist. She stood for a moment, swaying slightly, then attempted to walk down the hall in something approaching a straight line.

'Now *that's* more like it,' sighed Peter.

'She's drunk.'

40

'Aren't we all? You know what they say: *suivez la piste*, loosely translated as "follow that drunken woman". I'll be seeing you.'

John made a face. 'I give up. You're a sucker for punishment.'

'Never; I feel revitalized.' He punched John lightly on the shoulder then followed the girl, who was groping at door handles to assist her unsteady progress.

'Hello, let me help you,' he said.

'It's all right. I only want my coat,' she answered, her voice slightly blurred. 'It's in one of these bedrooms.'

Better and better, thought Peter. Aloud, he introduced himself. 'I'm Peter Verity, surgical SHO. I don't think we've met before.'

'No, we haven't. I'm not sure why, though: I work in the surgical office. Mr Masters helped me to get a job there after I'd done some other work for him, filling in for Mrs Deakin.'

Leo Masters's private secretary of thirteen years had been on maternity leave. 'I'm on Kevin Cox's team,' explained Peter. 'And you are . . . ?'

'Sonia. Sonia Ball.'

They shook hands, then she side-slipped alarmingly. Peter took the opportunity to place a steadying arm round her waist, and opened the nearest bedroom door. Annoyingly, there were six or seven girls in the double room, powdering their faces and combing their hair. The air was acrid with newly applied perfume.

'What does your coat look like?' asked Peter, indicating the pile of jackets and coats on the bed.

'Er, green. Woollen. Long.' She peered around helplessly. 'I don't remember this room.'

'Well, let's look anyway.' He carefully moved all the garments from one side of the bed to the other, but without success.

Sonia continued to stare vaguely, then suddenly a gleam of recollection shone in her eyes. 'I know. It was the little bedroom at the end.'

'Fair enough.' He took her arm and led her to the door. 'Goodnight, girls.'

They regained the corridor. 'I made a mistake,' said Sonia. 'I came late, and put my coat in the wrong bedroom. I can manage now, thank you.'

41

He hovered reluctantly outside the door as she went inside, concentrating hard on her tread. Almost immediately, however, she reappeared, giggling. 'I can't get it. Someone's asleep in there, and she's lying on it!'

Peter was about to look for himself, when she tugged at his sleeve. 'Let's go and have a drink, Dr Verity.'

Ah well, he thought. There were dimly lit corners in the room where the dancing was. They would have to do.

John Dyson had been watching Frances covertly at intervals ever since she had emerged from the kitchen for Leo's speech. She took her duties as hostess seriously, circulating among the guests, singling out those who were alone or who, conversely, were pinned against the wall by some determined bore. To anyone who didn't know her, she seemed witty, friendly and charming. To one who did, the façade was threadbare, and beneath it she was as tense as a tightly coiled spring.

It wasn't hard to guess the reason why. Robin was completely neglecting her, as usual. At this moment he was across the room, swaying to the music of a slow ballad, and Nurse Wentworth from Intensive Care was wrapped around him like a boa constrictor. Before that, it had been Staff Nurse Frazer from Theatre. The list was endless, and irrelevant. His partners had one thing in common: they were not his wife.

John suppressed the familiar anger. He knew perfectly well what Robin would say if anyone was stupid enough to challenge him. He would smile in a deprecating manner, and claim he was simply being a good host. Any further probing, and he would turn very nasty indeed – John had had personal experience of this.

As Frances left a small group of surgical secretaries with a nod and a smile, John seized his opportunity and stepped forward to claim her attention. 'Fran, you look remarkably cool in that blue silk, despite slaving over the proverbial hot stove. How do you do it?'

'I'm the original Snow Queen, John.' She lowered her voice. 'You should know.'

People were all around them, too close for the confidential conversation he would have liked. 'Dance?'

'No, but thank you for asking. I don't think Robin would be too pleased if it was you.'

'Hang Robin!' he snapped. She was going to move on; he could sense it. All evening he had been waiting to be with her, even for just a few minutes. He had to carry on talking. Something banal – anything would do. 'Have you found yourselves a house in Southampton yet?' he asked.

She shook her head. 'No. The hospital have offered us a temporary flat, so it's not desperately urgent. Selling's going to be our main problem.'

'True. Do you think you'll go back to secretarial work once you're settled in? Part-time, perhaps?'

'No. I mean, I don't know. Nothing's decided.' She seemed irritated by his questions, frowning and withdrawing from him. There was a sudden near-silence in the room as the taped music came to an end, and Robin deftly changed cassettes.

The new track started quietly, but with a distant hint of menace as the rumble of a thunderstorm sounded over the notes from the keyboard. John recognized the tune: 'Riders on the Storm' by the Doors. He knew the music well; it would last over seven minutes, unless Robin had edited it. Taking courage, he looked straight into Frances's face and held out his arms. 'Dance with me, Fran. Please.'

She hesitated fractionally, then glided forward, clasping her hands behind his neck. They were icy cold. As he tried to bring her closer, her elbows pressed into his chest, and he could sense the tension in every muscle of her body. Robin, he thought, what have you done to this lovely woman?

It was dark in their part of the room. The portion of John's brain which was not concentrating on Frances was pervaded by the music, by lyrics from a dead man which carried their own darkness. Echoes of his adolescence whispered past: his elder brother playing this track again and again, both of them either impervious in their youth to its bleak message, or simply complacently secure within their nucleus of family and friends. But now he wasn't twelve any more; he was thirty-four, and lonely.

Suddenly, a figure pushed past wearing a rustling costume – some kind of historical ball-gown. Frances lost her balance, and in steadying her John seized the opportunity to try to draw her closer. For several seconds she resisted, her limbs taut and unyielding, then Jim Morrison's voice vibrated richly above them: 'Girl, you gotta love your man.'

Abruptly, she seemed to sag. Her arms slid round his neck, clasping him tighter, tighter, and her cheek met his and welded into it. He could feel the fine bones of her face through the soft flesh, and the light flutter of her eyelashes as she closed her eyes. The slender body in the pale blue silk was pressing into his along its whole length; he tried to believe it, and found he could not.

Peter surfaced slowly from another cohesive clinch with the excellent Sonia, and drew a deep breath. What a find! There was going to be no nonsense here about 'coffee' meaning a steaming black beverage: this girl knew the score. He glanced surreptitiously at his watch. One thirty. Time to be moving. The party was breaking up now, anyway.

The girl gave a little cry of displeasure, and pulled his mouth back to hers with unexpected energy. For another minute he allowed himself to half-drown in the vortex, then gently but firmly pulled himself free.

'I think we should make a move,' he whispered into her soft pink ear. 'Why don't you collect your coat while I pay our respects and ring for a taxi?' He helped her to her feet and she smiled at him, her face flushed, a strand of blonde hair straggling across her forehead. Picking up her bag, she walked quite steadily to the door and out into the hall.

A small knot of die-hards stood chatting at the far side of the room, and Peter noticed Sue Pritchard nearby, collecting glasses from the window ledges. He sauntered over to her. 'Great party, Sue. Your cooking was superb. Have you seen Robin?'

'He was with Barry in the kitchen a few minutes ago,' she replied.

'Thanks. Look after yourself. No doubt we'll meet again.' He kissed her cheek lightly.

Peter entered the hall, but he never got as far as the kitchen. Down to his right Sonia was stumbling towards him, her face chalk-white, her mouth working soundlessly. 'Peter,' she croaked. 'Please come. Oh, God!'

'What is it?' His voice was tight with concern, as her expression was ghastly. He caught her shoulders. 'Do you feel ill?'

'No, no!' She shook her head wildly. 'Oh, Peter, you must come. It's that girl. I think – I think she's dead.'

Peter Verity felt as if he had been punched in the stomach. His heart began to pound, and there was a distant ringing in his ears. Concentrating hard, he chose words which would reassure the trembling girl beside him, who seemed to be on the verge of hysteria. 'Stay here. I'll go and look. It's probably someone who's had a little bit too much to drink and passed out.'

'No. I'm coming with you.' She grasped at his sleeve, dragging on it as they walked down the passageway.

The small bedroom at the end was dimly lit by a low-wattage ceiling light in a Chinese shade. There was no more music from the party, and the silence here was almost absolute. A figure lay motionless on the bed, partially covering a dark green coat which trailed on to the floor. It was a girl in a black dress, curled on to her left side as if she had just gone to sleep.

Peter took two steps forward, then stumbled as his foot caught in an object on the floor. Bending down, he picked up a black suede high-heeled court shoe; its fellow was on the floor, neatly placed at the side of the bed. Responding to the subliminal association, he turned his gaze immediately to the stockinged feet just above; there in the thin gleam of the overhead light, a golden ankle chain winked and smouldered.

With the shock of recognition, his heart thundered even more violently, and the drumming in his ears threatened to deafen him. 'Loretta!' he whispered.

He darted to an Anglepoise lamp on the bedside table, and illuminated the head of the girl lying on the bed. The face was half-hidden by glossy black hair. Gently, he turned her on to her back and sucked in his breath sharply.

Loretta's face was waxen, with a faint blue-grey tinge. Her

eyes were closed, the mouth very slightly open as if waiting for a kiss. The skin was cool. Peter stood rigid with horror, then his frozen brain clicked into medical gear. He pressed the side of her neck in the carotid area: no pulse. With his thumb, he lifted up each flaccid eyelid in turn, but the eyes were vacant, the pupils mute portals to a dead cavern from which all intelligence had fled. There was no change in their staring emptiness when he passed the lamp to and fro across her face.

'She's dead, isn't she?' Sonia was still rooted in the doorway.

He swallowed. 'Yes. Get Robin – quickly. You'll find him in the kitchen.'

He heard her blunder up the passageway, and forced his knuckles hard against his teeth. Seconds ticked away, then he heard the confused patter of several pairs of running feet. Robin burst into the room, wild-eyed.

'What's this story – my God!' He stood motionless for a moment, then pushed Peter out of the way and repeated his examination, shaking the body as if he could force life back into it. 'My God,' he said again. 'Take the feet . . . We must put her on the floor. Cardiac massage.'

Peter shook his head sadly. 'It's too late, Robin.'

'Jesus Christ! What are you talking about? We've got to get her to hospital. Someone ring for an ambulance!'

The group by the door stirred, and Peter saw a fleeting series of images – Barry Pritchard's thin arm holding the ladies back, his wife Sue wringing her hands together, the dazed eyes of Fran Winterley, the incongruous appearance of a French maid. They all wore similar expressions of shock, death-masks on the living.

There was a creak from the bed as Robin lifted Loretta's body into his arms. The limbs dangled, the head lolled back so far that a black curtain of hair hung down behind, and the pure line of her jaw and throat was clearly visible. He placed her carefully on to the floor then knelt down and inserted his fingers into her mouth. 'Nothing there,' he breathed tersely. 'Help me, Pete. We've got to do it.'

As he raised his fist in preparation for the heavy thump on the chest, Peter recovered from his trance. 'No!' he yelled. 'Stop this, Robin. Stop it now.' He threw himself on to Robin's clenched fist, and forced it down, inch by cracking inch, until it was pinned harmlessly against his knee. Robin snarled at him in fury, but Peter hung on until he relaxed.

'It's no good, Robin,' he said more quietly. 'She's been dead for some time. She's going *cold* . . .'

5

Detective Inspector Richard Montgomery yawned as his Sierra sped through the near-deserted streets of west Nottingham. At the age of forty-one, he had less stamina for night calls than he remembered possessing as an eager young constable. Nevertheless, the prospect of applying his brain to a case of suspicious death was imminent, and the public deserved an officer with all his faculties about him: he pressed a button and the driver's window slid down; cool air skimmed past his cheek.

'That's a help,' murmured William Bird at his side. The plump detective sergeant stretched in his seat then leaned forward to peer through the windscreen. 'Left here, I think, sir. It's the top flat of Willow Court. A Mr Robin Winterley is the owner and it was his party.'

'Who actually called the police?'

'He did. Two PCs from the nearest squad car were routed there. They found about twenty guests, all hospital people of one kind or another, and a dead girl in the bedroom. Dr Greaves is on his way over.'

'Good. I hope for their sake there was no drug-taking going on.'

Montgomery parked the car in front of the flats, and spotted a familiar Volkswagen nearby. 'Dr Greaves is here already,' he said. They hurried inside, and though Sergeant Bird looked longingly at the lift doors, Montgomery led the way up the carpeted stairs. In less than half a minute, he was ringing the bell of Flat 5.

A tall, dark-haired man opened the door. He was in his mid-thirties and handsome, but there was arrogance in the set of the grim mouth, and accusation in his level gaze. 'I'm Robin Winterley,' he said in answer to Montgomery's introduction. 'You'll need to meet my wife. Frances!' he called sharply. A pale, slender woman emerged from the corridor behind him. 'This is Inspector Montgomery, with Sergeant Bird.' She nodded wordlessly.

The detectives advanced into the hallway, where stale alcohol hung heavily in the moist air. They passed a row of brass hooks scantily burdened with coats, then a serpentine-fronted table which supported an attractive arrangement of carnations and roses in shades of apricot, saffron and cream, misted with gypsophila. Above the flowers was a large mirror; Montgomery caught a glimpse of his own lean face and dark hair stippled faintly with grey as he stepped forward to receive a résumé of the evening's events from the uniformed constables.

'. . . Apart from the Winterleys, there are eighteen other people here,' Constable Phelps finished up. 'Most of them are in the living-room. We've got all their names and addresses.' He ushered them through a nearby doorway.

'Ah, Montgomery!' Dr Greaves, an elderly GP who did duty as their police surgeon, hobbled towards them. Perhaps it was just the poor light, considered Montgomery, but he looked drained, an old man who should have been enjoying unbroken sleep. The doctor was nearly thirty years older than he was, and suffered from longstanding arthritis, but he showed little willingness to pass on the torch to his keen young partner, Ian May. Soon, however, he would be forced to retire.

'I just arrived myself,' he said. 'Such a lovely young girl . . .' He stretched out a consenting hand and stepped aside, allowing the detectives a first view of their subject. Montgomery saw a pool of black hair spilling across the carpet directly ahead of them, as if an inkpot had been upturned. Beyond, the body was neatly arranged, shapely legs emerging parallel from the dress's black kneeline tide, gold-embellished hands resting devoutly on the raven breast. He padded forward, almost as if she might wake, and looked down at the face. Dr Greaves was right: she had been beautiful.

'Carry on,' he said quietly, and stood with Sergeant Bird while the necessary examinations took place.

'She died between three and four hours ago,' stated the doctor minutes later, squinting at his thermometer. 'That is, some time in the region of eleven thirty.'

'And the cause? Is there any clue at all?' Montgomery knew Dr Greaves would be unable to specify. He had seen for himself that each creamy limb was unmarked, the throat unsullied, the back innocent of hidden stab wounds. Not so much as an appendix scar marred the smooth contours of the belly. Only the blue-grey tinge of the skin, and the extreme flaccidity of the muscles, would have told the casual observer that death had indeed visited this ordinary little room.

'We can speculate,' replied the GP, 'but only the post-mortem will tell us for sure. A young girl at a party . . . drugs must be high on the list: drugs and alcohol. I can't see any vomitus in the upper airways, but she may have inhaled and sucked it down.'

'What about natural causes?' asked Sergeant Bird.

'That's always a possibility. She may have a ruptured ectopic pregnancy, or there's unsuspected heart disease, pulmonary embolism, subarachnoid haemorrhage . . . none of these gives specific external signs. We need to find out if she complained of symptoms to anyone earlier in the evening. Constable Phelps has been trying to ascertain who last saw her alive.'

'That's right, sir.' The young constable materialised in the doorway. 'The latest sighting we have is from a Dr Verity, who was standing near her in the main party room until about ten fifteen. He's still on the premises: he was one of the couple who found the body.'

Montgomery nodded an acknowledgement. 'I'll go and speak to some of these people myself,' he said. 'Thank you for your help, Dr Greaves. I hope you get a bit of sleep tonight.'

The GP smiled politely, but made no attempt to leave the room. 'I'm just going to carry out one final examination,' he said.

A row of cowed, frightened faces greeted Montgomery as he entered the living-room. Only Robin Winterley looked bleakly furious, as if these events shouldn't have happened in his flat.

Most people's party finery was crumpled, as battered as their emotions, but in one corner a psychedelically costumed Donald Duck and a well-cantilevered French maid were incongruous in their splendour.

'Mr Winterley,' Montgomery said, 'we need to speak briefly and separately to everyone here in order to get the best picture of events. Is there a room you can put at our disposal for two or three hours?'

Robin shrugged and half-turned to view his own living-room, its litter of plates, glasses and audio cassettes, all the stigmata of an otherwise successful party. 'This is our main room,' he said. 'Two of the bedrooms are converted into studies for Fran and myself, but they're scarcely eight feet square.'

'One of those would be ideal. Perhaps you'd just show us the general layout of the flat first, then we'll start the interviews by discussing the background situation with you.'

The surgeon nodded, thin-lipped,and preceded the detectives into the corridor. The door opposite stood ajar, a rattle of dishes issuing from the other side; Robin pushed it open. 'The kitchen,' he said.

By the sink Fran Winterley and a shorter, less svelte young woman with wavy blonde hair paused with their tea-towels.

'Oh,' blurted out Fran's companion. 'Please don't think we're callous . . . We just had to *do* something . . .'

'A sensible idea,' said Montgomery. 'You are – ?'

'Mrs Pritchard. Susan. Barry and I are friends of Robin and Fran. We live across the courtyard.' She pointed out past the screened window.

'They kindly helped us to organize our party,' added Fran.

'I see.' Montgomery made a quick assessment of the room, noting the contents of the draining board, the culinary detritus on the breakfast bar, the fact that the only doorway was the one where he stood. He had already spotted the other side of the serving hatch in the living-room.

With Sergeant Bird at his shoulder he inspected the rest of the flat. The large, comfortable double bedroom had clearly been in use by party guests: the cream linen bedspread lay askew, hairs were scattered across the glass top of the dressing-table, and a lingering afterbouquet of perfume hung sweet-sour in the nostrils.

'We let people leave their coats on the bed,' said Robin tersely. 'That's why it's rumpled.'

The next two rooms were former bedrooms which had indeed been converted into studies. The first was particularly spartan, containing only a chair, a chipboard desk with a word processor, a filing cabinet and two wall-mounted bookshelves. Montgomery's gaze flicked across document wallets, dictionaries and a box of paper on the lower shelf. The walls were white, the carpet a blue and beige mix.

'Fran does freelance typing in here,' explained Robin. 'My study is next door.' He led the way into a much plusher room, decorated in brown and scarlet. Fitted mahogany bookshelves filled with journals and textbooks occupied the whole of two walls, and the matching desk had a brown leather inlay with gold tooling. The adjustable chair was thickly padded with soft chestnut leather, as was the three-seater sofa beneath the window. 'Use this room if you want,' offered their host.

'Thank you, I shall.'

This was the last room before the corridor turned through a right angle leading to the hall area. As they emerged and rounded the corner, Robin tried to pass an unobtrusive door on the left without comment, but Montgomery stopped him. 'What's in here?' he asked.

'Just the utility cupboard. Vacuum cleaner, ironing board, cleaning agents, light bulbs, candles. Here . . .' He threw open the door and flicked a switch, illuminating an area of five by three feet which smelt of polish. They moved on to the bathroom with its cream-coloured suite and springy, luxurious carpet. Montgomery paused by the mirror-fronted medicine chest. 'May I?' he asked. Given licence by a bare nod of acquiescence, he made a desultory examination of the various packets and bottles inside. Most were proprietary preparations, but an empty brown glass bottle on a small shelf above Robin's shaving equipment must have once held prescribed medicine. The label was torn, and barely legible.

'Do you know anything about this?' enquired Montgomery.

Robin frowned. 'Must be some old bottle of Fran's. I don't know why it's still in the cupboard. Shall I ask her?'

'No, I'll do that myself. Does everything here look in order?'

'I suppose so . . . yes.'

'You're sure?'

'Yes.'

'Good.'

As they left the bathroom Sergeant Bird, who had stayed out in the hall, approached Montgomery. 'Dr Greaves would like another word,' he whispered.

Montgomery turned to the surgeon. 'Perhaps you'll go with Sergeant Bird to your study, and I'll join you as soon as I can.' He waited until they had rounded the bend in the passageway, then walked reluctantly towards the death room. Constable Phelps stood aside as he reached the door and knocked gently; it opened immediately and again he saw the dark spread of hair and the long limbs, coffin-straight in contrast, that had been Loretta Dawes.

Even with the door closed behind them, Dr Greaves leaned forward confidentially, and kept his voice low. 'She was pregnant,' he said. 'There's no evidence as yet that this had a bearing on the cause of death, but . . . she was definitely pregnant. Three months gone.'

'Excuse me,' said Sergeant Bird from his seat under the window in Robin's study. 'I have you down as Mr Robin Winterley, yet I believe that you're a doctor. Does that mean you're a surgeon?'

'Yes.' Robin Winterley looked hostile and uncomfortable perched next to the desk on the chair they had commandeered from Frances's workroom. 'One loses the title of doctor on gaining the Fellowship exam; it's a rather archaic convention.'

'What level are you?' asked Montgomery, who was established at the desk.

'Senior registrar. I'm due to take up a consultant post in Southampton shortly.'

'How shortly?'

'Three weeks' time.'

'I see . . .' Montgomery remembered noticing a 'For Sale' board in the street outside the block of flats. 'Bad time for selling property,' he said.

'I know. Fran's staying on for a few weeks to try to get something arranged at this end. In the mean time, I've been offered hospital accommodation in Southampton.'

'Mm. Tell me about your party, Mr Winterley.'

'Well . . . It was essentially a leaving party. My boss, Leo Masters, made a presentation with the usual kind of witty speech, and I replied in the same vein . . . Everything was very jolly . . .'

'I've seen some people in fancy dress. Was that optional?'

'Yes, in a sense. You see, another party clashed with ours, and we said that individuals could come here afterwards if they wanted. Saturday would have been better for our do, but Leo had longstanding plans for visiting his son at boarding school this weekend. As it was, Barry Pritchard and I had to take a couple of hours off work to get things ready.'

'Was every guest here tonight invited specifically by you?'

'It started off that way, but then word spread and people began to ask their friends along, especially the nurses. In fairness, though, seven years as a surgeon in the same district, and mostly at the same hospital, means that you've built up relationships with staff from all sorts of departments, from Theatre to Administration. I was flattered so many wanted to come.'

'How well did you know Loretta Dawes?'

'Reasonably well. She was a third-year student nurse on Ward 7, where most of our patients are.'

'Did she have a specific invitation?'

'All the nurses from that ward did, from Sister Brocklebank downwards. Loretta came with her friend Alison Blake, who's another student nurse.'

Montgomery penned the name 'Alison' on his notepad, even though a perfectly competent scribe was at work by the window. 'Was Loretta engaged?' he asked.

'Er, no. Not that I'm aware of.'

'Going out with someone?'

'I've no idea.'

'A girl with her looks . . .' Montgomery flicked his cool blue eyes to Winterley's face. 'It would seem likely, wouldn't it?'

'Yes, but I'm not going to make guesses. You'll have to ask Alison. Or Paula.'

'Paula?'

'Another friend of Loretta's. They all live in the Nurses' Home.'

'Surname?' asked Sergeant Bird in the background.

'I'm not sure. Thompkins, I think.'

Montgomery took up a new position in the chestnut chair. 'What time did Loretta arrive here?' he asked.

Robin pondered. 'Eightish?' he murmured. 'No, they came after John and Pete. Perhaps eight thirty, or going up to nine.'

'Tell me her movements as far as you can remember them.'

Robin gave a helpless shrug. 'I'll try, but . . . there were probably a hundred and twenty people crammed in our flat at the height of the evening!'

'Do your best.'

'Let's see . . . Loretta and Alison started off in the kitchen, like most of the guests, because Fran and Sue were serving the food in there. It was a kind of risotto, easy to do in bulk. Then I saw them in the living-room . . . yes, Loretta was dancing with Pete at one point. I think I glimpsed her in the circle when Leo was presenting me with the decanter, but after that – I don't know.'

'What was she drinking?'

'White wine, I think.'

'Did she drink a lot?'

'I can't say. Barry and I were running the bar at the beginning, but later on people helped themselves.'

'Were there spirits on offer?'

'A few, but it was mainly wine and beer.'

'Mm . . . So you last saw her at the presentation. What time was this?'

'Ten-ish. I remember looking at my watch when some of the fancy dress crowd appeared shortly afterwards.'

'And you didn't see her again alive?'

'No.' The surgeon looked gaunt as Montgomery paused for thought. 'Is that all?' he asked.

'Just a few more questions. We'll take formal statements tomorrow. I'd like to hear about how the body was found: when, and by whom.'

'We told your constable . . . Sonia Ball, a young secretary from the surgical office, went into the end bedroom to fetch her coat. She found the body, showed Peter Verity, her companion at the time, then ran to the kitchen to fetch me.

'I went in. Loretta was on the bed . . . I lifted her on to the floor because the bed was soft. I was going to try resuscitation, but Pete stopped me. He said she was already dead – and he was right.'

'Had you thought she might be alive?' asked Montgomery quietly.

'I . . .' Robin's face looked grey. 'I think I was acting on instinct – a reflex, if you like. In hospitals we get used to intervening. We can't let go. I suppose I couldn't believe that a young girl could be dead like that, without any kind of warning . . .'

There was a pause. 'This Peter Verity,' said William Bird prosaically. 'Is that Mr?'

'No: Dr. He's Kevin Cox's senior house officer.'

'Mate of yours?'

'Yes. We used to work together for Leo Masters, but the SHOs rotate on to other teams.'

'I see. Thank you.'

Robin squared his shoulders and jutted out his chin, clear preliminaries to an attempt to close the interview.

'Just one more thing,' said Montgomery swiftly.

'Yes?'

'I hope you won't find this question offensive, but it's something we must ask . . . Did you see or hear of any drug-taking at the party, especially among members of Loretta's circle?'

'Certainly not! There was none of that sort of thing here. We weren't holding a bloody rave!' Despite Montgomery's caveat, Robin Winterley's neck was corded with outrage.

55

'You'll understand we have to explore all avenues when a young woman dies mysteriously like this. Have you heard any rumours at the Victoria of drug-taking among the nursing staff?'

'No. Nothing. And in any case, Loretta and her friends would never have involved themselves in things of that nature. They're all busy, happy girls.'

The sequitur wasn't, thought Montgomery wryly; these days it was not just the bored or disadvantaged who dabbled with the dubious pleasures of Ecstasy and its fellows. Still, Robin Winterley seemed sincere in these particular views. It would be most useful to question the girl Alison next. 'Loretta's friend Alison,' he said. 'Is she still here?'

'I'm afraid not. She went home early: got a lift with Sister Brocklebank.'

'What about the other girl you mentioned – Paula?'

'I don't know if she was here; I'll have to ask around. She's definitely not here now.'

'Very well. Thank you, Mr Winterley. We'll have a word now with your wife, if we may.'

As Robin left, they heard confused sounds outside, and a female voice raised in supplication. Constable Phelps leaned round the lintel. 'Mrs Pritchard would like to see you, sir.'

'Let her come in.'

Montgomery stood up as Susan Pritchard edged into the room, agitated and tearful, accompanied by a skinny young man with flaxen hair and a weak chin, whose left arm was nevertheless curved protectively around her shoulders.

'I'm sorry, Inspector,' she snuffled, 'I don't like to speak out of turn, but . . . would it be possible for Barry and me to be interviewed soon? It's Tommy, you see, my little boy . . . Mother is supervising both the children tonight, but he might wake up, and need me. And she'll be so worried herself. She always waits up. I rang her to say we'd be late, but that was hours ago . . .'

'Go home,' said Montgomery. 'Constable Phelps took your details, didn't he? We'll see you later on.'

'No – please. We want to help. Can't we do it now?'

Montgomery indicated the chair and Sue sat down gratefully, blowing her nose while Barry stood behind.

'Tell me what you know of Loretta,' invited Montgomery.

'I didn't know her very well, because I'm not at the hospital myself, but I met her at hospital dinners, and an evening here, and the review . . . she was beautiful, and very popular with the menfolk!' She gave a watery smile and squeezed Barry's hand. 'Barry saw much more of her, as he'll tell you. He used to say she had terrific legs.'

'Who was her boyfriend?' Montgomery eyed them both.

'Someone said she was seeing a chap called Gordon,' supplied Barry. 'A dental technician, apparently.'

'But he wasn't here tonight?'

'No.'

'Whom did she come with?' A little cross-checking wouldn't hurt.

'Alison Blake. They'd been student nurses together for three years.'

'Tell me what you saw of Loretta this evening: you first, Mrs Pritchard.'

'Oh . . . not very much. I was in the kitchen with Fran until the speeches. Let me think . . . John was sitting with us, so Loretta and Alison must have arrived after him – eight thirtyish, I'd say. We gave them each a plate of food, then they went through quite promptly to join the party. We carried on serving food and washing up until around ten, when Mr Masters presented Robin with a decanter, because he's leaving soon. I did see Loretta then; she was standing across the room, close to Peter Verity. And a bit later I saw her talking to a group of people in fancy dress who had just come in. But after that . . . I don't remember coming across her again.'

'Thank you. Dr Pritchard?'

Barry blinked nervously. 'It's as Sue said. The girls started off together, then they split up in the room where the dancing was. I saw them eating by one of the windows, then Loretta went to speak to Leo Masters. Later on she was dancing with Pete Verity. I can't say I noticed where she was after that, but the flat was very crowded.'

'What was she drinking?'

'White wine – Soave. I poured it. And Alison had pineapple juice.'

'Did either of you see her stagger, or look unwell?'

They shook their heads.

'She yawned a bit,' said Sue. 'During the speeches. They weren't boring – very funny, actually.'

'Right. Just one more thing . . .' Montgomery broached the ticklish subject of drugs, and received wide-eyed denials that any such thing went on among people they knew. He escorted them to the door. 'I'd be grateful if you would write down the names of every party guest you recognized tonight, and brief descriptions for any who were unfamiliar,' he said. He would be asking the Winterleys to do the same.

'Of course . . . anything.'

He turned back to Sergeant Bird, closing the door behind him. 'The pregnancy doesn't seem to be common knowledge, does it?' he murmured.

'No, sir. But her cronies from the Nurses' Home may well be in the know.'

'It's a pity they're not here. What's the time now? Heavens, four thirty. We must interview this Verity boy, the girl who found the body and Frances Winterley, but let's be as brief as possible with the rest. Have they taken the body away yet?'

A low rumble sounded in the corridor.

'They're just doing that now, sir.'

6

'This is awful,' said Peter Verity.

Like Robin Winterley, he looked Montgomery straight in the eye, and like Robin Winterley he was unfairly handsome, but then the differences began. Winterley's good looks were of the smooth, tanned, arrogant type, whereas Verity, despite his Roman nose, was much more boy-next-door. The senior registrar was in his mid-thirties, the SHO his mid-twenties; Verity conceded three inches in height.

He appeared completely dismayed.

'I agree,' said Montgomery. 'We'll keep this as brief as

possible. As you can imagine, we've been trying to ascertain how Loretta spent the hours before she was discovered, in the hope of finding clues to the circumstances of her death. She was seen in your company for part of the evening . . . Did you know Loretta well?'

'Yes.' The answer came without preamble. 'We were good friends. She was almost like one of the lads, despite her obvious feminine attributes. She used to come on CAMRA club outings – you know, real ale.'

'Did she have a lot of boyfriends?'

'Quite a few. With all she had to offer, it's hardly surprising. Lorrie and I had a brief fling ourselves a couple of years ago, but it was never anything serious. Since then, there have been various men in her life. The latest is a quiet little chap in the Dental Department; she's seemed really happy with him.'

'He wasn't here tonight, though.'

'That's not unusual. Lorrie liked to go out in a group with the other nurses, have fun in a general sort of way. People often attend hospital parties without their partners.'

'When you encountered her here, was she acting normally?'

Peter was briefly silent, considering. 'More or less,' he said. 'Her manner was a bit abrupt, but she relaxed when we had a few dances.'

'Did she say anything about feeling ill?'

'No.'

'Did she dance with reasonable vigour?'

'Nobody did in our part of the room: there were too many people. We just swayed on the spot.'

'What happened then?'

'Well, Barry turned the music off and announced that Leo Masters was going to address us. We shuffled into a rough circle, and Leo strode into the centre brandishing a heavy boxed gift for Robin, and began his peroration. Someone pushed Robin forwards; he pretended to be taken by surprise, but of course he knew all along, because his reply was much too polished. Everyone was laughing at the jokes, and I lost contact with Loretta at that point because a nurse I know from Theatre squeezed in between us.'

'Who was this?'

'Her name's Brenda Sykes. I ended up dancing with her shortly afterwards; Loretta had wandered off.'

'What time are we talking about here?'

'Ten-ish. Maybe half-past.'

'Did you see Loretta again?'

Peter Verity looked at him oddly. 'You mean alive? No.' His lips drew together.

'You were one of the first to find the body, I believe.'

'That's right. I was ready to go home about half-past one, and Sonia Ball, who was my companion by then, wanted to fetch her coat from the little bedroom near the front hall. She came out of the room very agitated, and told me she thought a girl in there was dead. I checked for myself, and it was true.'

He leaned forward earnestly. 'Sonia will be telling you this herself, but she actually saw Loretta in there at least two hours earlier, and thought it was someone sleeping off too much alcohol.'

'Indeed?' Montgomery added to his own list of personal notes with a stirring of interest. '*Did* Loretta drink a lot?' he enquired.

'Two or three glasses of white wine – nothing excessive.'

'Did she take any medicine in your company? Aspirins, or whatever?'

'No.'

'How about recreational drugs?'

'No. She was far too sensible.'

'Did anybody else take drugs?'

'Not that I heard of.'

'I see . . . Thank you for your time, Dr Verity. Please would you ask the young lady Sonia if she will come and speak to us?'

Peter nodded, stood up, then clapped a hand to the top of his head, murmuring, 'Christ!'

'Problems?' asked Montgomery.

'Yes: had a bit of a skinful myself, I'm afraid. "The wrath of grapes" . . . or in this case, hops.' He summoned a wry smile and left the room cautiously.

'Seemed sober enough to me,' muttered Sergeant Bird.

'I think his testimony will still be reliable,' agreed Montgomery. 'Of course, the bottom line will be the result of the PM

– but if drugs do prove to be the cause, we still need to know who was with her and who supplied them . . .'

Sonia Ball, pale and dishevelled, but nonetheless voluptuous, crept in to recount her story in a light and husky voice, but few new facts emerged. 'I didn't even know her name,' she told them sadly. Only when she had gone did it occur to Montgomery to clarify the arrangement for coats. When Frances Winterley took Sonia's place, that was the subject of his first question.

'We started off using those few brass hooks in the hall,' she said, 'but once their capacity was exceeded, we allowed people to leave coats and jackets on our own bed; it meant that the dressing-table mirror was available if anyone needed it, and our little wash-basin. There was a tacit understanding that the other rooms nearby were not for use – apart from the bathroom, of course.'

'Why do you think Sonia got it wrong?'

'That's easy to explain. Earlier on, we'd decided that either Robin or Barry would greet the guests on arrival, tell them about the food and where they could leave their coats. But later, they became involved with other things, and there was such a crush in the corridor that whoever was nearest the front door would open it. Sonia came just as the speeches started. She was given no advice, and must have simply chosen the first bedroom she found.'

'I understand. She left her coat on the bed, then some time later Loretta came and lay down on it. When did you last see Loretta yourself, Mrs Winterley?'

'I saw her with two of the influx of guests from the Radiology party, just before half-past ten. They were dressed as a cowboy and an Indian, and were both girls, although I can't give you their names because they were masked. I probably wouldn't know them, anyway, because I don't work at the hospital now.'

Ten thirty again, thought Montgomery. No one admitted to having seen Loretta after this time, except for Sonia Ball, who had found her sleeping, but alive, shortly after eleven o'clock. Now it was five o'clock, and everyone was desperately tired . . .

He possessed the main background information. The post-mortem to follow could well reveal some tragic, but perfectly natural cause of death. The time had come to wind up tonight's enquiries and await the result. He would see those few remaining guests in the living-room together, as briefly as possible.

'Thank you, Mrs Winterley,' he said. 'Sergeant Bird and I will just have a few words with the group still waiting, then everyone can go to bed. In the mean time, would you please check that nothing's missing from your medicine chest – Loretta might have borrowed something she shouldn't. I'd also like you and your husband to write down as many names of party guests as you can remember. I've asked the Pritchards to do the same.'

'Of course. Right now?'

'The names will do later.'

She nodded and glided out of the room, tall and faintly opalescent in the blue silk outfit.

'Handsome couple, the Winterleys,' said Sergeant Bird.

'Yes; this has put a black on their celebrations. I hope they weren't stupid enough to be involved with drugs.' Montgomery yawned, then stretched both arms up above his head until one shoulder joint cracked. 'Let's speak to Donald Duck and Co in a group, and simply ask if anyone saw Loretta after ten thirty.' He waited while Sergeant Bird heaved his large frame out of its chestnut leather cocoon and tucked his notebook into a pocket. As they turned to leave the room they had a fleeting view of Frances Winterley passing the doorway from the direction of the bathroom. Her face was oddly rigid with a look of fearful determination.

'You go ahead, Will,' murmured Montgomery. 'Make a start; I'll be with you shortly.' Something was jarring here. The Frances Winterley who had just been answering their questions had been a woman almost glacially composed. He peered up the passageway before the bulk of his sergeant blocked his line of vision; Frances had opened the door to the living-room, checked inside then immediately withdrawn. Now she was entering the kitchen.

As the living-room door closed behind Sergeant Bird, Montgomery prepared to knock on the kitchen door. His knuckles were inches from the wood when the muted sound of voices reached him.

'. . . tell you something.' Fran Winterley.

'Can't it wait? I've had as much as I can take tonight.' That was Robin.

'No. It's important. Please, Robin.'

'Go on, then. If you must . . . What have you got there?'

Silence for several seconds, then a shaky, almost unrecognizable voice . . . 'Do you remember, after James . . . I couldn't sleep for months and Dr Chadwick gave me various tablets. The only sort that worked were very strong . . . He – he told me to throw them away when I didn't need them any more, because they were dangerous to keep. You told me that, too . . .' A cough. 'Well, I *did* keep them. Very occasionally, I've needed one. But now – Robin, they've gone! They were in this bottle!'

'What are you talking about, Fran?' Robin sounded harsh and impatient. 'You probably finished them yourself. What tablets? This label's no bloody good.'

'Please listen to me. There were capsules in the bottle, and now they've gone.'

More silence, and a tension so strong Montgomery could feel it beating in waves against the door.

'Capsules,' repeated Robin at last. 'Let's get this straight. Do you mean those barbiturate capsules you were given four years ago?'

The monosyllabic reply was too faint to identify.

'The ones I specifically told you to destroy? You, a doctor's wife?'

'Yes.'

'How many were there?'

Nothing. 'Come on, Fran. I have to know. How many capsules were left – approximately?'

'The bottle was almost full.'

'Christ, Fran!'

'Robin, I'm so sorry. I never dreamt . . .'

'Be quiet. Let me assimilate this. If what you say is true, then perhaps it has a bearing on what happened tonight. But it doesn't make sense; it doesn't make sense at all. Are you sure you're not mistaken?'

'I wish I were, truly.'

The dialogue stopped, and Montgomery strained his ears, wondering what they were doing: examining the bottle, perhaps. Suddenly he heard an exclamation from Robin Winterley.

'Ah! I remember now. It can't have been full. Dr Chadwick only gave you a very limited number on each prescription, didn't he? Something like fifteen.'

There was a tiny sob.

'Isn't that so, Fran?'

'Yes . . . but – I stockpiled them. I saved them because there was a time when I felt as if I might want to take – a lot, all together . . .'

'Melodrama!' His voice was savage.

'It's true, I swear to you. The bottle was virtually full.' Steps sounded on the linoleum floor, then a muffled thud, as if someone had backed into a kitchen cupboard. 'Please don't be angry, Robin. I know everything's my fault. Tell me what to do. I can't think straight . . .'

'Do? There's only one thing to do! We've got to tell that Montgomery fellow right now, and take the consequences.'

Montgomery had flitted back to the study by the time the Winterleys sought him out. Fran's movements were stiff with reluctance, her face white with guilt and fear. Robin at first glance looked merely implacable, but as he stepped over the threshold the glint in his eye and the flare of his nostrils betrayed a cold fury.

'Inspector,' he said, 'my wife has something to tell you.'

7

'I can't confirm amylobarbitone as the cause of death,' said Frobisher, striding into the mortuary ante-room and peeling off his gloves. He eyed Montgomery and Sergeant Bird in turn over his half-moon spectacles. 'But that doesn't mean to say it wasn't. Only the blood samples and gastric contents analysis will tell us for sure.'

'Were there any indications at all?' asked Montgomery.

The pathologist flung himself into a chair and steepled his fingers. 'Indirectly,' he said after a moment's pause. 'I found a small area of inflammation in the stomach wall – that's non-specific, of course, but unusual in a young girl who appeared to have enjoyed excellent health. Now the barbiturates are weak acids themselves – much weaker than stomach acid. But chemically speaking, amylobarbitone in the form of sodium amytal is actually the salt of a weak acid and a strong base – are you with me? So when it hits the stomach, the alkali is released and it can strip the mucosa, the surface layer, causing erosions. I've seen it before: suicidal lad fifteen years ago swallowed nine grams of the stuff, and the capsules impacted in his oesophagus, making an awful mess of the tissues. But with him it was obvious. A lot of the capsular material was still present, some intact, some as a gelatinous sludge. And the turquoise dye had stained his stomach wall. I can't find any such signs in Loretta, though, at least not macroscopically. There was some partially digested food in her stomach; we'll examine it carefully for colour pigment and other excipients.'

'Excipients?' echoed Sergeant Bird.

Frobisher gave one of his fleeting, humourless smiles, a reflex twitching of muscles which rarely indulged in exercise. 'Packing material,' he said. 'Drugs manufacturers put substances like lactose or starch granules into their products in order to fill them out, make them a decent size to take. Some hormone preparations, for instance, have dosages in micrograms. The amount of active substance would be so small, you'd hardly be able to see the pill! Excipients can also aid the actual digestion of a drug . . .'

Montgomery watched Frobisher's face, and tried to imagine him teaching students at the university, which he still did on an intermittent basis. Like Dr Greaves, Frobisher was elderly and dry. One couldn't envisage him cracking jokes to liven up the proceedings, or creating memorable images. His lectures would be heavily didactic. Yet how often was it the bizarre illustration which lodged a point in a student's mind, sometimes for ever?

Changes were coming. Within two years, both Frobisher and Greaves would be retired. Montgomery had built up a solid relationship with both, and trusted their judgement and professionalism. A part of him wanted to hang on to this security, especially since whispers of upheaval in his own sphere of work were gaining volume, yet perversely another part found the prospect of new blood appealing.

'We don't often come across barbiturate poisoning these days,' Frobisher was saying. 'Along with morphine and the like, the barbiturates are Controlled Drugs, prescribable only in a strictly defined way. And there aren't many indications left for their use. The very short-acting forms like thiopentone are still used in anaesthesia, and the long-acting ones like phenobarbitone have a valuable role in the treatment of epilepsy, but the intermediate forms? They should only be prescribed for insomnia if all else fails, and even then only to patients already taking a barbiturate. Mrs Winterley isn't epileptic, is she?'

'No.'

'Then if you ask me, her GP was a fool.'

'Mr Winterley implied as much,' said Montgomery, with expedient understatement. Robin Winterley had actually delivered a biting tirade against fossilized GPs with antiquated prescribing habits, too arrogant or too incompetent to modify these habits in the face of new therapeutic philosophies . . . It was the closest he had come to a defence of his wife.

'Well, I'll contact you as soon as I get the toxicology results,' promised Frobisher. 'Then we'll know if we're barking up the right tree.'

When the telephone call came, Montgomery took it himself, and immediately left his office to track down his sergeant in the larger communal room shared by junior CID officers.

William Bird was at his desk, scowling into the computer monitor. Although he had finally been forced to face the demands of progress and acquire an elementary computer literacy, his attitude to the machines remained defiantly adversarial. He refused to regard them as friends. 'There,' he murmured, punching a key with a large blunt forefinger, 'see if *that* suits you any better!'

'If you break it, you certainly won't get the answer you want,' grinned Montgomery, drawing alongside the desk. 'You're not meant to attack each key like a piledriver.'

'Sorry. I got used to typing like that . . . Are you off to the canteen?'

'No. Frobisher's just been on the phone. The blood results are through: Loretta did receive a lethal dose of amylobarbitone.'

The sergeant pulled his lips together in a soundless whistle and nodded his head slowly, twice. His expression was abstracted. 'Are we looking at suicide, then?'

'I don't know. Remember what Frobisher told us about finding no material from the capsules? The lab have endorsed this in their analysis of the gastric contents. There's no trace of the dye, Patent Blue V, or gelatine, or silicone, or uncooked starch . . . Just the drug, the selfsame uncommon drug that has gone missing from the Winterleys' bathroom cabinet. That can't be coincidence, but what are we to make of it?'

They sat together for five minutes, pondering the ramifications of the forensic results. 'Something must have upset Loretta at the party,' began William Bird at last. 'Perhaps some aspect of the pregnancy. She gets emotional, rushes into the bathroom and rifles the cabinet for something to take: anything. She wants it to work quickly so she empties the contents of each capsule into a glass of water and flushes the shells down the loo. Then she drinks the solution, and returns to the party. Soon she feels drowsy – and wanders away to find somewhere to die . . .'

'There was no note,' objected Montgomery, 'accusatory or otherwise. I accept that dizziness might have overwhelmed her and rendered writing impossible, but the scenario has other problems, too. We've been told there was a constant queue for the bathroom . . . How long do you think it would take to prise open each of fifty capsules and make a solution of their contents? People would have been kicking the door down . . . And if she was upset enough for suicide – distraught, illogical, emotions heightened by alcohol – would she really spend time on something so fiddly, so precise? Wouldn't she just cram fistfuls of the capsules into her mouth, washing down as many as she could?'

'I suppose so,' conceded Sergeant Bird.

'And why did no one *see* her looking so upset? The most anyone noticed was an expression of "pique" early on in the evening.'

'We haven't been asking that specific question, sir. We asked if she complained of feeling ill.'

'Well, we'll ask it now.' Montgomery stood up, uneasy, determined. 'We'll speak to all the names on that list of Winterley's, and find out who those fancy dress people were. We'll also interview all Loretta's work colleagues, whether they were at the party or not. There's more to this case than meets the eye.'

Ward 7 was a long, old-fashioned ward with a row of curtained beds on either side of the central nightingale. Sister Brocklebank, a sturdy, pleasant-faced woman of fifty, greeted the two detectives in the doorway of the cramped ward office; the ward clerk in the background, on hearing their names, paused from her filing and glanced their way with surreptitious curiosity.

'I've earmarked the relatives' waiting-room for us,' said Sister Brocklebank. She led the way up the corridor and held open the door to a small, orange-carpeted room with easy chairs and magazines. 'Sorry about the smell of smoke. You said you wanted to discuss Loretta?'

Montgomery appreciated her directness. 'Yes,' he replied. 'Tests have shown that she died of barbiturate poisoning. We need to establish if these were self-administered.'

'Good Lord,' said Sister Brocklebank softly. 'Barbiturates . . . that's quite a shock: we were all expecting to hear that she'd had a brain haemorrhage, or defective heart valve, or something.'

'You didn't think she might have overdosed on drugs and alcohol?'

'No – she wasn't like that. She was eminently sensible. Calculating, almost.'

'We want you to tell us all you can about Loretta, her work and her character. I believe she did much of her training on this ward.'

68

'That's right. She started off with us as a first-year student, rotated through various other departments then came back here in the spring. She was always very quick to learn, and confident both with procedures and with people. When she asked me recently if I would be a referee for the purposes of her job applications, she said she felt ready to manage a ward herself, as a staff nurse.'

'Did she ever discuss personal matters with you? Boyfriends, money problems?'

'I've tried to encourage all my nurses to look upon me as someone they could talk to, who would be discreet. There is a personnel department, of course, but the people there are remote from most working units. Several nurses have asked me for advice over the years, but I can't say Loretta was one of them. She joined in with the general chat, as you'd expect, over lunch or when staff were gathering to hear the Report. People would discuss their weekend activities, or plan forthcoming events, just as they do in any workplace. Loretta always seemed to have an active social life.'

'Did she have a boyfriend?'

'Her name was sometimes coupled with that of Gordon Mudge, one of the dental technicians, but I don't know if he was a boyfriend as such. Her peers will probably know.'

Montgomery nodded. 'Yes; we intend to see her friend Alison Blake. Can you tell me anything about their relationship?'

Sister Brocklebank gave a faint smile. 'They were an odd couple in many ways: Loretta, outgoing and devastatingly attractive, Alison, shy, awkward and worried about her weight. But I've seen it before. It's like marriages of opposites: both parties gain from the whole the pieces they lack themselves. At least, I believe that's the theory.

'They went through their training together, and even though they sometimes worked in different wards or departments, they remained close friends until a few months ago, when I got the impression that Loretta had – moved on, as it were. She seemed to find more in common with Paula Thompkins. Alison was very down. But then Loretta and Paula had some sort of quarrel, and she picked up the threads with Alison again.'

'They arrived at the party together,' said Montgomery.

'Yes.'

'But Alison left early.'

'I gave her a lift. She was in the hall, waiting to phone for a taxi, but one of the registrars was monopolizing the telephone.'

'What time was this?'

'Around ten thirty. A few minutes after the speeches.'

'Did she say why she wanted to leave?'

'Not in so many words. But she looked tired; Alison often has migraines. She commented that the music was very loud . . . I think she'd just had enough.'

'Did either of you mention Loretta?'

'I did. I asked Alison if Loretta was staying, and she said something like, "Lorrie's in safe hands. I don't want to intrude."'

'Did she specify?'

'No.'

'Did you see much of Loretta at the party yourself?'

'Odd flashes and a few words in the corridor, that's all. It was *very* crowded. She seemed to spend most of the evening with Peter Verity.' Her face suddenly clouded. 'Poor Peter; he found the body, didn't he?'

'Mm. They were old flames, I gather.'

'Yes. Peter has always been popular with the nurses. He's both good-looking and approachable – but splendidly amoral. A love 'em and leave 'em type. Every hospital has at least one. It doesn't seem to stop the girls from trying their luck, though. They all think they'll be the one to tame him. In many ways, I felt that he and Loretta made a good couple.'

'You say he's popular; what about Loretta?'

The pause before Sister Brocklebank replied told its own story.

Staff Nurse Janet Harper replaced her colleague and regarded the detectives sourly. 'I don't know why you asked for me,' she said. 'I only worked with Loretta.' She looked thirty: thin, dark and disappointed, her left hand bare of rings.

'That's why we felt you could help,' Montgomery said mildly.

'But we weren't friends,' she insisted with an air of challenge.

'I'm not going to give her an encomium just because she's dead.'

'We wouldn't want you to.' Witnesses such as Janet Harper could be very valuable.

'I wasn't even at the party.'

'We're simply examining sidelights on Loretta's character at present. I gather she could be calculating . . .'

Recognition flared avidly in her eyes. 'Yes,' she hissed. 'Whatever Loretta wanted, Loretta made sure she got.'

'Can you give an instance of that?'

She seemed momentarily discomfited. 'I was talking generally,' she said.

Montgomery's intuition was equal to the occasion. 'She went out with Peter Verity, didn't she?' he asked in tones of vagueness.

Her mouth became a sharp, bitter line. 'Some time ago.'

'Ah. Who was her current boyfriend, then?'

'She was seeing Gordon Mudge, one of the dental technicians, but I don't think he was a boyfriend as such, unless it was a stopgap. Loretta has always wanted to better herself: she comes from a large family who live in a Mansfield slum. Gordon's prospects would have been too limited for her.'

'We understand that her main girl friends were Alison Blake and Paula Thompkins. What can you tell us about them?'

Janet Harper gave a dismissive shrug. 'Alison is a social no-hoper who consoles herself with religion. Loretta knew that she made the perfect foil whenever they went out together. Paula was more her type, though.'

'But they quarrelled. Do you know why?'

'No, I don't.' She sounded regretful. 'Paula was ideal for Loretta. *Hers* is a family of *nouveaux riches*. They live in Leicestershire in a huge house with a swimming-pool.'

'Have you been there yourself?' asked Sergeant Bird.

'I've seen photographs. Her father's in truck haulage, or something.'

'Does Paula work on this ward?'

'No; she's in Accident and Emergency – Casualty.'

The questions continued.

*

Sergeant Bird pulled a wry face when Janet Harper had gone. 'Full of the milk of human kindness, that one,' he murmured.

'Useful, though,' grinned Montgomery.

'She can't have known about the pregnancy.'

'My thoughts exactly. Can you imagine her holding back the derogatory comments? Never. But who did know, I wonder? Did Gordon Mudge?'

'Pregnant?'

Gordon Mudge gaped at them in a stupor, then sank slowly on to a chair alongside his work-bench. 'Are you sure?' he croaked.

'Certain.'

'Oh . . .' His pallid face was shapeless with distress. Absently he picked up an acrylic prosthesis from a collection nearby, and turned it over in his hands. 'How – how old was the child?' he said at last.

'Three months,' supplied Montgomery.

'Oh . . .' He seemed incapable of further speech.

'How long had you been going out with Loretta?' asked Montgomery.

There was a pause, then Gordon's mild blue eyes began to lose their dazed look and slowly kindle with a new lambency: wariness. 'About four months,' he said carefully, his gaze oscillating between the two detectives. 'The child isn't mine, though. You must believe me. We weren't on those sort of terms.'

'What "terms" were you on?'

'Friendly . . . affectionate. We went out to plays, and concerts and films. Only the cheap seats, but we both liked to see what was going on.'

'Did you regard her as your girlfriend?'

Gordon nodded miserably. 'Yes. I thought we were just – taking things slowly. I didn't want to crowd her, you see . . . She was so beautiful, any man would have been proud to be with her.'

'How often did you go out?'

'Once a week . . . sometime only once a fortnight, because of her studies.'

'You weren't at the party with her.'

'No . . . like I said, I didn't want to crowd her. I knew it would put her off, make her feel suffocated. So I didn't mind if she went to parties and things with the other girls – in fact, I was always pleased when she did, because I felt that gave me, er . . .'

Brownie points for tolerance, thought Montgomery. 'Did Loretta ever mention another man friend to you?' he asked.

'No . . . that is, nobody *concurrent*.' Gordon's rather childlike mouth twisted. He gripped the prosthesis tightly, then seemed to realize what he was doing; carefully he replaced it on the bench and gave a gusty sigh. 'I should have guessed,' he said. 'People like Loretta don't end up with people like me. That's not the way things work, is it? I was just kidding myself . . .'

'Where now?' asked Sergeant Bird minutes later as they left Oral Surgery. 'Alison in the Nurses' Home?'

'No – here's a sign for A and E. Let's try Paula Thompkins first.'

Montgomery strode down a squeaky-clean green corridor, pushed through a pair of glass-panelled doors and asked the sister in charge if he could speak to Paula.

'I'm sorry,' she said with a regretful smile. 'It's her day off. But she'll be working an early shift tomorrow.'

Montgomery rejoined his sergeant clutching a piece of paper which bore a Leicestershire telephone number and address: 'The Grange, Danton-on-the-Wolds, Leicestershire.'

'Paula's not here,' he said. 'Alison it is.'

8

Detective Sergeant William Bird was a kindly man. Although ruddy-cheeked and solidly built, in the typical image of a policeman, he had a character which invited confidences. A widower with no children, he could offer a genuinely sympathetic ear to people who were anxious, in trouble or bereaved. Those who underestimated him, however, usually lived to regret it. He could be as astute and efficient as Montgomery, who had invited him to lead the interview with a young nurse reputed to be shy.

As introductions were made in room 23 of the Nurses' Home, Sergeant Bird studied the girl who had just admitted them. Alison Blake was slightly below middle height and overweight, with mousy hair curling beneath her round chin and earnest eyes of an indeterminate shade of grey.

It was the mouth which rang a warning bell in an otherwise ingenuous face. The subtle twist of bigotry was there: whether moral, religious, or from some other provenance Sergeant Bird could not discern, but he recognized it with the instinct of years.

Her small study-bedroom was nevertheless welcoming. In a building so uniformly drab, functional and ill-lit, effort had been made to create a cosy oasis. Patchwork cushions were scattered over the chairs and bed. Above a shelf of books, another shelf supported a bone china teapot and cluster of matching mugs. A huge rag doll sat in the corner. Family photographs, and posters of birds, beasts and Arthur Rackham's fairy people covered the walls; he half-expected to see a tapestry with the message 'Home Sweet Home' hanging over the bed.

'I'm just admiring your room, Alison,' he told her. 'Did you make the cushions?'

She blushed. 'Some of them, Sergeant Bird, yes. My mother did those two on the chair, and she made the brown and orange rug over there by the wardrobe. She's very clever with a needle or crochet hook.'

'Evidently you take after her. Is that her picture on the desk?'

'Yes.'

'And on this one she's with your father?'

'Yes. He – he doesn't live with us any more.' Her mouth pursed primly.

'I'm sorry to hear that. Have you any brothers or sisters?'

'No, there's just Mother and me. I see her as often as I can. We were about to go for a holiday in Grasmere, and then . . . then this happened to Lorrie. It's terrible. I still can't believe it.'

'I need to ask you a few questions about Loretta, Alison. I know you were a close friend of hers. Would that be all right?'

'Of course. I want to help. I'm sorry . . . please sit down. Would you like a cup of tea before you start? I've got some Earl Grey.'

'My favourite. But later, thank you, if you don't mind . . .' Gently he probed Alison's understanding of the cause of her friend's death; she appeared to be as shocked as Sister Brocklebank when he told her what had happened. No, Loretta had never taken drugs to her knowledge: the odd aspirin, maybe, but that was all . . . Alison chewed agitatedly at her thumb nail, a look of bovine incomprehension on her face.

'I gather you trained with Loretta,' said Sergeant Bird as she assimilated the information.

'Yes, for three years, although we weren't always on the same ward.'

'She was a little older than you, wasn't she?'

'Yes; she did a year at technical college before she decided to become a nurse. I think she had good GCSE and A levels. Certainly she was bright. She sailed through all the nursing exams.'

'What was she like, though, personality-wise? Was she popular with the other nurses?'

Alison thought for a moment. 'Yes and no. She was lively, and could be very good company, but sometimes she would annoy people by being thoughtless. I don't think she meant any harm, she just forgot that others perhaps weren't as quick-witted as she was. She would get impatient with them.'

75

Sergeant Bird decided that Alison was speaking from personal experience. Fleetingly his mind considered the contrast between the two girls, as noted by the other witnesses that morning. The bright girl and the plodder, the leader and the follower, the extrovert and the pale, insipid shadow. Symbiosis, they assumed . . .

But didn't resentment sometimes build up in the more passive partner, slowly, insidiously, until one day something went bang? Maybe the trigger would be quite trivial, in the nature of a last straw. He wondered if Alison were capable of that kind of emotion.

'. . . and the cinema, sometimes,' Alison was saying. 'We might go out with the other nurses for a meal – you know, Chinese or Italian. Those are fun. Of course, she had a lot of boyfriends, so there were periods of several weeks when I hardly saw her except in the canteen.'

'Have *you* got a boyfriend, Alison?'

For the second time she blushed, a mottled stain spreading up her neck to the lobes of her ears.

'Oh no,' she said rapidly.

'Tell me about the people she went out with. Were they from the hospital?'

'Yes, most of them. You see, with us living in, and spending so much time on the hospital campus, it's inevitable that we mainly meet hospital people. And there are a lot of parties. I don't go to many myself, but Lorrie liked to.'

'So did she go out with doctors?'

'One or two. Then medical students, and most recently a dental technician called Gordon.'

'Can you tell me any of their names, Alison?' Sergeant Bird reached for his notebook.

'I'll try. How far back do you want to go?'

'Let's say the last twelve months, plus any former boyfriends who are still working here.'

Alison gave him a list of names hesitantly, adding various comments or qualifying riders to some of them. At the end she tailed off, and sat biting her left thumb nail, a picture of indecision.

'Did you regard Gordon Mudge as Loretta's current boy-friend?' asked the sergeant.

'I . . . yes, I did, but . . .' Alison chewed the nail more fiercely than ever.

'You felt she was lukewarm?' he prompted.

She stopped chewing, her muffin face frozen and oddly desperate.

'Perhaps there was someone else . . .'

The hand fell down to her side as Alison made up her mind. 'Sergeant Bird,' she began, 'I wasn't sure whether to tell anyone this, but – about a week ago, Lorrie hinted that she was having a relationship with – a married man. She didn't say who, but she seemed quite gleeful about it, really happy. I'd never seen her quite like that before. She said it would cause a stir when people found out . . . but she might have been teasing me, you know, pulling my leg because I was prying. It might not have been true at all.'

'Did she say whether he might be at the party?'

'No.'

'Who *was* she with at the party? You, initially, I know, but what about later?'

'She – she spoke to various people. Sister Brocklebank, Mr Masters, Robin Winterley . . . but mainly Peter. She was danc-ing with Peter.'

'This is the Peter Verity you've mentioned? Her old boyfriend?'

'Yes.'

'What was the time when you left with Sister Brocklebank?'

'Oh . . . I don't really know. It seemed late, but it was before eleven, I think.'

'Did you tell Loretta you were going?'

Alison's face registered an alarming series of chameleon colours, ending in a heavy, unbecoming puce. The dimpled arms, the straining flesh beneath her too-tight nurse's uniform, might have rendered her a figure of fun in other circumstances, but neither Sergeant Bird nor his inspector felt the remotest desire to smile. There was misery in the room: reminiscent misery ebbing and surging in thick dirty waves.

'Perhaps you didn't want to bother her?'

Alison stared fixedly at the rag doll. 'I couldn't find her. I looked, but she wasn't there, so I decided to get a taxi because I was on my own and you sometimes meet rough people on the buses at night . . .'

'But Sister Brocklebank gave you a lift.'

'Yes.'

'She said you told her Loretta was in good hands.'

The puce colour deepened. 'I – I assumed she was. Peter's jacket was still on the hook . . .'

'You thought they were together? In a bedroom, perhaps?'

She nodded mutely.

'Even thought they were no longer a couple?'

While Alison licked her dry lips, Sergeant Bird wondered at the stillness of the building, the thick-walled soundlessness all around. Beyond the gay orange curtains straggled a drooping north-facing shrubbery, kept in permanent shade by the branches of a mossy elm tree and the towering walls which enclosed it on three sides.

'Yes,' she said at last. 'Things – can't always be neatly defined, put into compartments . . .'

'I understand. Alison . . .' He spoke gently. 'Did you know that Loretta was pregnant when she died?'

The grey eyes swung his way, wide and stunned, and he heard her sharp intake of breath. Her hand strayed out, seemingly of its own volition, to touch a book on the bedside cabinet, but then jerked back as if its leather cover was electrified.

Across the cover were letters stamped in gold: HOLY BIBLE.

'We've got the names, sir.'

Detective Sergeant Brian Jackson and his colleague, Detective Constable Graham Smythe, converged on Sergeant Bird's desk where Montgomery was discussing aspects of the case in the late afternoon.

'Well done. I suppose the party was bristling with married male doctors.'

'Twelve to be precise,' agreed Jackson. 'But only five are regarded as having worked in close proximity to Loretta over the last few months. Three are surgeons: the two consultants, Leo Masters and Kevin Cox, and Robin Winterley himself, the senior registrar; then there is a Dr Patel, an anaesthetist who does a lot of theatre work with Masters, and finally Barry Pritchard, who was in Casualty with Loretta but has now moved on to a dermatology job.'

Montgomery folded his arms thoughtfully. 'At face value, this is a good lead, and we should run with it,' he said. 'Let's not forget, though, that Loretta might have been feeding Alison a story, provoking a display of moral indignation – or conversely, it may be Alison who is spinning the tale.

'On the assumption that it's genuine, what are our facts? Loretta died during a party at Robin Winterley's flat. Frobisher reckons the fatal dose of amylobarbitone was taken not more than three hours before her death, so she was on the premises at the time. She was three months pregnant, but had withheld this knowledge from those of her friends we have so far interviewed. Her GP knows nothing of the pregnancy, but has confirmed that she was a healthy girl who took no medication – in particular no barbiturates – except for the contraceptive pill.

'We can rule out accidental death. Our choice is either suicide, or murder, and the unborn child could well have been the key factor. Yesterday, Will, you suggested that someone might have upset Loretta at the party. It's possible. Perhaps the father of the child suddenly and shockingly rejected her, and she acted before she had time to calm down. The practical difficulties, however, remain: why did no one see her looking devastated, and why would she waste time dismantling all the capsules?'

'Perhaps it was a planned suicide,' postulated Sergeant Bird. As Jackson and Smythe frowned in puzzlement, he continued: 'She might have waited for Winterley's party in order to make a statement in his own home. A note would therefore have been unnecessary: *he* would have known. And she had visited the flat on a previous occasion, so she could have taken the capsules then, and prepared them in advance.'

'Why bother with that at all?' demanded Jackson.

'Because she was a nurse. She would know the outer coating would delay digestion and absorption of the drug, making it possible that someone would find her in time . . .'

'Feasible, Will,' nodded Montgomery, 'but of course we don't *know* the man involved is Winterley. It could be the consultant Masters, or Kevin Cox. There's also the question of Loretta's own character. She doesn't sound like the sort of girl who would commit suicide just because a man has turned her down. Even the father of her child. So let's now consider the other option . . .

'Sister Brocklebank described Loretta to us as "eminently sensible, calculating, almost." Staff Nurse Harper, admittedly less disinterested in her analyses, told us that whatever Loretta wanted, Loretta got. It's reasonable, therefore, to imagine that Loretta was a girl who would fight for her rights. If someone had treated her badly, she wouldn't just conveniently remove herself from the scene. She had a bargaining chip sitting right there in her uterus. So she would make bargains, or even threats . . .'

'Blackmail,' murmured Jackson.

'Exactly. If the father was a prominent member of the medical hierarchy, she could have ruined him professionally, even in these more liberal times. The night of the party may have been his only chance to act first.'

Graham Smythe had been listening to all this with a mournful expression on his sensitive face, his moist brown eyes gazing at each speaker in turn. 'He may have promised her things, to keep her sweet until he was ready,' he said. 'Or he may have given her presents as a – an earnest of future security: anony-mous-looking gifts, money perhaps.'

'Anything is possible,' agreed Montgomery. 'We need more facts before we can hypothesize any further. Did Loretta keep a diary, letters, cards? They'll either be in the Nurses' Home or in Mansfield. Did she confide in her mother, or Paula Thompkins? We must ask. How significant was the quarrel with Paula? Remember Leo Masters is Paula's uncle . . .'

'DNA fingerprinting would tell us who the baby's father is,' stated Jackson.

'True; the foetal tissue is in storage. But asking for samples is an awfully jackbooted way to start an enquiry. The father may be blameless anyway. It's better if we see how far good

80

groundwork and co-operation will lead us. We don't want a backlash from the medical establishment.'

'"Softly, softly".'

'That's right. Minimally intrusive, minimally invasive – until we're sure of our direction. But you've given me an idea, Brian. Some of those medics will be blood donors. If you can find out even their basic details from the records, it could exclude some of our putative candidates.'

Jackson brightened. 'Will do,' he said.

Janet Harper hauled her bag of laundry up the basement stairs of the Nurses' Home, thin-lipped with displeasure. The washing powder had left white streaks on her navy cotton shirt; she had been obliged to repeat the rinsing cycle – and then that Sykes girl had pipped her in the lunge for the drier. The chore should have been finished an hour ago, not at this time of night, a quarter to twelve.

On the ground floor she staggered along the polished arterial corridor, then turned down a narrower passageway into the north wing of the building. What a dismal place, she thought sourly. High ceilings, dim lights, too many women. Funny, she had never envisaged still being here at the age of thirty. Others had managed to secure the bright rooms and neat flatlets in the hospital's modern tower block down in The Park, but not Janet Harper. Her life was spent commuting between one disinfectant-reeking Victorian edifice and another.

Light footsteps sounded behind her, footsteps in a hurry. As Janet half-turned, Paula Thompkins strode past on the left and muttered an acknowledgement.

Janet wanted more than this. 'Have you been out all day?' she piped.

The question forced Paula to slow down and swing round. Her legs were birdlike in black leggings, and a rucksack was slung between her slender shoulders. 'Yes.' She continued to walk backwards as she replied. 'I went home. But I'm on an "early" tomorrow, so I thought I'd sleep here tonight.'

'You missed the police, then.'

Paula's eyes narrowed. 'What?'

'The police.' Janet put down her laundry bag and stationed herself in the centre of the passage. 'They were asking all sorts of questions about Loretta.'

'Do they know how she died?' Paula's voice sounded restricted; she looked pale.

'Yes.'

'Well, come on, then, tell me. You obviously know.' Now her tone had sharpened.

Janet leaned forward confidentially, even though the corridor around them was empty as far as the eye could see. 'It was drugs,' she hissed. 'Barbiturates.'

'*Rubbish!*'

'It was! The police have been speaking to everyone who knew her, asking about her character, her habits . . . They wanted to know why you fell out with her – was it over drugs?'

Paula stared at her, speechless with contempt.

'You might not like it, but it's true,' insisted Janet. 'I always knew she was no good. Cocksure, grasping, ruthless . . . but this time she went too far.'

'I don't know how you can say such things.' Paula sounded weary. She resumed her walk along the bilious green floor, but the elastic had gone from her tread. After four yards, she turned again. 'Did they say if it was an accident, or what?'

'Must have been.' Janet hadn't moved. 'You don't OD on purpose, do you?'

'Unless . . .'

'Suicide? You know as well as I do, Loretta was far too selfish.'

The squeak of linoleum nearby precluded any further conversation. Seconds later, a short, plump figure bustled into view, voluminous in a fluffy pink dressing-gown.

'Oh – please come,' she gasped.

'What is it, Alison?'

She looked at both of them, then haltingly addressed Paula. 'It's – it's Lorrie. She's come back. I *heard* her.'

Paula and Janet found themselves exchanging glances. 'What do you mean, Alison?'

'I – I heard her. I'd just asked God to send her back again, then there she was, in her room.' Alison's teeth chattered; her cheeks seemed to have taken on the greenish hue of the floor and surrounding walls.

'You *saw* her?' Paula, too, was a strange colour.

'No . . . but I know it was her. The door is locked. It couldn't have been anyone else – and I'd prayed for her to come.'

'Why?' Janet made the question sound like an accusation.

'I – I wanted to tell her I was sorry. It was all my fault. I – I should have waited for her at the party, made sure she was all right. Now she's dead, and the poor little baby, and I didn't even *know* . . .' She clutched the sugar-pink winceyette around her and stared at them with tormented eyes.

'You say you heard something,' Paula said slowly. 'Surely it was the pipes, or someone up above?'

'No! I've lived next door to Lorrie for three years. I know when sounds are coming from her room!'

'What sort of noises did you hear?' asked Janet.

'Scraping sounds . . . furniture being moved.'

'Obviously not a spirit, then,' she said briskly. 'It must have been another room. Let's get you back to bed.' She pushed the laundry bag to the side of the corridor and guided Alison back to the turn-off from which she had emerged, a gloomy cul-de-sac housing rooms 22 to 24.

The three girls passed Alison's room and paused outside number 24, craning towards the dark stout door with its faded brass numerals. Around them, the gaunt building settled ponderously for sleep with random creaks and clicks, but close at hand nothing stirred. Janet held her breath and pressed her ear against the cool wood: beyond was silence. She knocked sharply, then rattled the handle; the door was locked.

'No one in there,' she said. 'How long ago did you hear these noises?'

Alison had shrunk into her fluffy robe, pulling the sides of the shawl collar tightly together under her chin. 'I . . . twenty, maybe thirty minutes ago.' She looked shamefaced. 'I was scared at first. I sat and blocked my ears. Then after the noises had stopped, I waited in case they started again, then came outside to find someone.'

'If you thought you'd got what you asked for, why were you afraid?' The sneer was unmistakable in Janet's voice.

'I suppose I hadn't anticipated an answer – not so soon.' Alison reached into the pocket of her dressing-gown and pulled out her bible, which she grasped with both hands. 'Mother always told me not to petition God directly for things for my own benefit, and in a way this was something for me, to make me feel better. I knew it was wrong, but there are passages in the Bible which made me think that perhaps God wouldn't mind. The Psalms, for instance – they're all about trusting Him, asking for His help in adversity . . .

'But I never expected anything to happen. When I heard Lorrie come back, I suddenly thought: she'll be angry with me. I caused trouble for her, and then I deserted her when she needed me . . .' Her eyes flickered uncertainly towards Paula before she resumed. 'I know you'll think I'm mad, but I'm not. It was her.'

9

'We've just looked through Loretta's possessions in the Nurses' Home,' said Jackson to Montgomery the following morning.

'Any joy?'

'No. She had a few letters and postcards stashed away in a shoebox, but they were mainly from other girls, old school-friends and the like. Two anonymous valentines, one of them rude . . . The letters only relate to this year, so any older ones have either been destroyed, or they're in Mansfield.'

'What about a diary?'

'There was one: called itself the "Good Grooming Guide". But she'd only used it sporadically to scribble down engagements.'

Montgomery gave a grim smile. 'Loretta was probably so busy doing things, she didn't have time to write about them. Were there any names at all?'

'Very few. She tended simply to make a note of destinations

and times. The initial "G" cropped up on three or four occasions – for instance, "Meet G Playhouse 7 p.m." – but we've checked with Gordon Mudge and he was her escort on those particular nights. The last entry said "R's party". That's Robin Winterley; no mystery there.'

'I suppose we should have expected this,' mused Montgomery. 'An illicit affair is more likely to be conducted in snatched hours than pre-booked evenings. Nevertheless . . . girls usually like to keep something from an admirer: a card, a pressed flower, a piece of jewellery . . . What about her financial status?'

'One bank statement, one building society passbook. The figures seemed consistent with her situation.'

'Check that there were no other accounts, no secret nest-egg. Will and I are off to Mansfield this afternoon; we'll enquire about Loretta's personal papers there.'

'Letters? Yes, she kept those. She took a box-full up to the attic just after Christmas. I'm not sure about the more recent ones, but we'll certainly look.'

'Thank you, Mrs Dawes,' said Montgomery. '. . . No, later will do fine.'

She sank back into the chair, a tired, pleasant woman with typical Midlands working-class features. Loretta hadn't received her startling beauty from her mother, he thought. Only the fine legs, perhaps, though the impact of the pair before him was blunted by thick Lycra stockings and flat-heeled sandals.

The detectives had been honest with the Dawes family about the circumstances surrounding Loretta's death; today they saw that the pain and shock had transmuted into a gritty determination on the part of the parents to help all they could.

'Like I said, we were happy for Loretta to live her own life,' went on Mrs Dawes. 'After all, what was there for her here? Seven of us in this leaking house – eight with Loretta – and no jobs locally for the young. We hadn't expected her to opt for nursing, but we were thrilled when she did. It's not a job, it's a whole career. I'm just a shop assistant, and Dan here works for the council.'

Her husband, muscular in a checked shirt, nodded his florid face in accord. 'But our girl knew she was always welcome here,' he said. 'She'd come home some weekends and kip down with her sisters. And she spent Christmas with us. Bought us lovely presents, she did, even though she wasn't that flush herself. See that stainless steel lighter on the mantelpiece? That's what she got for me. Box o' Swan has always done me fine, but Loretta wanted her old dad to have the best.'

'Did either of you know anything about the pregnancy?'

Mrs Dawes hesitated. 'I wondered,' she said. 'Loretta and I went shopping in Nottingham three weeks ago, and she seemed – different to me. There was a kind of glow in her face . . . Inspector, I've had six children myself, and that gives you an instinct, especially when it's someone close. Long before the more obvious signs. So, yes, I wondered, but Loretta spoke of other things, and I knew she'd tell me when she was ready, so I didn't raise the subject myself. We met her friend Gordon in a tea-shop, and I found I couldn't imagine them as a couple. I – I actually started hoping that she'd got back with Peter, and the baby was his.'

Her husband sent her an interrogatory look, his heavy face perturbed. 'You didn't let on to *me* about any of this!' he grated.

She rested a conciliatory hand on his knee. 'I wasn't sure. It was just a feeling.' She turned to Montgomery. 'You said that a married man might be the father.'

'It's possible.'

'Do you know who it is?'

'We were hoping you might.'

'Oh . . . I'm sorry. I've got no idea.'

'Did she speak a lot about any of the doctors – appear to hero-worship anyone?'

'Not after her first year. She used to tell us everything in detail: every ward procedure from dressings to lumbar punctures, stories about patients and their stroppy relatives, which consultants had thrown a tantrum, which nurses were incompetent. But then the work became less of a novelty, and she came home less as well, so when we did see her she wanted to hear the news from her brothers and sisters.'

Sergeant Bird leaned forward. 'Might she have confided in them?' he asked.

Mrs Dawes shook her head doubtfully. 'I don't think so. She was the eldest by four years. Talbot is seventeen, Harold is fifteen, and Dickie is just ten. No, she wouldn't have told the boys. As for her sisters . . . Cheryl is thirteen, and Chloe twelve. It's unlikely. I expect she discussed it with her Nottingham friends.'

'Whom did you have in mind?' asked Montgomery.

'Alison, Paula . . .'

'Have you met them?'

'Yes. Only Alison has visited us here, though, apart from Peter.'

Mr Dawes gave an unexpected guffaw, which he turned into a cough.

His wife managed a faint smile. 'It was a Saturday. She came for a meal. It was – interesting.'

'Alison is very prim and proper,' explained her husband. 'We're sat at the table and I've just filled me gob wi' sausage when Alison starts saying Grace. So I can't chew and I don't say "Amen", but she turns and looks at me disapproving like, so I mumble "Amen" and drop half the sausage on me plate . . .'

'Loretta was embarrassed,' said Mrs Dawes. 'Unfortunately, that wasn't the end of it. Dickie had a practical joke kit – one of those rubber bladders with a tube and bulb attached, which you position under the table-cloth and pump up with air when a plate's on top of it. He put it in Alison's place, and made her plate wiggle. She just wasn't amused. He was only a little boy, and the gravy didn't spill in her lap, or anything, but she didn't play along. The meal was awkward after that.'

'What about Paula?'

'I met her once briefly, in the Nurses' Home. She seemed all right: friendly, confident. More Loretta's type, I felt.'

'And Peter?'

Definite warmth in the memory. 'We liked Peter,' she said. 'We could talk to him and not feel – ashamed of where we live, or the way we speak . . . He made us feel as if we contributed something to society, just like him. I could see that Loretta was really fond of him. She'd always told me she wanted to marry someone like a scientist or a doctor, and I thought: yes, duck, you're going to get your wish. But later she told me they were just mates and were going to stay that way.'

'Cheryl said she hoped he'd stay on the market till she was a bit older,' said Mr Dawes.

'Would it be possible for us to have a brief word with Cheryl, if she's not too upset?'

'She'll *want* to help.' He lumbered towards the door. 'I just heard her come in. She's been at school today: we've tried to keep everything as normal as possible for the youngsters.'

'A private word would be best.'

The two detectives were left with Cheryl in the kitchen. She was a well-developed teenager, dark like Loretta, but totally lacking her sister's sculpted bone structure and slender elegance. From behind a thin parapet of wariness, she answered their questions with growing candour. No, she hadn't liked Alison, but thought she might have been shy. Why? Because she bit her nails all the time. Paula? She'd met her at Easter – spent a whole day in Nottingham with Loretta, saw the castle, then the wards, the Casualty Department and the Nurses' Home. She was wondering about becoming a nurse herself. Paula had been nice, told her stories about a patient who'd hidden virtually the entire contents of a bar in his locker, but then Loretta had read out a newspaper story and they'd ended up arguing . . . over *politics*, of all things! It was so boring. Disappointing, too, because she'd hoped to see Peter again.

Special men? That drippy Gordon wasn't up to much. Loretta should never have let Peter get away. He gave her that lovely gold ankle chain. Did they mean, who was the father of the child? She didn't know, but Loretta had always promised to marry someone rich. Someone rich who had earned their own money . . .

Montgomery stood with Sergeant Bird in the front doorway after a less helpful exchange with Talbot, the eldest son, unemployed at seventeen. The housing estate around them was a relentlessly dreary sprawl of grey council semis, each small plot of garden a repository for broken tricycles, overflowing plastic bin-bags and rusting car spare parts. A torn newspaper flapped weakly between the wooden bars of the Dawes's front gate.

'Loretta was growing away from us, despite what we've said,' acknowledged Mrs Dawes wistfully. 'It was right and proper: she had real brains and a striking, exotic beauty. She took after her great-aunt Maria, who was half Spanish; none of the others did. We always knew she'd make something of herself.

'I said to her once, you're getting beyond us, duck. She smiled and promised she'd never leave us behind. But she has done . . . sooner than any of us expected.'

Desolation unrolled across the group like a carpet, extinguishing all spirit except for the anger of Mr Dawes. His stance became truculent; he challenged Montgomery squarely: 'Our Lorrie had everything to live for. No way has she killed herself. You are looking for a murderer, aren't you?'

'Oh, yes,' Montgomery replied.

'Sorry, Paula left an hour ago. She did the early shift.' The nurse in Accident and Emergency pulled a regretful face at Montgomery. 'She's gone to her parents' home,' she added helpfully.

Montgomery consulted his watch as he strode away with Sergeant Bird. 'Leicestershire: a thirty, maybe forty-minute drive,' he said. 'I'm going anyway. It's time we saw Paula. Do you want me to drop you off at the station first, Will?' That lay in the opposite direction.

'No need, sir. I don't have a train to catch, and Sam's used to getting his dinner mid-evening.' Sam was William Bird's adopted cat, an elderly animal who had thrived following his liberation from the kindly but limiting security of a Cat Rescue Centre. Montgomery knew that his colleague spent most evenings at home with his music and books, alone except for this bundle of surprisingly single-minded black-and-white fur.

They left the city centre and drove south across Trent Bridge, Montgomery at the wheel of his own Sierra. The late afternoon traffic on the A60 was heavy, but moving well. Soon Nottingham's outer suburbs were behind them, and a landscape of gently undulating farmland swelled to either side.

'The Grange, Danton-on-the-Wolds,' murmured Sergeant Bird. 'Sounds as if they have money.'

'Yes. Janet Harper commented that Paula's family were "*nouveau*" . . . If I remember rightly, Mr Thompkins is in truck haulage.'

The village of Danton had its share of moneyed residents, they discovered. Beyond the modest brick cottages with their pantile roofs was a hinterland of substantial dwellings, their gardens high-walled for privacy, their broad driveways replete with Range Rovers and BMWs.

The Grange proved to be a gabled Victorian house, with a tumbling rockery at the front studded with alpine plants. A thin woman in her late forties knelt by the side of the gravel drive, prodding at the earth with a trowel. Montgomery parked in the road nearby, and the detectives approached her on foot.

'Mrs Thompkins?'

'Yes.'

They introduced themselves; she looked taken aback.

'It's about the death of Paula's friend Loretta,' explained Montgomery. 'We're hoping Paula can help us with some routine enquiries. Is she here?'

'She's just over the road, swimming with a friend. I'll go and fetch her, if you'd like to wait a moment . . .' She seemed uncertain whether or not to invite them into the house: her hands, bare of gardening gloves, were stained with soil as were the knees of the corduroy trousers she wore. Unexpectedly, she wore a considerable amount of make-up.

Sergeant Bird caught a glimpse of blue tiling in the distance. 'You have a pool yourself?' he asked rhetorically, nodding in the direction of the rear garden. 'Perhaps we could wait round the back . . . I love gardens.'

'Please do.' Reassured, she hurried away, and he strolled with Montgomery up the side of the house, enjoying the colourful shrubs and the early evening air. As they passed a huge bay window, Montgomery tapped his arm. 'Look at this, Will.'

The room beyond was furnished eclectically: antique pieces, apparently genuine, nestled around a modern three-piece suite glaringly upholstered in a material with diagonal blue stripes.

'Carole would kill for that ottoman,' whispered Montgomery, pointing towards a Gothic-looking carved wooden box whose lid was covered with scarlet embroidery.

'Do you think it's genuine?'

'It's Victorian, made in medieval style.'

'What about this table under the window?'

'I can only just see one of the feet, but it looks like a drum table to me. Rosewood, probably Georgian.' Montgomery had imbibed a certain amount of knowledge from his wife's hobby. 'You see the drawers round the edge?'

'Oh yes . . . do they taper?'

'No; every alternate one is a dummy.'

'But they've all got keyholes!'

'I know. Clever, isn't it?' His pale brow darkened slightly. 'Look what they've put on top!'

Sergeant Bird peered at the rocket-shaped glass cylinder with its central swirl of red globules. 'It's a lava lamp!' he exclaimed. 'I thought those things went out with the seventies.'

'And over there, Will. On the tripod table . . . it's one of those electrical arcing lamps.' He groaned. 'That really is a crime. These people have money, but no taste at all.'

Further evidence in support of this perception was apparent when they reached the rear garden. The plot was long and wedge-shaped, lawn flanked by mature trees, but any harmony it had shared with the mellow old house had been destroyed by the starkly modern swimming-pool abutting the patio. Its dry tiles glared ultramarine in the westerly sunshine, and the diving-board and water chutes stood bright and solid as children's toys. One edge was fringed with tall, globular lamps.

'Seems incongruous,' murmured Sergeant Bird, gesturing from the pool towards a small bed of roses nearby where the blooms, various floribunda, clustered around an old brass sundial on a weathered stone plinth.

'I agree.' Montgomery walked slowly forwards, hands in pockets, until he had reached the edge of the empty pool; he stood and contemplated the layer of garden debris covering the bottom. 'I suppose if there are children you want the pool near the house where you can keep an eye on them . . . but I think they could have chosen a more sympathetic design. Still . . .' he sighed, 'what people do with their own property is their affair. At least it's out of sight at the back.'

'We're just jealous,' grinned Sergeant Bird.

They turned as a figure in a lime-green robe rounded the corner of the house and approached them barefoot. They divined that this was a girl only because they were expecting Paula; the wet black hair was boyishly short, plastered down like a skull-cap, and the narrow hips and flat chest formed no contours beneath the towelling robe.

'I'm Paula,' she confirmed, and gave each of them a brisk nod in response to their own introduction. 'Why not sit down?' She led the way to a wooden table with bench seating on the patio.

'We're trying to establish the facts surrounding Loretta's death,' began Montgomery without further preamble. 'To that end, we're interviewing all her friends. We're especially keen on identifying the father of the baby – you knew she was pregnant?'

'I've heard. But not from Loretta. Hospital gossip, today.'

'Not even a hint from Loretta? I thought you were close friends.'

'Not all that close.'

'Is this since the quarrel?'

She gave him a cool stare. 'We didn't quarrel.'

'People have suggested that you did.'

'"People"? Who, exactly?'

'Colleagues of yours.'

'Much they know. We've been busy with exams and projects, that's all. No time for socialising.'

'We wondered if your political differences might have been the cause?'

'Pardon?'

'You had opposing views in certain political areas.'

She rolled her eyes in mock incredulity, but a faint pink stain was creeping up each cheek. 'Wowee,' she drawled. 'Show me a group of colleagues who don't disagree over how the country should be run. I suppose you think because we're young, and we're women, we don't have opinions on these matters!'

Montgomery ignored that. 'What was Loretta's position?' he asked.

'I don't see . . .'

'It could be important.'

She shrugged. 'Loretta's from a staunchly socialist family of limited means, who have never managed to leave their disadvantages behind, while my father did well during the enterprise culture of the eighties – as you can see. We differed over the old "incentive to work" chestnut, that's all: how much an individual should be allowed to hang on to themselves.'

'And the NHS,' put in Sergeant Bird instinctively.

'Well . . . yes; there's been lively discussion in all quarters. You'd expect that. Loretta was rightly proud of the whole concept of the NHS, and I agree with her there: it's the best thing the socialists ever did for this country. But she considered it sacrosanct, never to be changed in any way. She couldn't accept that it had become a creaking gravy train, riddled with waste and inefficiencies. We've just assumed Trust status at the Victoria, and as with any transition, there are problems; many of them reflect old defects that no one ever grappled with before. But Loretta got very hostile, said running a health service like a business showed crass ignorance of the nature of illness, said people and their problems couldn't be condensed into items to be bought and sold . . . I agreed with a lot of that, but when I tried to modify some of her points, she accused me of betraying the patients.' Paula's eyes glittered. 'That did annoy me, because I believe in the NHS and its basic philosophy myself. I'm loyal and I intend to continue working within the NHS for as long as I'm a nurse!'

'So you did have a *minor* tiff,' murmured Montgomery.

'Hardly merits the term.'

'So you made up your differences and were friends again?'

'Of course.'

'Did you share the usual things when girls live under the same roof – make-up, clothes?'

'Yes.'

'Girl-talk: tales of boyfriends and the like?'

'To a degree.'

'Who do you think is the baby's father?'

Paula shied away from Montgomery's mild but unwavering gaze. 'I – I don't know. Gordon, I suppose. But . . .' She made a helpless gesture.

'You're not convinced, are you? You don't feel that Gordon's the right candidate . . . Paula, who else was she seeing?'

'I don't know.'

'Are you *sure*? Girls together in the Nurses' Home . . . Loretta, training with you, sharing your clothes, bringing her young sister to meet you . . . ?'

'She said nothing.' Paula looked edgy and upset.

'Think carefully . . . Did she particularly admire any of the married doctors? Do you think she could have been having an affair?'

'I – I've told you, I don't know.'

'All right.' Montgomery paused for a moment to take stock, and spotted Mrs Thompkins watching them from behind a curtain. 'Leo Masters,' he said, 'is he your mother's brother, or your father's?'

The girl's discomfort increased. 'Mother's,' she said, and swallowed.

'Does he have children?'

'Yes; my cousins, Laurel and Edwin.'

'I don't imagine he gets much time for a home life, being a busy surgeon.'

'Well, Laurel's at university now – Oxford, and Edwin's away at boarding school. But he's a very good father when they are together. They still go on family holidays, skiing usually, and he visits them whenever he can during term.'

'Do your two families get together much?'

'The adults don't . . .' Paula lowered her voice, even though her mother was twenty yards away behind double glazing. 'Auntie Cynth and my parents don't get on. It was a mix-up to do with wedding invitations. One mistake, and high dudgeon all round. You know . . .'

'Your mother looks concerned,' said Montgomery. 'Perhaps

you'll just go and reassure her, Sergeant? Tell her we won't be very long here.'

As William Bird plodded round to the front door, Montgomery saw that Paula's agitation had intensified. Doubtless she suspected that her mother would be questioned – but there was nothing she could do about it. 'What does your Auntie Cynth do?' he asked her.

'Oh – she stays at home most of the time. She's hard of hearing, and it's affected her confidence. But she does work in the Oxfam shop one morning a week.'

'Deafness can be very difficult.'

'Yes – it was such a shame. They went to the Gambia four years ago. Uncle Leo and a small team from the hospital were doing some specialized surgery in Banjul; some of them travelled to remote villages to encourage patients to come forward. Auntie Cynth didn't have any medical skills, but she wanted to be with him, so she went as a kind of general factotum. Unfortunately she caught a viral infection – it turned out to be similar to Lassa fever – and it affected the nerves in her ears. We were just glad she was alive.'

You're very fond of your aunt, aren't you? thought Montgomery. It was all there in her face. 'So she paid for his enterprise,' he said.

'Yes, but – neither of them looks at it like that. They're always helping others. Uncle Leo is so generous with his time and money. He's there for the patients, for his junior staff . . . he never delegates the unpleasant tasks, he does them himself. And all the best hospital fund-raising ideas are his.'

An asset to the community, like the cobbler who ensured that everyone but his family was well shod . . . Did Cynthia too walk barefoot? wondered Montgomery.

'I've heard that he has a witty line in speeches,' he said.

'He has a good memory, backed up by a series of little reference books,' she smiled, resting her forearms on the wooden table.

'Did you hear his speech on Saturday night?'

The wariness was back in an instant. 'No . . . I didn't go to Robin's party. I went to the Radiology one instead.'

'Ah . . . Did your aunt go, perhaps?'

'Er, no. She doesn't like crowds and loud music.'

'I saw some of the people who had been to the fancy dress party; they all wore masks. Can you give me the names of anyone you know who attended both events?'

Paula thought for a minute, then named the Donald Duck and French maid couple. 'Sorry; I can't think of any others,' she said. 'A few left early, but may have gone somewhere else. You'll have to ask Robin.'

'Indeed.' Subsequent questioning revealed no further useful information; Montgomery rose gracefully to his feet as Sergeant Bird reappeared with Mrs Thompkins. 'Thank you for your time,' he said to Paula. 'I hope you didn't get cold. Are you going back to the pool?'

'Yes.' The robe swung open as she levered herself up from the bench seat; a navy blue one-piece swimming costume clung to her flat stomach and meagre chest.

'Pity about yours,' he added.

'Oh, it's got a crack in it. It'll be okay for next year.' She slicked back her half-dry hair with a casual gesture and led them up the side of the house to the front garden. An eight-year-old Jaguar was just crunching to a halt on the driveway. 'That's Dad,' she said. 'You didn't want him, did you?'

'Not at present, thank you.' They strode on past the vehicle, glimpsing inside a well-fleshed occupant with a square, pugnacious jaw. Paula seemed unable to leave their side; at the end of the drive she turned and regarded Montgomery narrowly.

'I don't suppose it's occurred to you,' she said, 'that *Loretta* may not have realized she was pregnant?'

'I suppose it's possible,' mused Sergeant Bird as Montgomery drove northwards at a steady fifty miles per hour. 'She might have put it down to exam worry, or an illness, or even too much sport.'

'I don't believe that,' countered Montgomery tartly. 'All our evidence has painted Loretta as a healthy, confident girl. But why does *Paula* want us to consider ignorance as an option? There's something odd here . . . What did you get from Mrs

Thompkins? I trust you grilled her on the state of the Masters's marriage?'

'I tried to. She says the families don't meet very often, although the children keep up the links. Cynthia fell out with her once, years ago, over some mutual cousin's wedding. They passed over Laurel as a bridesmaid, asked Paula instead, then came back to Laurel at the last minute when Paula had to drop out. There was some mix-up over the invitations, as well. All in all, it rankled with Cynthia – who had actually accused her sister-in-law of a pre-emptive strike – and you know how these things fester. Apparently the girls themselves got over it quickly, and have remained good friends since.

'Mrs Thompkins also claims that Cynthia has been disdainful about their lifestyle and some of their acquisitions, although Leo isn't at all judgemental. She describes him as "a brother in a million". I think it's fair to say overall that Cynthia is uncomfortable with her in-laws' *nouveaux-riche* pretensions and lack of social graces, while they view her as both condescending and envious.'

'Envious . . . I wonder . . .' Montgomery tapped the wheel lightly with his fingers as he waited at traffic lights. 'What did you think of that Jag?'

'Old, but not vintage. Only fair condition.'

'Exactly. And if there's one thing the successful self-made man likes to flaunt, it's his car – right?'

'Yes . . .'

The lights changed; Montgomery let in the clutch and pulled away smoothly, but his mind was only nominally on the driving. 'You know something, Will?' he said. 'I didn't see any crack in that swimming pool.'

10

'Someone told us that Loretta spoke to Leo Masters during the party,' said Sergeant Bird the next morning.

'It was Barry Pritchard,' remembered Montgomery. 'He saw

her with Masters, then later with Verity. The question of "opportunity" obiously arises, but I don't want to go too deeply into that until I've got everyone's version of the evening's events.'

'It was surely a poisoned drink, though.'

'I don't know. At this stage one can only say probably. I've always found those Agatha Christie-type scenarios where something lethal is dropped into an existing drink totally unbelievable, but if she was handed a *new* drink, no one would suspect.'

'Wouldn't it taste foul?'

'Not if she was eating highly spiced food at the same time. There was tabasco sauce on the breakfast bar, which has a hot chilli taste . . .' He paused for a moment, his blue-grey eyes taking on a distant focus. 'We're still left, though, with the problems of who had prior knowledge of the barbiturate capsules, or the time and privacy to doctor them on the evening in question. I'm hoping Frances Winterley can help us with some of that, but before we bother her again I'd like to see Leo and Cynthia Masters for myself. Were you able to make an appointment at the hospital?'

'Of sorts. Masters is in theatre all morning and has meetings this afternoon and evening: he suggested lunchtime.'

'Mm. Where does he live?'

'Wollaton; near the park.'

'Then let's call on Mrs Masters.'

'I'm Mavis Beecham. I'm the housekeeper here, and have been for fourteen years.' The middle-aged woman who admitted the two detectives had sharp eyes in a jowly face with deep grooves linking nose and mouth; her manner was a strange mixture of obsequiousness and self-importance.

'Ah – they must be happy with your services,' said Montgomery.

'I like to give satisfaction . . . Have you come about the young nurse from the Victoria Hospital?'

Montgomery made a vague affirmatory sound.

'I thought so. Tragic, that. I saw it in the paper. Such a lovely young girl – like a Spanish princess. What must her parents be going through . . . ?'

'We wondered if Mrs Masters is at home,' interjected Montgomery.

'No. It's her morning for the Oxfam shop. Has to have something to occupy her, poor soul.' The glint of malevolence between the pouchy eyelids seemed to belie her sympathetic tone.

'We heard that Mrs Masters has, er, problems,' said Montgomery delicately.

Mavis Beecham pursed her lips and nodded heavily. '"Let him who is without sin", I always tell myself . . . but then there's the other side of that coin: a citizen's responsibility towards Officers of the Law. So I'll *say* nothing, but – follow me . . .' With an elaborate gesture for silence, she led them up the stairs to a bedroom at the rear, opened the door of a fitted closet, and retreated as if to dissociate herself from its contents. 'Behind the Lego box,' she hissed conspiratorially.

Sergeant Bird met Montgomery's eye for the briefest of seconds before he leaned forward to peer into the dim cavity. He felt an irreverent urge to laugh.

'Next to the Action Man!' added the housekeeper as his fingers brushed against the smooth cold hardness of glass. It proved to be the neck of a vodka bottle; two more lay beside it.

'Of course, it's not for me to comment on these things,' sniffed their informant as she bustled down the stairs again, 'but I'm sorry for Mr Masters. He doesn't need extra burdens, with all the long hours he puts in. What does he come home to, I ask myself?'

'One would hardly blame him if he looked elsewhere,' murmured Montgomery.

'That's what I say to my Walter: he's carrying her out of a sense of duty. He's a generous man, you know: gives me a little something extra whenever Walter's taken bad.'

'I suppose Walter has frequent attacks,' said Montgomery, straight-faced.

'He does, that. He . . .' The door bell interrupted her, shockingly loud. A concession to Cynthia Masters's deafness, reasoned Montgomery. He waited while Mrs Beecham accepted a parcel from the postman, the laser gaze from her flinty eyes fastened to the return address.

'Do you have any duties here at the weekends?' he asked when she had placed it on the hall table. 'You don't. What are your actual hours of work at this address?'

'Ten till twelve, Tuesday and Thursday mornings.' She went on to outline her cleaning plan.

'I see.' "Housekeeper" seemed a decidedly glorified term for such part-time domestic assistance. He suspected she had coined it herself. Without question, the woman had no business rummaging in wardrobes – but what else might she know? 'Did Mrs Masters mention what time they got back from the party on Friday?' he hazarded. His list may have been inaccurate, and Paula hadn't sounded certain about her aunt's whereabouts.

'She doesn't tell me much about their social life.' Mrs Beecham answered sourly. 'I said to her on Tuesday, shame about that pretty young nurse, and all she said was "Yes". Didn't describe the party, even though the *Evening News* had said that several consultants from the Victoria were present. But last week I'd reckoned she was going somewhere, because this long yellow ball-gown had been hanging out, and it wasn't for her daughter's use. Laurel hasn't been home for weeks.'

'May we see the gown?' asked Montgomery.

'Sorry. I don't know where she's put it; it's not back in the usual place.'

'Never mind. Tell me . . . did Mrs Masters seem upset about the nurse?'

'Hard to say, Mr Montgomery. She walked out of the room abrupt, like.'

'Are you sure Laurel didn't take the gown to Oxford?' asked William Bird softly. 'How do you know she didn't come home?'

''Cause Florrie told me.'

'Florrie?'

'Lives across the road. That house, there.' She pointed out through the living-room window. 'It belongs to her daughter, but Florrie has a room at the front. It's like a bed-sit. I visit her from time to time – to take her things: pots of jam, books.' Mrs Beecham straightened her back virtuously.

100

'So Florrie knows the various cars,' said Sergeant Bird.
'That's right. She's very good with colours.'

'Yes,' said the lady in question, a bony, alert-looking senior citizen. 'I've got sharp ears. People don't expect it from someone my age. This glass is so *thin*,' she tapped against the window with impatient knuckles, 'that I hear all the car engines, and Davy's motor bike at number 5, and the lawn mowers and hedge trimmers . . . You never used to get summer Sundays ruined so comprehensively.

'The cars at Mr Masters's house? Well, he has the big grey one and she has the little white one, and when Laurel is home there's a red one tucked next to the white one on the drive. Edwin's too young, of course, but no doubt when he's seventeen he'll be wanting one. Youngsters think of them as a right these days, not a privilege. I'm proud that I've never learned to drive. All that noise, those fumes! Yes, my daughter takes me out in her car . . .

'Friday? Yes. I didn't like the television programmes so I came up here for some quiet music on the radio. I saw Mr Masters drive off at twenty-past seven, and Mrs Masters followed a few minutes later. No, I'm sorry, I don't know what she was wearing. I didn't hear her come back, but when he returned – what? oh, about half-past eleven or a quarter to twelve – her car was already on the drive. Yes, definitely. The white one.

'What? Oh . . . pleasure. I always enjoy a bit of company. Even gentlemen like yourselves.'

A low jingle sounded as Montgomery pushed open the door of the Oxfam shop, but the light-haired woman at the back continued her task of attaching price tags to the garments without interruption. He strode forward to the counter as Sergeant Bird closed the door, and cleared his throat loudly: 'Ahem!'

She swung round with startled eyes. 'I'm so sorry . . . I didn't hear you. I was concentrating . . .'

Montgomery proffered his warrant card. 'Montgomery, CID,'

he said. 'And this is Sergeant Bird. We've been looking into the death of Loretta Dawes on Friday night, and wonder if you might be able to help us.'

'Help you?' There was white all round her irises, like a horse that was about to bolt.

'We're speaking to everyone who went to the party, in an effort to trace Loretta's movements throughout the evening. We wondered if you or your husband noticed anything unusual?'

She lifted a small hand, palm outwards as if to ward him off. 'I'm sorry,' she said. 'I didn't go. I was invited, of course, but I'm not fond of loud music so I stayed at home.'

'When did your husband return?'

'I think it was going up to twelve.'

'Has he said anything about Loretta's death to you?'

'What do you mean? Why should he?'

'I meant, did he mention seeing anything remarkable at the party? Loretta staggering, perhaps. Or maybe he expressed an opinion about what happened?'

'Surely it was some sort of accident! That's what we thought.'

'The dose of the drug was very high indeed. Other interpretations have become more likely.'

'Suicide? No, Inspector . . . I've only met her twice, but Loretta didn't strike me as that kind of girl. She was too . . . vigorous.'

'So Leo saw nothing abnormal?'

'Not that I'm aware of.'

'How did you spend the evening, Mrs Masters?' Montgomery spoke loudly and enunciated with care; he had noticed her watching his mouth intently.

'Partly sewing, partly packing a tuck box and some little gifts for Edwin, our son. He's at boarding school in Somerset. We visited him on Saturday.'

'Did you go out at all in your car that evening – the Friday?'

'No. I had nowhere special to go.'

'You're sure?'

'Quite sure.'

'I see. Thank you.'

*

'Take a pew,' said Leo Masters cheerfully, indicating an uneven row of chairs in the theatre ante-room. He was dressed in green overalls and rubber boots; at his side Robin Winterley, in similar overalls and clogs, flashed them a dark glance of acknowledgement over the rim of his teacup.

'Sorry to drag you up here,' went on the consultant. 'The list is overrunning, and lunch is as ever a waning prospect. You can share our tea, though, and if you're lucky someone might bring you something mummified between two slices of bread.'

The detectives sat down. 'As you can imagine,' began Montgomery, 'it's about Loretta . . .'

Leo Masters's face was instantly sober. It was a strong, virile face, but also a caring one. When he pulled the cap from his head, thick brown hair sprang up at the temples; not even the lankening of sweat could contain it, nor hide the streaks of gold twisting through each strand. Leo by name, Leo by appearance: he had a solid neck and large square teeth.

'That poor girl,' he said. 'She had so much potential. It's a sheer bloody waste – an inexplicable waste.' Robin nodded in silent agreement.

'Did you see her at the party?'

'Yes. She looked stunning. That's one of the reasons we're having difficulty taking it in.'

'She spoke to you, I believe.'

'Just briefly. I'd told Sister Brocklebank that I'd be happy to provide Loretta with a reference if she wanted one for her staff nurse applications. Loretta thanked me, but said she didn't need it. I wasn't surprised; she had no lack of people to speak highly of her work.'

'Did she say anything else?'

'No. She wandered off – then a couple of minutes later she was with you, Robin, wasn't she?'

'We exchanged a word or two. Nothing significant.'

'I heard you telling her not to drink so much, or something like that.'

'It was said in jest. She seemed to be knocking it back a bit at that point.'

'Was she unsteady on her feet?' asked Montgomery eagerly.

'I don't recall that,' said Robin. 'She was dancing with Peter a few minutes later.'

'Who else was nearby?'

'Kevin Cox, Barry Pritchard . . .'

'And what time was this?'

'Now you're asking. Nine o'clock, a quarter past . . . some time around then.'

'Where exactly did she go when she left you?'

Robin pondered, a deep cleft appearing between his eyebrows. 'She went into the corridor, but reappeared quite promptly and made her way to the window where Peter and Alison were standing.'

'Thank you.' Montgomery turned back to the senior surgeon. 'Did your wife attend the party?'

'No. She's deaf; she prefers quiet, intimate gatherings.'

'How about your niece Paula?'

'I think she did come, late on. I got a glimpse of the yellow dress a few minutes before I left.'

'Yellow dress?'

'Yes. One my wife made for Laurel four or five years ago; we call it the Hanoverian dress.'

'You're sure? You recognized the garment?'

'Yes.' Leo Masters seemed almost amused by Montgomery's vehemence. 'Cynthia spoke of lending it to Paula for the Radiology fancy dress party. Of course, she wore a wig and a mask on Friday; her own hair is cut short, like a boy's.'

'Did Paula speak to you?'

'No; as I said, it was just a glimpse – across the room.'

Across the room.

The light was fading fast as John Dyson eased his Orion to a halt in the small courtyard adjoining the Doctors' Mess. His mucles felt luxuriously stretched, the result of an hour's play at Westwood, and his skin still glowed from the hot needle-point shower at the finish. A dusky squash-ball-shaped bruise throbbed on his left calf. He pressed the central locking release, and Peter scrambled out of the passenger seat.

'Thanks for the lift, John.' He opened the rear door and

leaned to recover his kit from the back seat, his face, too, lustrous from the evening's exertions. Gripping the handles of the sports bag, he hesitated. 'The night's still young. What is it, nine o'clock? Fancy a game of chess at my place?'

For John, the desolation had just begun to close in. It was something to do with the gaunt, irregular bulk of the hospital rearing above them like a giant hand, with Loretta, with twilight, with the prospect of his own cold and lonely house. No Jackie, no Fran, no comfort of any kind. He had planned to kill the hours in the Mess bar, one of the sad ones, peripheral in his non-acute specialty, no real reason to be there. He would have sat with a low-alcohol lager until he was too tired to care.

'Whaddya say?' Peter flashed him an encouraging smile; perhaps he guessed at John's depression but it would not be mentioned – they had their own tacit interdicts.

John roused himself to banter. 'If you're such a glutton for punishment, who am I to deny you? I thought you might prefer to go and lick your wounds.'

'Phoo. You only won three–two tonight. Just wait till next time . . . And as for the chess, be warned. I've been practising on Barry Pritchard's computer. I can swing a draw on level 5 . . . still want to chance your luck?'

'Lead me to it.' John locked the car and they made their way round the side of the building to the paved terrace walk. Lights twinkled far below in The Park, but the deepening dusk distorted spatial perception; over the parapet the drop seemed infinite. Peter lived in Tower House, a residential block constructed alongside the rock on which the hospital stood, vertically parallel like the Old Man of Hoy; access from the terrace was via a covered walkway linking to the fourth floor.

As they passed the tall curtained windows of Ward 7, they saw a dumpy figure standing immobile in their path.

'Peter, is that you?' The voice was soft and faltering.

'Me or my double. Greetings, young Alison.'

'And John?'

'The very same.' Even as he spoke, John knew that her hesitancy was a façade: she had heard their conversation from the other end of the terrace, and had waited here to waylay them.

105

She wore her cap and uniform.

'I see you've just come off duty,' said Peter. 'How's Ward 7? Have you managed to discharge that schizophrenic with the fistula yet?'

Alison shook her head sorrowfully. 'No. His relatives were on the ward tonight. They refuse to have him home. We're going to ring the social worker tomorrow.'

'So the bed's still blocked?' He sighed. 'Kevin will demolish us on tomorrow's ward round. He's getting tetchy about his waiting lists, and we're always first in line for the flak.' He turned to John. 'It's all right for you pathologists in your ivory towers.'

'Well, you know what they say: if you like the human race, be a psychiatrist, if you don't, be a pathologist. The choice is there.'

'Don't believe him,' said Peter to Alison. 'This air of misanthropy is a front. He's like a broody hen with his student group down at the university; he even gave them extra sessions when they got near their exams.'

'Lest they show me up,' said John, drawing a chuckle from Peter and a feeble flicker of amusement from Alison's tight lips.

'Well, take care, Alison. We'll see you around.' Peter lifted his hand in a valedictory gesture, but the girl made no effort to move aside. She hung her head, then looked up at them with an expression of embarrassment sprinkled with apprehension.

'Please, I . . .' She glanced at the curtained windows of Ward 7. 'I'm sorry to intrude, but would it be possible for us to talk somewhere, just for a few minutes? Somewhere private?'

John felt an unworthy sense of irritation – pure selfishness, he knew. Some echo of the sentiment was dimly present in Peter's tone, although his words were friendly enough: 'Course we can. What did you want to discuss?'

Now Alison did move. She edged outwards across the terrace to the very parapet, and in the gloaming they could see the agitation in her eyes. 'It's about Loretta and Mr Winterley's party,' she whispered. 'People have been saying such terrible things. I've tried not to listen, but you know what it's like in the Victoria at the moment. Those with the least knowledge

106

seem to have the most to say . . . I thought I could ignore it all, but – they've succeeded. They've made me think again. I wondered . . . you were both there that night . . . could we talk?'

John's vague feelings of annoyance crystallized into a deep seam of reluctance. So much ill-informed gossip had sparked from the tongues of colleagues that week. Doctors, nurses, technicians, porters, cleaners – everyone was speculating, with varying degrees of ghoulishness, on the events of Friday. Many of them hadn't even known Loretta. Their prurience repelled him, and he found himself suspecting Alison's motives in raising the subject.

'Is it urgent, Alison? Is there something new?' Peter was speaking, attempting now to back-track. Perhaps his antennae, too, were twitching.

'Not new, exactly. It's just . . . Oh – ' She bit her thumb nail savagely and they saw that she was trembling. 'It could be my fault,' she choked. 'All of it. It could have happened because of me. But I don't *know*, and if it isn't, it's better if I don't say anything . . .'

Peter grimaced covertly at John before taking her elbow in a firm grip and steering her towards the covered walkway. 'Alison, we're starving,' he said. 'Come to Tower House with us and share our toast. Then you can tell us what's on your mind.'

Peter's room in the quiet residential tower block was a typical bachelor pad, functional but spartan. The bookshelf was crowded with medical tomes and journals, with a small row of paperbacked thrillers along the top. Beer-mats and nameless electronic spare parts adorned the desk and window ledge, while next to the bed stood two traffic cones and a 'humpback bridge' sign. John had a long familiarity with these accoutrements, but the recent police activity made him appraise them in a new light.

'Er, Pete,' he said as they licked butter from their fingers, 'I don't think I'd keep these road signs hanging around if I were you.'

'Perhaps not,' agreed his friend blandly, before turning to the girl perched next to him on the edge of the bed. 'Now, Alison,' he commanded, 'spill all your woes.'

'I – I don't know if I can.'

'You've eaten my toast. You must.'

She nodded gravely, as if such a bargain made sense. 'Well . . .' she began, then swallowed. 'I'll be blunt. People are saying that Lorrie was killed – murdered. They say she was given a large dose of barbiturates, so massive that it couldn't have been an accident. The only other alternative was suicide, and nobody believes that.'

'What about you?' asked Peter.

'I feel the same, don't you? We've both known Lorrie for years. She'd never have done such a thing. But in that case they're right, and she *was* killed, which is a *grotesque* idea – unless it was an accident after all.'

John felt himself frowning. 'What do you mean?'

'I mean – perhaps Loretta was never meant to have been the victim. Perhaps the poison was intended for *me*.'

'*You?*' John hadn't meant to sound so disparaging, but the word burst out of him, sharp with scepticism.

'I shouldn't imagine you have an enemy in the world, Alison,' said Peter.

'Oh . . . I could be wrong. That's why this is so difficult. But . . . there's someone in the hospital who might have an important secret, and if he has, he knows I know about it . . .'

'Why do you say "might" and "if"? Is there some doubt?'

'Well . . . I was reassured. But that might have just been to fob me off. Supposing it was true, though, and something made him decide to act, despite the passage of time . . .'

'Alison, you're babbling. Can't you be more specific? I don't know what you're trying to suggest. Whom are we talking about here?'

She drew back. 'I can't name names. I might be quite wrong, and then the consequences would be awful!'

Peter eyed her sternly. 'More awful than murder?'

'I – I can't! Really!'

'Then I don't see how we can help you.'

'Oh . . .' She tore at the side of her thumb with the nail of her middle finger, then gnawed at the loose tag of flesh, creating a bloody gouge.

'Drink your tea,' said Peter hastily, passing her a green mug. His ribs rose as he took a deep breath. 'Now, then . . . Let's say for the sake of argument that someone *does* have it in for you. Why should that result in Loretta being killed?'

Alison took a grateful gulp and cupped her hands round the mug. 'Because of the method,' she said. 'I've thought a lot about this. People have just assumed that something was put in her drink, but I can't accept that. She was drinking Soave – very pale, very clear. Even if the drug could have been added without her noticing, there would have been a *sediment*. So I considered the food instead, and I remembered: Lorrie ate most of mine. I don't like prawns, you see, so I only had a bit of the rice, then left the plate on the window-sill till Lorrie came back. Someone could easily have scattered the drug over the risotto while my back was turned. I tried a bit more, then I felt sick.'

Honestly, thought John, slumped unorthopaedically in the hard chair by the desk. Attention-seeking fantasies. Aloud, he said, 'Barbiturates wouldn't have made you feel sick. Drowsy, perhaps, but not sick.'

'Well, I only had a few mouthfuls. Loretta ate all the rest. And the plate was unattended for at least fifteen minutes . . . What do you think, Peter?'

'It's an idea,' he said carefully, 'but I think we're best leaving theories to the police.'

'But that's the point: they weren't considering murder when they spoke to me. None of us was. They've no idea that Loretta ate my food. Do I tell them, or what?'

He shrugged. 'That has to be your decision.'

Alison subsided, scouring her thumb again, the flesh already raw as steak. 'I don't know what to do.'

At eleven o'clock John went home, but Alison hung back in such a way that only a breach of good manners could have evicted her. Peter yawned and stretched, hoping the hint would be taken and not resented.

'Well, young lady . . .' He spoke lightly. 'Are you on an

"early" tomorrow? If you are, you'll have the joy of seeing Kevin Cox chew me up and spit me out.'

She looked distressed. 'Those chronic patients aren't your fault.'

'Try telling him that. If you'll excuse me, I think I'll go to bed and have nightmares about it.'

He stood up, but Alison remained seated on the bed.

'Peter . . .'

'Yes?'

'I – I wanted to ask you something.'

'Go on.'

'I . . .' She flushed and scraped furiously at the tortured thumb.

Peter crouched down in front of her, balancing on the balls of his feet, and gently separated her two hands. 'It's about the man, isn't it, the man with the secret? I understand why you didn't want to name him while John was here, but you can tell *me*. We're old friends, aren't we?'

For a second she looked blank, then she nodded vigorously. 'Oh, yes.'

'I don't mind saying I'd like ten minutes alone with whoever did it. Loretta meant a lot to me.'

Alison grasped his fingers tightly. 'Peter, I feel the same. And Lorrie wants justice – that's why she came back in the night! It was her way of telling me to find out. And I owe it to her, because I got her involved in all this.'

Slowly, smoothly, Peter extricated himself from her frenzied grip. He sat in the chair vacated by John, but brought it closer to soften the blow. 'I'm listening,' he said.

Alison looked at him once, then riveted her gaze to the nearest traffic cone. 'I don't know how to start,' she said. 'Perhaps I can describe a *hypothetical* situation . . . Say there was once a consultant who had private as well as NHS patients, but who blurred the lines a bit between the two groups. Say he wrote prescriptions for his private patients on NHS forms, for instance.'

'There was such a consultant,' interrupted Peter with a snort. 'Dr O'Reilly. He was sacked.'

'Yes. I know. This story isn't about him, but his case illus-

110

trates what can happen . . . Say this other consultant is questioned by a nurse one day. He reassures her that all is correct and Trust accounting will keep it that way, and she doesn't want to make trouble because basically she respects him, so she leaves it at that . . . But then three months later he and the nurse are together at the same social occasion, and another nurse dies who has eaten from her plate . . .'

'Alison. Are you accusing Leo, or Kevin?'

'This is *hypothetical*,' she insisted. 'I just want to know what you would conclude.'

'Well . . . I'd have to ask if the nurse told anyone else about her discovery.'

'No one in authority, because she was giving him the benefit of the doubt. But she did discuss it with a friend.'

'Ah. I don't suppose this was the friend who died?'

'It was.'

'And did the friend tell anyone else?'

'I think it's possible.'

Peter had been reflecting earlier on why Alison had chosen him as her confidant, in preference to someone more accessible from the Nurses' Home, such as Paula. Now a shadowy understanding stirred. If she truly believed that Leo Masters was implicated, she could hardly debate the matter with Leo's niece. Loretta, however, with her staunchly socialist credo, may have had no such qualms . . . Indeed, this could have been the cause of their rift . . .

'Peter, what should I do?'

He sighed. 'It would really help if you could be frank. Is the consultant Leo Masters?'

'I'm sorry; I can't tell you.'

'All right, then. Whoever it is, you've got to think carefully whether or not there was convincing evidence of an offence with the prescriptions. If there wasn't, and he's innocent, then we could end up triggering a messy internal enquiry for no good reason. Even if there was, it's still a wild extrapolation from a bit of fiddling to help a patient, to murder. So weigh up the pros and cons scrupulously. Having said that, I think the police should know that Loretta ate from a plate which had been sitting around on a window-sill.'

'Will you explain it to them?'

'No; it would be hearsay from me.'

'Oh . . . then perhaps I should, when I've thought it over some more.'

'I agree. Don't leave it too long.' He rose and picked up a bunch of keys from the desk. 'Glad that's settled. Now let me escort you back to the Nurses' Home.'

She looked up at him, flushing slightly, as he prepared to open the door. 'Peter . . . there was something else I wanted to say. The girls from Wards 7 and 8 were planning an outing before all this happened – just to the Playhouse to see *St Joan* next Tuesday. We decided to go ahead with it, because everyone needs a break, something to take our minds off this horrible enquiry. The others are taking their boyfriends along. I wondered . . . would you like to come with me?'

Hell, thought Peter. This was all he didn't need. He remembered a time two years before when he had just moved to the district from Sheffield, a time of innocent 'outings' with a much slimmer Alison. Long after his inevitable progression to Loretta, Janet Harper had warned him of Alison's enduring sheep's eyes, but he had chosen to discount her opinions. Now, however, he acknowledged that she had been right.

'That's a very kind offer,' he said, 'but unfortunately I'll be on call. I've swapped a duty with Manjit.'

'Oh . . .' She seemed slowly to crumple, then rallied, a tiny splinter of hope visible in her grey eyes. 'I understand,' she went on. 'I know you're busy. Mother's coming to Nottingham a week on Sunday; she'll be staying here for a few days instead of our Grasmere trip. We thought the police might want me again. Will you come to tea with us?'

Peter almost groaned. He suspected she had never propositioned a man before in her life, especially with so little encouragement. Pity stirred inside him. Poor Alison. To refuse would be to kick someone who was already down, to accept would set a precedent both dangerous and unfair.

'I'm flattered that you want to be seen with a reprobate like me,' he said, 'but perhaps it's best if I keep a low profile. I've been neglecting my girlfriend a bit recently.'

This time the message did hit home. Her face congealed in a

purple mask of hurt, grief and shame, and she turned to scrabble feebly at the door handle. 'Sorry to have bothered you,' she said woodenly as he opened the door for her. 'You don't need to walk me to the Nurses' Home; I'll be quite all right.'

'You're sure? It's no trouble.'

'Yes, I'm sure. You stay here.'

He let her out of Tower House's fourth-floor outer door, then wandered back along the airless corridors, hearing the faint echo of her feet in the elevated walkway. He knew he had handled the problem badly, but raising false hopes could only have led to more misery. Physically tired, but wide awake, he took an apple from the bowl on his shelf, crunched a piece from it, and chewed. Girlfriend, he had said. At present, that meant anyone and no one. Work, squash, beer, chess, those were his palliatives while normality was so dislocated. And yet . . .

He found himself thinking of Sonia.

11

'We're going to miss you,' said Sue Pritchard, smiling wistfully at Fran over the coffee table in the Winterleys' flat. 'If it wasn't so mean and selfish, I'd start hoping for hitches in your property transactions.'

'The market's flat enough without hitches.' Fran held out a plate of home-made Cherry Bakewell slices to her friend. 'My dread is that we won't be able to sell at all. I don't want to stay on my own once Robin's gone south, but uninhabited properties invariably lose value . . .'

That wasn't the only reason, she knew, and Sue probably guessed. Robin had never felt constrained by his marriage vows. The intense, claustrophobic maelstrom of hospital life had kept his bachelor values to the fore: he thrived on the clatter of the corridors, the tension in the operating theatres, urgent bleeps, adoring secretaries – and the steamy parties. It was a short step from these to squalid little liaisons in on-call rooms. For years, Fran had made all the sacrifices, years of spoiled dinners and endless waiting. Still she loved him, selfish liar though he was. Southampton was both a fresh start and a last chance. Letting him spend time alone there would be like playing Russian roulette.

'I was wondering which side of the Solent you'd live,' said Sue. 'The east is more convenient for the city, but the west has so much natural beauty, what with the New Forest and Lymington. We went to Exbury once on the Beaulieu estuary; it's really nice – all creeks and salt-marshes and watery views. You should write to the Tourist Board and get some brochures.'

'It's meant to be a new home, not a holiday,' laughed Fran.

'I don't see why the two should be mutually exclusive. Seriously, Fran . . .' Sue's expression became sober. 'Barry and I both wish you well. You deserve some luck. I often think how much we have, with Tommy and Christine . . .' She blinked. 'This is great cake, by the way. You must give me the recipe sometime.'

'How is Barry enjoying his dermatology post?' asked Fran politely.

'He appreciates the dearth of out-of-hours emergencies,' said Sue, 'and I enjoy having him around more, but – well, it all sounds a bit dull. I think I was getting vicarious kicks from his stories about Casualty, but I can't get excited over someone's mole or patch of eczema! Still, he'll need to know all about skins when he's a GP.'

'That's definitely what he wants?'

Sue nodded, relaxed, complacent. 'Yes. He's fixed up a psychiatry post for February. And there's talk of a partnership in the Kegworth practice next year. Everything seems to be falling into place.'

'Well done.' Fran sipped her tea and put down the cup. Part of her was glad for Sue, but the other part longed to advise vigilance, alert her to the treacheries of life. Sue looked so mellow there, so satisfied. She had an affectionate husband who loved his babies; she saw no need for questions.

I was happy once, Fran wanted to say. *How do you know your world's secure?* She rose to make more tea.

*

Four miles away, Cynthia Masters was sifting through papers in the top of the bureau. She had found the key at last, lurking in a small Indian polished stone pot where Leo kept his cufflinks, but now that she had access to the household documents, she was still unable to find the file of bank statements. The only other lockable repository in the entire house was Leo's own desk drawer; if he had moved the file there, his motive could not be innocent.

With increasing unease she moved aside manilla envelopes, blotting paper, bottles of ink. Leo always kept his cheque-book with him, so that was no viable alternative. There was nothing useful here, unless . . . Suddenly she saw a white paper with the bank's name at its head. Trembling, she withdrew it, and scanned the columns of figures; several moments elapsed before she realised that this was the statement she had already seen.

Another one lay behind it. Just one; presumably they were here pending filing. She hardly dared look. In some ways it was already too late, but she still needed to know . . .

It was there. Third line down. A cheque debited, for five hundred pounds. No odd figure of pence. Five hundred pounds exactly.

At police headquarters, Montgomery's junior officers had just assembled for another briefing.

'We are now in a position to trace Loretta's movements on the night of the party quite fully,' he told them. 'She travelled along the Derby Road by bus with Alison Blake, then walked from the nearest stop the four hundred yards to the Winterley flat. The girls arrived at eight forty p.m. and were admitted by Robin Winterley who suggested they get some food in the kitchen then join the party in the living-room. They left their jackets in the double bedroom and took his advice, spending five minutes or so in the kitchen chatting with John Dyson, the pathologist, Frances Winterley and her neighbour Susan Pritchard. Peter Verity came in for a second helping of risotto and left with the girls for the bar in the living-room, but there they parted company.

'Barry Pritchard served Loretta with a glass of Soave and

Alison with a pineapple juice, which they carried across the room to a window-sill; they stood here together eating their food. Loretta then left Alison and spoke to Leo Masters – allegedly discussing job references. Robin Winterley was nearby, and she conversed with him next. He says she was drinking rather quickly, but we haven't ascertained whether or not her glass had been topped up at this point.'

'What was the blood alcohol from the body?' asked Sergeant Bird.

'Seventy. Would have been an amber if she'd been tested for driving.' He leaned against the desk. 'Loretta then went out into the corridor, but we don't know why. Perhaps she was checking who had arrived, or wanted something from her jacket pocket. Or perhaps she went to the bathroom, but no one remembers her standing in the queue. Suffice it to say she met Sister Brocklebank shortly afterwards, who asked her to take a message to Alison.

'She returned to the living-room, found Alison with Peter Verity, delivered the message then began dancing with Peter. They stayed together for forty minutes or so until the presentation at ten o'clock. The guests formed a circle around Masters and Winterley – a cramped, three-deep circle; Loretta was initially standing next to Peter Verity but another girl, Brenda Sykes, pushed between them. Loretta was not holding a drink.

'After the speeches, Loretta was seen in the corner speaking to two of the masked fancy dress people who had begun to filter in from the Radiology party. These were a cowboy and an Indian, but we have identified the two girls involved and they are not considered suspect. Two of the others still remain a mystery, however: a cavalier and a woman in a yellow ball-gown. This ball-gown may be significant for reasons I'll come to later.

'The very last sighting of Loretta on her feet was in the corridor at ten thirty. At ten past eleven, the secretary Sonia Ball crept into the small bedroom to collect her coat, but saw Loretta apparently sleeping on it, and left to rejoin the party. When she came back again at one thirty, Loretta was dead.

'I want us to consider opportunity first, motive next. No one believes Loretta committed suicide, and it seems from our itinerary that there was only the narrowest window of time when she could have taken the drug herself – namely, the five minutes or so between leaving Robin Winterley in the living-room and meeting Sister Brocklebank in the corridor. Certainly there was insufficient time to open all the capsules in the way we described before . . . and if someone else did that on the actual night of the party, it is difficult to conceive how they found the time *and* the privacy to make these preparations.'

·The most likely answer in my mind is that the capsules were taken from the medicine chest on an earlier date. Frances Winterley has admitted that she hadn't swallowed one in years, and had virtually forgotten they were there. The label was worn, but just legible. We know that several of Robin's hospital colleagues had been entertained in his flat over the preceding months . . .'

'Who in particular?' asked Jackson.

'I intend to get a definitive list from Mrs Winterley this afternoon. But certainly Leo Masters and his wife have had dinner there . . .

'Let's assume just for now that someone at the party already had the capsules prepared. This could have been as a whitish powder, or as a solution. If the "excipient" hadn't been filtered out, the fluid would have been cloudy. So how was it adminis-tered to Loretta? We've not been impressed with the idea of something added to a glass in her possession, but perhaps our killer had concealed a glass of tainted wine in the room, ready to hand to her when an opportunity presented itself.'

'Or exchange for hers when her back was turned,' proffered Smythe.

'Indeed. If, on the other hand, a powder was used, then Loretta must have left her plate unattended, or been thoroughly distracted whilst holding it.'

The detectives nodded.

'You can work out for yourselves which people had the best opportunities to poison Loretta that night. But let's move on to motive. We know Loretta was pregnant; someone raised the point that she might not have been aware of it herself . . .'

'She was, sir.' Jackson was emphatic. 'There were baby clothes in her bottom drawer.'

'Little blue matinée jackets and bootees,' added Smythe.

'Right. So she knew. We were fairly sure she did. The father is said to be a married man, but her old boyfriend Peter Verity may also be in the frame, since it's been hinted that he continued close relations with Loretta on a sporadic basis. Whoever it is, Loretta may have been applying pressure – blackmail, even.

'We have Masters, Winterley, Cox, Patel, Pritchard and Verity to choose between. I'm hoping the register of blood donors will help us whittle that down a bit. Did you find out, Brian?'

Jackson indicated one of his colleagues. 'Robert has a contact in the haematology lab,' he said.

Montgomery swung round. 'You've spoken to this contact?'

'Yes, sir.' Robert Allen, a lean detective sergeant from Scotland, had lived south of the border long enough to lose the word 'aye' from his vocabulary. 'He explained everything to me. We've had a piece of luck, in that the foetus is blood group AB. That's quite rare, and it means that he received the gene for A from one of his parents and the gene for B from the other. The letters denote blood antigens, apparently. Now, Forensic say that Loretta was group B, so she's definitely responsible for the B gene, whether or not her full genotype was BB or BO. If she'd been an AB herself, things would have been more difficult.'

'So the father is group A,' said Montgomery.

'Yes.'

'Why didn't you just *say* so?' groaned Jackson.

'I thought you'd like to know how the conclusion was reached. Blood grouping's actually much more complicated than that: there's the Rhesus system, the MNS system, various eponymous antigens – but ABO is the most important, where O is the absence of A or B.'

'In that case, what percentage of the population is blood group A?'

'Forty-two per cent.'

Jackson howled his derision. 'A great help!'

'If you're really interested, A subdivides into A^1 or A^2, but on our present information we are looking at forty-two per cent.'

'Let me see the list, Robert,' said Montgomery, holding out

his hand. Uncharacteristically flushed, Allen handed it over. 'They're a public-spirited lot,' went on Montgomery. 'It appears that all our suspects except Barry Pritchard give blood. We've got Leo Masters, A positive, Kevin Cox, O positive, Dinesh Patel, O negative, Robin Winterley, A negative and Peter Verity, O positive. How important are these positives and negatives for our current crude analysis, Robert?'

'The Rhesus "factor"? We can ignore it. Loretta and the baby were both Rhesus positive and the gene – well, three genes actually – dominates, so the father's Rhesus status doesn't matter.'

'Then we're down to Masters or Winterley!' enthused Jackson.

'Hold your horses, Brian.' The quiet, deep voice was Sergeant Bird's. 'The real father is only part of the issue. It's the person who *believes* they were the father that counts. If the married man turned her down flat, she may have rekindled her affair with Verity in order to turn him into the consolation prize.'

'I got them to check Gordon Mudge, by the way,' said Allen. 'He's group B.'

'He wasn't at the party anyway,' said Montgomery. 'But Barry Pritchard was – we can't rule him out just yet. Masters, Winterley, Pritchard, Verity: all four had dealings with Loretta that night. Pritchard actually handed her a drink, the others spent time in conversation with her, or dancing.

'There's one more element we must discuss, and that's the yellow dress. Leo Masters thought his niece Paula was present because he saw a masked guest in a yellow ball-gown identical with a dress of his daughter's which his wife had lent to Paula. Curiously, though, Paula had denied going to the Winterley party when William and I had interviewed her earlier. She claimed she had stayed at the Radiology bash. Was this the truth, or not?

'There are discrepancies, too, in Cynthia Masters's own account of her movements on the Friday night. She asserts she stayed at home for the entire evening, but a reliable-sounding witness across the road states that she saw Cynthia leave the house shortly after Leo, and arrive back sometime before him. Now, Cynthia may indeed have done this, but for an innocent reason she wishes to keep dark. Or our witness may have been wrong after all. But the third alternative can't be disregarded: was Cynthia Masters herself at the party? Did she really pass on the gown to Paula, or did she use it herself? It's far-fetched, but perfectly possible.

'William and I are going to visit Frances Winterley after this review, and hopefully Susan Pritchard as well. We shall ask about the yellow dress, and we'll also try to ascertain who could have had prior knowledge of the barbiturate capsules . . .'

A knock sounded at the door, and WPC Rosalind Winger stepped inside, holding a cardboard shoebox tied with string. ''Scuse me, sir,' she said to Montgomery. 'A young man called Talbot Dawes left this for you at the front desk.'

'Ah . . . thanks, Ros.' Montgomery pulled on a pair of disposable gloves, slid the string off the edge of the lid and lifted out the contents *en masse* as she left the room. Photographs, letters, cards and three small booklets spilled across the desk. His colleagues crowded round as he lifted one of the booklets, a diary, from the pile and flicked through its pages. Unlike those of Loretta's most recent diary, they were well filled with biro-scribbled handwriting. He read three random entries then moved on to the photographs, separating them with his protected fingers: Loretta out in the Peak District with Paula and a dog, Loretta at a party with a group of grinning girls, Loretta at another party with Peter Verity's arm round her shoulder, Loretta alone in close-up three-quarter view, a cigarette between her carmine lips, the knowledge of centuries in her eyes . . .

He turned to Jackson, who had leaned over the desk for a closer look. 'Little job for you, Brian,' he said.

Frances Winterley's naturally pale face looked apprehensive as she admitted the detectives to the flat, and Montgomery sought to reassure her. 'The flowers are doing well,' he said lightly as they passed the golden display in the hall. 'You'd think they were picked yesterday.'

'Sue brought them for the party,' Fran replied. 'She arranged them herself. She's very clever like that.'

'If it's clever you're after, try some of Fran's Cherry Bakewell.' Sue Pritchard appeared in the corridor with a crumb-laden plate. 'I'm sure there's brandy in it.' She smiled. 'Hello, Inspector, Sergeant. I was just keeping Fran company until you came. Mum is supervising my two terrors until five o'clock, so I actually feel human this afternoon.' She turned to Fran. 'I'll put this in the kitchen, and leave you to it.'

'Don't go on our account,' said Montgomery. 'In fact, it would be most useful if you stayed.'

'Well . . . if you're sure. Perhaps half an hour.'

'Come into the living-room,' invited Fran. 'Would you like some tea and cake?'

Sergeant Bird's jaw opened on the mannerly equivalent of *not half*! but Montgomery was too quick for him. 'Later, thank you,' he said. 'Perhaps we can start in the kitchen . . . ?' Without waiting for a reply, he followed Susan Pritchard; they all stood by the breakfast bar as she deposited her plate in the sink. 'We've traced Loretta's movements throughout the night of the party here,' he said, 'but we're just a bit hazy about the very beginning. Who was in this room with you when Loretta and Alison came in?'

The women's eyes met in a reflex of mystification, and Sue gave a loose shrug. 'Well . . .' she said, 'as far as I can recall, there was only John Dyson. He was sitting over there by the cooker, wasn't he, Fran?'

'Yes.'

'Does he know Loretta?'

'Slightly. They've been to the flat for dinner before.'

'Ah – I wanted to ask you about that. But first, let's clarify what happened on Friday. Can you tell me exactly what everyone did while Loretta was here in the kitchen?'

Fran, her expression still mildly puzzled, began thoughtfully: 'John was on a stool; he stood up and chatted when the girls came in. I think he offered them a drink, but they were actually served later on next door . . . Er, Alison said something about being on a diet, so I only gave her a small portion of the risotto, and a more generous one for Loretta. I was here, Sue was over there. Then Peter came in, asking for seconds, and they all three left together . . .'

'Were there any side dishes for people to help themselves?' asked Sergeant Bird.

'Just a couple of bowls of salad under the hatch, with napkins and forks.'

'Nothing else added?'

'Only extra sauce if anyone wanted it,' said Sue. 'There was already some in the risotto.'

'What kind of sauce?' Montgomery was interested now, though the focus as yet defied definition.

'You could choose: either tabasco or soy.'

Tabasco . . . hot chilli, a masker of flavours . . . He still didn't know quite what to make of it. 'Were the bottles freely available?' He addressed Fran.

'Not really; we were using them ourselves, for the cooking. I simply asked people if they wanted extra, and put it on for them if they did. I don't quite see . . .'

'Did any sauce bottles find their way into the living-room?'

'I don't think so, no.'

'Let me see them anyway.'

Frowning, Fran knelt down to a low cupboard; there was a chink of glass, then she handed up the narrow-necked bottles, one by one.

'I'd like to take these away, if you don't mind,' said Montgomery. 'Purely for routine purposes.'

'Routine? Well – if it helps.'

'Thank you. Now, this John Dyson. Can you tell me about him? All I know is that he's a medic, and single.'

'He's a widower,' said Frances. 'His wife Jackie used to work in the same office as I did – we were medical secretaries. She died of leukaemia four years ago; it was so sad. I don't think John's recovered fully, even now.'

'What is his field?'

'Pathology. He's a senior registrar. He works at the Victoria mainly, and occasionally at the university.'

'I see. Does he visit the flat often?'

'He used to, but more recently his visits have tailed off.'

'When was the last time? Aside from the party, I mean.'

'That would be a dinner we held earlier this year: March-time. We invited some of Robin's team over, doctors and ward staff, and asked John along as well. If I'm honest, it was partly for goodwill and partly to make up the numbers. The surgeons know him in any case; he reports on the specimens they send. They had plenty to talk about over the dinner table – shop, of course.'

'Is there any chance you can remember exactly who was here?'

'It shouldn't be difficult. Let me see . . . Leo Masters came with his wife Cynthia, and Kevin Cox and his wife Marie, then there was the registrar Tim Heald – he's left now, he's in London – Peter, Sister Brocklebank, Loretta and Alison. And John, as we've said. The other nurses were on duty. We had twelve guests in all, counting Barry and Sue.'

'Right.' Montgomery spotted Sergeant Bird supporting his back against a cupboard, miserably eyeing the kettle, and for once took pity. 'I don't suppose we could now accept your offer of tea?'

Frances Winterley saw them to the door half an hour later, ten minutes after her friend had left to resume responsibility for her children. 'I'm sorry I couldn't help you with the yellow dress,' she said.

'No matter,' answered Montgomery. 'Our talk has been very useful.'

'Good.' She didn't look particularly gratified. Her face was gaunt, lips and skin no longer glowing pearl but the flat white of pallor; at her elbow Sue Pritchard's flower arrangement bloomed with a contrasting health that was almost obscene.

'Inspector . . .' she said hesitantly, 'I've had the feeling from the direction of your questions that you don't think Loretta killed herself, or died as the result of an accident – do you agree?'

'Our minds remain open until we've solved the case.'

She nodded slowly, as if he had been more specific. 'Robin doesn't say very much, you see. Not here. I imagine they've all discussed it in the hospital, but here I'm isolated – in the very place it happened.' She raised her blue eyes to his. 'I don't suppose you'd tell me if you have any leads, if you've made

123

any progess? No; I understand.' Her jaw clenched. 'I wish we could sell this flat. Tomorrow. At a loss, even. Because try as I might, I can't ignore the fact that someone died here.

'Right here, in our home.'

'Oh . . . come in.' Susan Pritchard seemed startled to find the detectives at her own door in the flats across the courtyard. 'Mum's in the living-room with the children; I hope you don't mind another kitchen?' She led the way, adding 'Barry isn't home yet, I'm afraid.'

'No matter,' said Montgomery. 'We were hoping you could perhaps amplify one or two of the topics we covered in Mrs Winterley's home . . .' He came quickly to the point. 'It was clear that a variety of drinks were served, some quite complex ones with ice and lemon, etc. Was this Frances's idea?'

'No; as a matter of fact, it was Robin's. Fran suggested champagne cocktails for everyone, to keep things simple, but Robin overruled her.'

'I see. And the food?'

'I'd say that was a consensus between the four of us. Fran and I had done that dish before, with gratifying success. In case you're wondering, it has no specific regional connotations, so that's why we were able to offer either tabasco or soy sauce to pep it up. It works well with both.'

'Ah. You had company in the kitchen for a good hour, didn't you – John Dyson.'

Now Sue smiled, revealing a small and endearing overlap between her front teeth. 'We couldn't get rid of him,' she agreed. 'He's always been fond of Fran. It goes right back to the days when she shared an office with Jackie. And when Jackie died, Fran was kind to him: made sure he was included in things.'

For a moment Montgomery felt a sharp *déjà vu*, back to that nightmare period when William Bird's wife Jean had been killed outright in a car smash, a stupid, unnecessary accident brought about by the selfishness of a drunken driver. He remembered the shock and rage, then the helpless realization that whatever he did for Will, he couldn't bring Jean back. The best they could all manage was to 'make sure he was included in things'. Five years on, he wondered if his self-contained friend was sometimes guilty of accommodating *him* . . .

'She said his visits to the flat had tailed off recently,' he recalled. 'Do you think that was simply the natural course of events?'

'Well . . .' Sue looked uncomfortable. 'Not exactly. It was that dinner party, really, the one Fran told you about . . .' She hesitated, then took a deep breath. 'I wouldn't betray a confidence, but anyone present could tell you this, so it might as well be me. The evening was unusually embarrassing. I've been present at three or four dinners that Robin and Fran have hosted for fellow members of staff. They've gone like clockwork: Fran is a superb cook, and her conversation is invariably courteous and charming. She never looks out of place, even when the others insist on discussing medical politics. Robin can be most entertaining with a drink or two inside him, and I've always had the impression that the other guests have enjoyed a good evening.

'This particular occasion, though, didn't gel at all. Fran did her best, and so did Peter Verity and Sister Brocklebank, but somehow it all seemed to be an effort. I think one spectre at the feast was Leo Masters's wife, Cynthia. I hadn't met her before, myself; he'd come alone the previous time. She seemed very stand-offish: I tried to speak to her twice, and was rebuffed both times. Then, worse than ever, I saw that she was getting drunk. Leo bundled her away early. I've since found out that she's deaf, but why on earth didn't she *explain*? We would all have been more thoughtful then.

'Anyway, when they left, Robin began acting as if it was Fran's fault. He hectored and carped, and seemed determined to humiliate her in a score of little ways – criticizing the food, whatever. I got the feeling that he'd been trying to impress his consultant, but the evening had gone wrong and he was now looking for someone to blame. Fran eventually rose to clear the table – still gracious and serene, outwardly at least – and John followed her into the kitchen. They didn't return for a few minutes, and Robin went to find them. It turned out John had made a clumsy pass at Fran. She told me later she could have

125

handled it herself, but Robin thundered into the room at the wrong moment. Both the men were well tanked-up with ethanol: an almighty row ensued.

'We could hear everything in the living-room. I suppose it's funny now, to think how we maintained polite conversation about the best way to make Cumberland Sauce, and the preponderance of Irving Berlin songs in the hospital review, when all along our attention was elsewhere. You couldn't ignore the shouting. Robin accused John of abusing hospitality, John riposted by calling him a dog in the manger who didn't deserve any wife, let alone one like Fran. Robin then pulled the 'don't darken my door again' line, and John stormed out, slamming the aforesaid door.

'For a few weeks after that evening, I gather relations between the two were decidedly sticky, but eventually they reached some form of truce. I think they realized that they couldn't go on acting like sulky schoolboys when they had a professional relationship to maintain. They were always meeting up at clinico-pathological conferences and such. Then latterly, when Southampton became a certainty, they must have decided that hanging on to residual hostilities was futile.'

A fair appraisal, thought Montgomery. He was careful nevertheless to separate in his mind the facts of Susan Pritchard's story from the heavy overlay of hearsay and interpretation. Suddenly, a key rattled in the front door and someone entered the flat. They heard the screech and chuckle of infants as the living-room door was opened, then the low murmur of an adult voice; seconds later, Barry Pritchard appeared.

'Er, Inspector,' he stammered, 'I wasn't expecting . . . that is, have you been waiting to see me?' His weak-chinned face was tense and watchful; Montgomery was absurdly tempted to reply, 'I think you know the answer to that.'

'Not specifically,' he said, and saw clear relief on the other's features. He wondered why. 'We were just talking to your wife about the general arrangements for Dr Winterley's party, but perhaps you could spare Sergeant Bird five minutes of your time?'

'Yellow dresses?' murmured William Bird as he left the kitchen with the young dermatologist.

Montgomery nodded, then faced Susan Pritchard once again. 'I know that you're a close friend of Robin and Fran,' he said, 'and you'll feel loyalty towards them, but in an investigation of this kind, the truth must come before all other considerations . . . Would you be prepared to describe for me the state of their marriage as you see it?'

She gave a rueful smilé. 'We never know the full truth about someone else's marriage, do we? We just think we do. All I can say is that Fran has always loved Robin, despite his bouts of bullying, and she's looking forward to making a go of Southampton. I can't speak for Robin himself. There have been rumours, but over eight years of traumas the two have stuck together, so perhaps that tells its own tale.'

'Rumours?'

'Oh . . . odd bits of gossip Barry heard at the hospital, about Robin and a secretary, or Robin and a nurse. This was three or four years ago. I don't know if Fran ever knew; certainly she never mentioned it to me. But she's proud, so who can say?'

'What about Loretta?'

'No. He wasn't linked with Loretta. At least, not that we heard.'

They became aware of a scrabbling sound behind them, then the door, already ajar, swung open. A little girl of eighteen months or so in a tartan dress toddled forwards, grasped Sue around the knees then lurched back, tugging at her skirt. Sue crouched to the level of the small bright face. 'Mummy's coming soon,' she said. 'Then we'll all have tea. Granny made your favourite pudding this morning.

'This is Christine,' she told Montgomery. He smiled at the child and admired the dress, then Sue continued, 'I know it's presumptuous and interfering of me, but I've often thought a baby would have helped Robin and Fran. They did have a son, James, four years after they were married, but he was premature and his lungs couldn't function properly. He only lived an hour. I don't know if they've tried again, or not . . . those aren't the sort of things Fran will discuss.

'But I feel guilty sometimes because I have so much. I've got Christine, and Tommy, and Barry. The babies are healthy, and Barry's a wonderful husband. Even when Christine was born, and Mum warned me I was neglecting Barry, he was so uncomplaining and supportive. He used to bring me presents "because it was Wednesday", or some such silly reason . . .'

She bent and picked up her daughter, so that one chubby leg dangled to either side of her hip. 'I appreciate it all,' she said. 'But when I think of people like Fran, and John . . . it just doesn't seem fair.'

12

The crash of the 'tin' in an adjoining court dimly registered in Montgomery's mind as he wiped the runnels of sweat from his face and neck with a thick terry towel. His lungs heaved; he was feeling his age. Only his determination to beat Patrick Lord before the next pair of players came to claim the court kept him going. For Patrick Lord was a cheat.

There was nothing tangible to provoke an open confrontation. Montgomery had played the powerful uniformed inspector on four previous occasions, and had lost the first two matches with no suspicions of gamesmanship. The third, however, his own victory, and the fourth, a draw, had left him with the distinct impression that Lord was a bad loser. Now, at two games all and five-two up in the fifth, he found it was happening again; Lord was both using his own lumbering body to obstruct at every turn, and calling a rash of doubtful lets on Montgomery's strokes. Montgomery was clear about his immediate plan of action. First, he would beat the man. Then he would never play him again.

He wiped his damp palms and the racket handle, then returned to the service box. Concentrate for the whole of each rally, squash-playing lore went, then deliberately make yourself relax in between. In particular, don't think about what has just passed . . . Easier said than done.

Ten minutes later Montgomery had reached match point, and his opponent was florid-faced and wild-eyed above his flamboyant moustache. Finesse had overcome raw strength; every lob, every drop shot, every trickle boast had been models of accuracy and timing. All Lord had been able to do was swear and carp about 'women's play' – receiving in return an enigmatic smile. Now, in the last rally, Montgomery suddenly spotted Lord's racket head trailing near the ground. With a final surge of energy, he drove the ball off the front wall straight at the hulking figure as it crouched on the T. Lord, in a tangle of misplaced limbs, was unable to make the volley.

There was a smattering of applause from the casual onlookers in the gallery above, but no gracious words of congratulation from the vanquished. Montgomery nodded briefly towards Lord then picked up the squash ball and collected the rest of his gear together. Stiffly they walked from the claustrophobic court into the cool air of the corridor outside.

'Bit o' luck, eh?' began Lord.

'Always helps,' said Montgomery equably.

'That cut drop in the third game was jammy, wasn't it? I reckon it was a misstroke. And that let at seven-four in the fifth . . .' He blustered on, but Montgomery wasn't listening. He had just spotted a familiar face: surely that was Dr Verity and a companion entering the glass doors of the show court? They drew level, and he looked again. Yes, Peter Verity was bending to place his sports bag in the corner while chatting with a tall, athletic-looking man who had a neatly trimmed brown beard.

Montgomery carried on past the strengthened glass wall, showered and downed his usual quart of dilute orange juice, but he left the beer-drinking Patrick Lord at the earliest opportunity and wandered back to the courts. He sat on a bench behind a couple dressed in squash whites, and watched the remainder of Verity's match over the girl's shoulder.

It was soon evident that the bearded man was the more experienced player. He varied his pace, he could hit to a length, and his confident use of angle shots had Verity charging up and down the court like an over-excited terrier. He also disguised his shots in a masterly way. Yet Peter refused to give up, and eventually he was rewarded: his opponent began to make mistakes. A mistimed volley, a drop shot that failed to gain a nick, a lob to the back corner which fell short . . . Minutes later the match was Peter's.

He was grinning as he came off the court, and the grin widened when he spotted Montgomery. 'Hello,' he said. 'I didn't know you were a member here. Are you in the League?'

'I took my name out because of work commitments,' replied Montgomery, 'but I came here for a friendly this afternoon. Sunday's a good day.' His eyes strayed in a vaguely interrogatory manner to the panting man at Peter's side.

'Sorry – this is John Dyson, a mate of mine from the hospital.'

The pathologist, thought Montgomery immediately. Frances Winterley's admirer. 'Richard Montgomery,' he introduced himself.

'Detective Inspector,' added Peter.

'Not today,' smiled Montgomery. 'I'm off duty. But I *did* want a few further words with you. Would there be a convenient time tomorrow when we can talk?'

Peter wrinkled his nose. 'Not really. My team's on "take" – that means emergency admissions all day and night. There might be a slack period, but it's not very likely. Do you want to ask your questions now?'

'If you don't mind, that would be most helpful.'

'Just give me ten minutes for a shower, then, and I'm all yours . . .'

Within the allotted time the three were sitting at a quiet table at the back of the bar.

'Fire away!' urged Peter, freshly scrubbed and still buoyant from his win.

'I wanted to ask you about a yellow dress,' said Montgomery. 'We are trying to identify a woman who attended Robin Winterley's party in a Hanoverian-style ball-gown. She was also wearing a mask. Did you see her?' He was addressing Peter, but spotted a spark of interest kindle in John Dyson's watchful eyes. 'Either of you?' he added.

Dyson spoke; his was a deep, mellow voice. 'I did,' he said. 'I was dancing with Fran about – oh, I'd say eleven fifteen, when someone in the kind of dress you've described pushed past us. I only caught a glimpse – not enough to work out who it was.'

'Do you think it could have been Paula Thompkins?'

130

'I'm sorry. I've heard of Paula but I've never met her. We're not exactly at the social hub of things in the Path Department.'

Montgomery was already regretting the leading question. 'Perhaps you can remember the woman's physique?' he said carefully. 'Was she tall or short? Well-built or boyish?'

'Oh – definitely not boyish.' Dyson permitted himself a faint smile. 'The dress was quite revealing at the neck – lots of lace ruffles: *décolletage*, I think it's called – and there was no lack of flesh behind it. I suppose she was about five feet five or six, but I'm not sure what height her heels were.'

'Had you noticed her earlier?'

'No.'

'What about afterwards? Did you see her again?'

'I can't say that I did.'

'Dr Verity?'

'I wish you'd call me Peter. No, I've no recollection of this woman at all. I'm afraid I was with a rather interesting blonde, so it was a case of tunnel vision.'

'Did either of you come across Leo Masters's wife at the party?'

An odd look flashed between them. 'No,' said Peter after a pause.

'But . . .' supplied Montgomery.

'Rest assured you haven't missed your vocation, Inspector. The "but" is: we saw Mrs Masters in the street outside, but she never came in.'

Montgomery poked his chin forwards. 'When was this?'

He shrugged. 'Early on. Eight o'clock.'

'Was she walking past, or standing?'

'She was sitting in her car. We would have spoken to her, but she leaned forward just as we drew level. I thought she was changing her shoes in the driver's well.'

'Did you see the colour of her clothing?'

'Sorry, I can't remember.'

'Was she alone?'

'Yes. When we got to Robin's flat, Leo was already there.'

Montgomery frowned, digesting this information. 'Thank you,' he said eventually.

Across the table, Peter's expression of engaging frankness had slowly metamorphosed into one of doubt. 'Is that all?' he asked.

'Yes. Thanks for your time.'

'Do you mind if I ask you something?'

'Not at all.'

Peter chewed his lip. 'It's about Alison,' he said. 'Alison Blake. Has she, er, spoken to you recently?' At his side, John Dyson half-lifted his head, then let it sink again in an attitude of pseudo-detachment.

'What about?' asked Montgomery.

'Well, if she had, you'd know.'

'. . . And if you've some information for me, the direct route is best.'

'Sorry. Forget I spoke.'

'They say that in courtrooms: a jury is directed to ignore a barrister's outburst, or a piece of irrelevant testimony. Do you think they do, Peter?'

'You win . . . I can't tell you much, though. Just that Alison has a theory concerning Loretta's death. She was going to see you about it, but perhaps she chickened out.'

'Were you impressed with this "theory"?'

'I don't know. At first, I thought she was just seeking attention . . .'

'*Your* attention,' murmured John.

'. . . But then I wasn't so sure. It was something about Loretta's plate of food being left unsupervised on a window-sill before she finished eating it. I think you should see Alison again yourselves.'

'Thanks for the tip.' Montgomery stood up and the two doctors followed suit, Peter stretching and flexing the fingers of his right hand.

'We must have a game, Inspector,' he said. 'If I can beat John, I can take on anyone.'

'Some day, perhaps.'

Peter escorted him to the door while John went to replenish their drinks at the bar. As they stepped into the car-park, where a light breeze eddied through the leaves of surrounding trees, he turned to face Montgomery. 'It's over a week since Loretta died,' he said tersely. 'She certainly didn't commit suicide, and no one seems to believe it was an accident. Have you any real clues? Is this yellow dress a lead?'

'It might be. We don't know as yet.'

'I want to help, you know. Loretta was a good friend of mine.'

'So I gather.'

Something in Montgomery's tone caused the young doctor to flush. 'I told you about our affair,' he said. 'It was the kind of thing that happens in a hospital community. In the early years of a medical career you're often so itinerant that there isn't time to build up a platonic friendship first. It can follow a dead affair, though.'

'But your affair didn't die entirely, did it?'

Peter Verity regarded Montgomery appraisingly, his mouth slightly open, his head cocked to one side. A ray of afternoon sun buffed his black hair into liquid iridescence. 'I didn't want to confuse you,' he said after a moment. 'People with conventional jobs and their own homes tend not to understand.'

'Try me.'

'Well . . . Busy general hospitals are a community in themselves. Nurses and junior staff from other departments live on or near the site. Working hours are all over the place; you're as likely to meet someone you know in the middle of the night as during the day.

'Say a young lad is brought into Casualty after an RTA – a road traffic accident. He's been thrown from his motor bike at seventy miles per hour. The neurosurgeons have done their bit, but there's an added problem – he's losing blood into his chest from a ruptured aorta. The vascular surgeons take him to Theatre and spend four hours trying to fix it. They've just closed up the wound when there's a sudden red spurt in the chest drain and the bottle turns crimson in front of your eyes. You speed up the drips, but it's no good: within two minutes he's dead. A lad of seventeen. You change your clothes and make your legs walk round the corner towards the cluster of frantic relatives. You tell them . . .

'It's late at night and you can't remember when you last had anything to eat. You know you can't get out of the hospital for

133

another twenty hours. You cross the courtyard and there's a nurse you know well just coming off her shift. You talk a bit. She offers you some food. You end up in her room. No one else matters; you're not married, and neither is she. Whatever happens happens in isolation. There's no extrapolation. Next day each of you might be with someone else . . .'

'Cheerfully amoral,' Sister Brocklebank had said of Peter, and where the seduction of innocents was concerned she was probably right. But Peter's relationship with Loretta had been different. In this abnormal community where the young bore such grotesque adult pressures, it would be natural to seek the comfort of a trusted friend. Even Montgomery, ruefully aware of his own overdeveloped tendency to moralize, could accept that.

'I've heard about the baby,' said Peter candidly. 'It's not mine. We were always very careful.'

'Mm.'

'I meant what I said.' In the slanting sun, his dark eyes were brilliant. 'I want to help you if I can. Tell me if there's anything I can do. And don't forget about that game of squash . . .'

Montgomery made another non-committal noise, then turned to walk towards his car. He liked Peter Verity, and in other circumstances he might have taken the proposal of a game seriously. But for now, any idea of an association was untenable: Peter was at best a witness . . . at worst a suspect.

The door to the inner office squeaked as Peter slowly pushed it open. It was Monday afternoon, and he had shared the bustle of emergency admissions with the housemen all day so far, but now there was a blessed hiatus, and he had decided to pay a visit to a particular surgical secretary.

The widening gap revealed a froth of saffron curls before Sonia's profile came into view; she was tapping at a computer keyboard while listening through earphones to a tape of dictated notes: her expression was one of rapt concentration.

Peter watched her amusedly for a few seconds, then crept forward and stretched out his hand. A single red rose slid across the desk in front of her.

'Oh!' She tore off the earphones and swivelled round in the chair. 'Peter!'

He had forgotten how small and breathy her voice was. She wore a creamy short-sleeved top of lambswool blended with fluffy angora, and looked infinitely cuddleable. 'The very same,' he said.

'I didn't think you'd come. You said you'd ring: I waited all last week. In the end, I felt that perhaps you associated me too closely with that nurse's death, and you'd never want to see me again . . .'

She was partly right. 'I'm sorry,' he said. 'I've been very busy.'

Sonia sniffed the rose, her face alight with pleasure. 'It's so fresh – did you buy it? I thought you were on take today.'

'You're not supposed to ask questions like that. Let's just say it came from a local source.' He raised his eyebrows to forbid further questioning on the topic; one of the hospital-owned houses in The Park had now spread the favours of its garden to a wider, more appreciative audience.

'I'm glad you came. You've only seen me drunk. I'm not usually, you know . . . it's just that I was so *bored*, with nobody nice to talk to.'

'Thanks!'

'No – I meant, until you came along.'

He leaned over her desk, supporting his weight on one arm, and idly scanned the words she had typed on the computer screen. It was a discharge letter to a GP. Suddenly, he began to laugh.

Sonia threw him a hurt little look. 'It's not *funny*. It's very sad. This poor lady has lost her leg.'

Peter gulped, and contained his mirth with an effort. 'You can't send this, Sonia,' he said, and pointed to a line in the second paragraph.

'". . . necessitating a Baloney amputation",' she read. 'What's wrong with that?'

'It should be "below-knee".'

'That's what I've put.'

'No . . . at – a – level – below – the – knee.'

'Oh!' She went a becoming shade of pink. 'How silly. I

135

thought it was some Irish operation. Usually they have names.' She tapped out a correction, then scrabbled among her stock of tapes and inserted a new one into the machine. Listening intently, she manipulated the buttons until she had found the right place. 'Perhaps you could help me with this,' she said. 'It's Dr Mace. He always sounds adenoidal.' She lifted the ear-piece so that Peter could hear. A disembodied monotone spoke of 'advanced didease with bodorong due to nymph edeba.'

'Breast cancer, I presume,' said Peter.

'Yes. But what on earth is "bodorong"?'

'I'd guess he's saying *peau d'orange*, which you probably know is French for orange skin. When the lymph channels are blocked, the tissues become swollen and the external surface with its widened pores can resemble orange peel . . . It's an accepted medical term.'

'And nymph edeba – ah! Lymphoedema!' She penned a rapid note. 'Thank you; it all makes sense now.'

'Let's just listen again to be sure.' As Peter leaned forward, his face was inches from her soft neck, with its faint scent of l'Air du Temps. Ignoring the tape, he pressed his lips lightly against her skin.

She flushed once more, but gamely waited until the end of the report before laying the machine down. 'I've got my tea break when Mrs Wilkinson comes back,' she said, indicating the adjoining empty desk. 'Would you like to come to the canteen with me?'

'I'm afraid I can't. I should be back on the ward now. But there was something I wanted to ask you.'

'Oh?' Anticipation shone in her wide blue eyes.

'You told me you worked for a spell as Leo's private secretary, doing a locum while Mrs Deakin was on maternity leave.'

Her disappointment was painfully apparent. 'That's right,' she said quietly. 'It was for a few weeks around Easter.'

'Have you any recollection of a nurse asking to speak with Leo in confidence?'

'As a patient, do you mean?'

'No. Someone who wanted to discuss accounting matters with him – a short, plump junior nurse.'

'Nurse Blake!'

Peter's heart gave a jolt. 'That's right,' he said calmly.

'Yes, I remember her. All rigid and intent, like some sort of biblical martyr . . .'

The bleep in Peter's pocket made a piercing intrusion into their conversation. 'I'll answer it outside in a minute,' he said. 'We need to talk as soon as possible. Are you free tomorrow night?'

'Er, yes, but . . .'

'Have dinner with me. Luigi's, at eight o'clock.'

She hesitated. 'If it's only information you want, there's no need to buy me dinner.'

'It isn't only information I want.'

'Oh . . . then, yes. Yes, please.'

'Good.' He made as if to leave the desk, then bent down again to whisper in her ear. 'Crohn's disease is a problem for men, too, you know.'

'What?'

Grinning, he pointed to the sheet at the top of the pile of printed letters: *A diagnosis of Crone's disease was made*, she had typed. 'I think you need me,' he said.

She giggled, a delighted tinkle of uncomplicated happiness. Instantly the door opened and the other secretary, a middle-aged woman with vinegar features and dark, utilitarian clothes, made a straight-backed progress to the other desk.

Peter nodded at both, and left.

Two hours later, John Dyson was feeding his own final histology report on to a small rotating spool. In the background he heard a telephone ring, but his concentration was on the stained slide as he moved it to and fro under the microscope.

There was a click of high heels and a rap on the door. 'Come in,' he said.

Miss Stoddard, the department secretary, stood on the threshold. 'Sorry to interrupt your work, Dr Dyson,' she said. 'There's a Nurse Blake on the telephone, asking for a word with you. She sounds upset. Shall I put her through?'

The old feeling of reluctance resurfaced. Alison – ringing *him*. Why? 'All right,' he said tersely, and crossed to pick up his own receiver. 'John Dyson.'

'Oh . . . Dr Dyson. I'm so sorry to disturb you. I thought you might have gone, since it's five o'clock . . .'

'What's the problem, Alison?'

'I – oh, this is awful. I don't know how to say it. I – I've received an anonymous letter.'

'A *what*?'

'An anonymous letter. It's really horrible.' Her voice shook, and slid to a higher pitch. 'Someone's threatening me!'

'Surely not.' John instinctively made his own voice slow and soothing. 'Have you got it with you? Are you in a private enough place to read it out?'

'I *can't* do that. I'm sorry, I just can't!'

He could feel the force of her threatened hysteria down the telephone line, and cursed himself for a fool. 'Don't worry,' he said hastily. 'It doesn't matter. Just tell me the gist.'

'It's only a couple of lines . . .'

'The gist if you can manage it.'

'Well . . . it says it could have been me, and I should keep quiet.'

'What could have been you?'

'I don't know. It's too vague. Oh, Dr Dyson, what do you think I should do? I feel so scared.'

He hesitated. 'I think you've no choice but to tell the police. Are you in the Nurses' Home now? Then ring Inspector Montgomery and see what he says. I'm sorry I can't come and help you with this myself; I have to dash off in a minute for a meeting up at the District. It's one I can't get out of.'

'Oh, you mustn't miss your meeting. Thank you so much for advising me. I really didn't know who to turn to. I'll ring the police as you say – I'll ask for Sergeant Bird . . .'

As she prattled on, John Dyson listened with mixed feelings. One question kept recurring in his mind and would not be suppressed: why was she telling him? Why not Peter?

13

'"It could have been you. Do yourself a favour and keep your mouth shut,"' read Jackson. 'Charming!'

The message – an ugly little concoction of bonded notepaper and strips of pasted newsprint – lay on Sergeant Bird's desk. In some parts, individual letters had been used; in others, entire words. Only the envelope bore capital letters printed by hand.

'First class stamp; posted in the city centre on Saturday,' said Montgomery. 'Address written in blue biro, newsprint inside from a quality paper: I'd say *The Times*. You saw Alison, Will. What was your impression?'

William Bird sighed and pulled a face. 'I can't make her out,' he said. 'She was scared, but stubborn – wouldn't tell me why anyone should threaten her like that. I brought up Verity's point about the food on the window-sill, and she agreed she'd discussed that with him, but she couldn't offer any suggestion as to why someone would want to poison her food.

'She said she didn't feel safe in her room any more. You've seen the place, sir – that corridor cul-de-sac is certainly creepy for a young girl on her own. And it seems she might be having mental problems: I met Janet Harper on my way out – you remember, Ward 7's staff nurse – and she told me Alison had been in quite a tizzy last Monday night, claiming that Loretta had come back from the dead to demand justice.'

'What – she saw Loretta?'

'Not exactly. She had been willing her to return, apparently out of some sort of guilt, then she heard a few odd sounds in the block and interpreted them as Loretta. Janet and Paula went to investigate; they didn't find anything. Loretta's own door was locked.'

'Paula . . . I wish we knew where she fitted in.'

'I asked Janet again about Paula's rift with Loretta. She knew nothing of a specific quarrel, but was keen to postulate reasons for a broader cooling-off between the girls. She repeated her opinion that Loretta had always been a cheap little social climber – doesn't mince words, our Janet – and even a *nouveau* would appear to be a step up to a working-class girl. But apparently there's now some gossip that Mr Thompkins's truck haulage business has been in big trouble recently, and the family risks losing the house. So Paula would have been no more use to Loretta, and Alison, the safe option, was always there to fall back on.'

Montgomery was thoughtful. 'I never did see a crack in that swimming pool,' he said, 'and their car had clearly been traded down . . . We must talk more about Paula soon. But first,' he became brisk, 'we've got this letter to sort out.'

'I reckon Alison sent it to herself,' said Brian Jackson, who had been examining the crude message with interest. 'She seems to have been seeking attention from the other nurses and doctors; the post box is within walking distance from the hospital; she couldn't offer Will a plausible reason as to why someone should try to harm her.'

'That certainly crossed my mind,' agreed Montgomery. 'We don't want to get side-tracked from our main investigation if it *is* a hoax – but we can't make assumptions just yet. We must test the envelope for prints and saliva, and identify which newspaper was used as a source of words and phrases . . . Robert, would you find out the arrangements for rubbish disposal in the Nurses' Home and every other hospital residence? Also see if there are any communal newspapers in places like the Mess, with a view to tracking down the mutilated paper. Thank you . . .' He turned his attention again to the envelope, where Alison's name and address were neatly printed in slanting capitals. 'This is the only bit of handwriting,' he mused. 'I wonder if it has features in common with any of Loretta's mementoes?' He switched his gaze to Jackson, who looked mildly uncomfortable. 'You inspected the correspondence that Talbot Dawes brought in for us, didn't you? Did you find anything significant?'

'Er, no, sir.'

Montgomery knew Jackson's evasiveness of old. 'You *did* go through the box, didn't you?'

'Just briefly, sir. I'm afraid I was in court yesterday morning, then I had to meet Packy Murphy in a pub because he promised a hot tip . . .'

Which didn't materialize, despite hours of liquid persuasion, thought Montgomery. Aloud, he said, 'Bring me the box. And the diary we had originally. I'll double check the documents myself.'

Minutes later, in his own office, Montgomery was ruminating furiously. He had found a small card, bearing a photograph of wild flowers reflected in water, and inside was written: *I can't stop thinking about you – B*. Not only this; the diary had revealed another puzzle that Jackson had missed . . .

There was a tap at the door, and William Bird entered. 'Forensic have just been on the phone,' he said. 'Those sauce bottles were clean. Nothing in them but culinary ingredients. They also said . . .' Here he looked slightly abashed.

'Go on. I can take it.'

'They said you would need at least ten mls of water or twenty mls of alcohol in order to dissolve the lethal dose of amylobarbitone, so if it was administered via a sauce bottle, someone would have had to have shaken an inordinate quantity on to Loretta's food.'

Montgomery grimaced in return. 'Ouch,' he said. 'I suppose I *did* get carried away. It seemed a reasonable idea at the time. Oh, well . . . come and tell me what you think of this.' He indicated the card.

Sergeant Bird pursed his lips. 'The writing's not very similar,' he said.

'Not the writing, Will, the sentiment. Who is this "B" who was besotted with Loretta? There's no one on Alison's list whose name begins with B.'

'I don't know, sir, but the card could be any age. There's no date.'

'All the material in this shoebox relates to the last two years.'

'Ah, then – what about Barry Pritchard?'

'Exactly.'

They stared at each other in silence.

'No,' said William Bird at last. 'Anyone with his solid family credentials would have to be mad to send a card like this. Think how nurses under one roof must gossip.'

'You're forgetting, Will: this is one nurse who managed to conceal not only the father of her child but the actual fact of her pregnancy from her family and all her colleagues. The relationship with "B" might have been a bit of discreet fun for her.'

Sergeant Bird examined the card, careful to hold it by the edges only. 'We can check fingerprints against Alison's letter,' he said. 'Are there any more cards?'

'Not that I've come across. But there's this . . .' Montgomery pushed Loretta's diary across the desk to his sergeant; the open double page equated to seven days in May. 'What do you think?'

'They're just appointments, like Brian said.'

'Look more closely.'

Sergeant Bird peered down at the entries. 'I can't see – oh, wait. There's a little dot against one of the dates . . . no, it's an asterisk. And here's another. Are these what you meant?'

'Yes. But look at that second one again. Are you sure it's an asterisk?'

'Oh – it's a tiny letter T.'

'Now turn the page.'

'Here's another.' He raised his head. 'Some sort of code for lovers' trysts?'

'Not necessarily. When we discussed this before, we concluded that Loretta was unlikely to be able to record concrete evening appointments with a married lover. But what say these are *potential* meeting opportunities: supposing the dates are nights when he was on duty in the hospital?' Montgomery leaned forward; he was feeling both excited and smug. 'The letter T occurs on every sixth day, the asterisks more randomly. Now, if you remember from the Philippa Rowe case up at the District Hospital, the team of doctors responsible for the day's emergency admissions in medicine or surgery is said to be "on take". That state lasts for twenty-four hours, until the next morning, and the entire team, from consultant to house officer, is likely to be involved.'

'So you think "T" might stand for "take"?'

'There's a good chance. The "take" rota puts each team of doctors in the hot seat at regular intervals. *Individual* on-call duties, by contrast, are more random.'

'Hence the asterisks . . . that's clever, sir; I hope you're right. If we can get hold of the doctors' rotas, the diary could lead us straight to Loretta's mystery man!'

'I'd like to think so. We deserve a break. I propose we give Brian a chance to redeem himself: he can track down the duty rotas for Masters, Winterley, Pritchard and Peter Verity, while you and I call on Cynthia Masters.'

'Again?'

'Yes. I'm fed up with this yellow dress nonsense. If it's all a storm in a teacup, it's time we found out and moved on to other things. Likewise the discrepancies in Mrs Masters's story for Friday night. She may have lied to us about her whereabouts for reasons that are far from felonious, but until we ask her, we aren't going to know.' He stood up and stretched. 'Today we cut out the dead wood, Will. I'm determined.'

One door of Leo Masters's double garage was open as the detectives approached the large, detached house; somewhat to their surprise, the consultant himself emerged, clad in oil-stained blue overalls.

'Day off,' he explained with a friendly smile. 'I'm catching up on some DIY: treating myself to an extra bank of garage shelves.' He glanced down at the overalls. 'Just like theatre garb, aren't they?' he chuckled. 'I don't think you've ever seen me in my civvies. Come into the house . . .'

In the cool hallway Montgomery divulged that it was Cynthia they were hoping to interview.

'Oh.' A shadow passed over Leo Masters's face. 'She's in the kitchen; I'll fetch her.' He paused. 'Look, Inspector. I'd appreciate it if you could be patient with Cynthia. She hasn't been herself over the last few days, and her hearing is a struggle at the best of times . . .' He left them and returned with his wife, who did indeed look anxious and strained. 'I'll just pop out and remove these overalls, then I'll be with you.'

'You don't need to.' Cynthia's voice was faint. 'Finish your shelves . . . It's only me they want.'

'Nonsense!' he said solidly. 'Can't have you entertaining officers of the law unchaperoned. Besides – I might have the odd two penn'orth to contribute myself.' Now he was genial, tacitly offering moral support. He squeezed Cynthia's shoulder and strode away before she could protest. Within minutes they were all seated together in the elegant, green-toned drawing-room.

'We spoke before about a yellow dress belonging to your daughter,' remarked Montgomery to Cynthia. 'You told me that Paula had borrowed it for a party, but there seems to have been some subsequent confusion as to which party, and who was actually wearing it. Where is the dress now?'

'Here. She returned it yesterday.'

'Did she state categorically that she had worn it?'

'Well . . . not in so many words. But she gave that impression.'

'Was it altered?' asked Sergeant Bird.

'Not permanently. She said something like "It was fine with a few tacking stitches." We didn't speak at length; she was in a hurry.'

'Did Paula say anything about attending Robin Winterley's party?'

'No; she described her party as a "Radiology bash".'

Leo Masters was frowning. Montgomery turned to him. 'You told us you spotted the same dress at Mr Winterley's flat. Are you still confident that it was the garment your wife made?'

'Well . . . I *thought* I was. It's a pretty distinctive gown, with all those ruffles – but surely, you can ask Paula about this if you're in doubt?'

'We try to confirm our facts from more than one perspective whenever possible,' smiled Montgomery reassuringly. 'Mrs Masters, are you certain you didn't see the dress yourself while you were in the vicinity of Willow Court?'

'I beg your pardon?' Cynthia cupped a hand behind her ear, but there was shock in her face: she had heard the question.

Montgomery repeated the gist; she stared at him, wide-eyed. 'You – you're mistaken, Inspector,' she stammered. 'I was never there. We've already discussed all this; I stayed at home that evening.'

'I'm afraid I have to contradict you, Mrs Masters. You were

seen outside Robin Winterley's flat by two reliable witnesses at eight o'clock on the night of the party.'

Leo inhaled sharply. 'Cynthia?'

'This isn't right. They must have seen someone else. I was here all night . . .'

'Mrs Masters, we know that isn't the case.' Montgomery was gentle, but firm. 'You were spotted leaving in your car by one of your neighbours a few minutes after your husband had left. We know you went to Willow Court. Were you watching the party guests, or did you actually go inside?'

Cynthia Masters looked stricken. She turned to Leo in supplication. 'I'm sorry, Leo. I shouldn't have lied. He's right: I did go out. It was a lip-reading class. I wanted to surprise you . . . I didn't want you to be always ashamed of me, making excuses . . .'

'Ashamed?' He gaped at her.

'Where was this class?' asked Montgomery.

'Sheriff's Crescent. I just parked outside Mr Winterley's flat *en passant*, as it were. Pure idle curiosity.'

'Mrs Masters . . .' Montgomery enunciated carefully. 'Willow Court is nowhere near the direct route from here to Sheriff's Crescent. Now, we've established you were there. I'd like to repeat my question: did you go inside?'

'No!' Her voice shook; Leo, clearly perturbed, darted an accusing glance at Montgomery.

'Tell me what you did, then.'

Cynthia twisted her fingers together in a restless cat's cradle. 'I – I watched for a few minutes, that was all.'

'What time did your lip-reading start?'

'I'm sorry? Oh – what time . . . eight o'clock. The session was eight till ten.'

'So you made yourself late in order to watch guests coming and going at a party to which you had been invited, and presumably could have attended after ten if you had so wished.'

'It wasn't as simple as that – but you don't believe me anyway, do you? Please wait here . . .' She rose with quiet dignity and left the room, returning after a short space of time with a book, a notepad and a document wallet. 'This is my manual – and these are the lecture notes. Here's the receipt from the college, with the class number on it . . . Leo is often out on a Friday. I was going to tell him when I'd achieved some competence . . .' She gave a faint smile. 'Actually, I hoped he'd notice for himself.'

'Fair enough. You went to a lip-reading class. But you still haven't explained why you lingered opposite Willow Court first. I'm afraid "idle curiosity" simply won't do as an answer.'

Cynthia bit her lip, stared at Montgomery's granite features, and went red then white in rapid succession.

'I must protest,' burst out Leo. 'Can't you see how you're upsetting my wife? So she had a strange whim; people do, you know.'

'It's all right, Leo,' she whispered. 'The inspector is quite correct. I went there for a purpose . . .' Her tortured gaze reverted to Montgomery's face. 'I – I'd got a foolish idea in my head. I thought Leo might be having an affair – no, please, Leo, let me go on. I watched for a while in case he left the party early with someone, and then . . . then I went to my class.'

'But why?' Leo was incredulous. 'How could you ever imagine such a thing?'

'Oh . . . it seems so silly now. I know I was wrong. It was little things . . . a night I couldn't contact you at the hospital, that button in your car . . . Nothing to speak of. I suppose being alone here so much, I magnified the incidents out of all proportion.'

She gave Montgomery an eager, tremulous smile, but his own facial muscles refused to respond: there was more to this than she had so far revealed, he was convinced.

Leo unwittingly put the question for him. 'Cynthia, love, there's nothing there to turn into suspicions of an affair. I can't believe you'd think that of me. What's the real reason? You must tell me.'

She was dumb.

'*Please*,' he urged. 'For all our sakes.'

'It was the money,' she said draggingly. 'That five hundred pounds. But it doesn't matter now; I know I was wrong.'

'Five hundred pounds? What – oh, I see.' He dismissed the issue in an instant. 'I understand why Cynthia was misled,' he

146

said to Montgomery, 'and I'm happy she now knows the truth. Is that all you wanted to discuss?'

Money, and a nice round sum . . . 'Could you just enlarge a little on this question of money that worried Mrs Masters?' Montgomery asked pleasantly.

'It was a miscellaneous cheque to cover supplementary school fees for Edwin: cello lessons, tennis coaching, that kind of thing. I paid it without consulting Cynthia, then she spotted the entry on our bank statement weeks later.'

'Just a one-off sum?' Out of the tail of his eye, Montgomery saw Cynthia open her mouth, then close it again.

Leo Masters gave a jerky nod.

'Mrs Masters . . .' Sergeant Bird's voice was soft and mellow. 'You have taken courage and told us that you thought Leo might leave the party early with someone . . . did you have a particular person in mind?'

'I – no. I suppose I thought maybe some nurse . . .'

'Loretta Dawes, for instance?'

'No! Definitely not Loretta. I had no one in particular in mind. My suspicions were diffuse . . .' Rainbow hues chased across her face once more; the more emphatic her pronunciations, the less convincing she sounded.

Leo's golden head was bowed.

Montgomery negotiated his Sierra through the teeming traffic with automatic precision while the bulk of his mind pondered the events of the previous hour. 'Cynthia's not convinced, is she?' he murmured to Sergeant Bird.

' "The lady doth protest too much, methinks," ' was the reply.

'My sentiments exactly. That's Shakespeare, isn't it?'

'*Hamlet*, sir.'

'I can only remember bits of *Macbeth* from school . . . but yes: that's the feel of it. Cynthia wanted to persuade herself as much as us that Leo wasn't involved. I feel she was waiting for an unequivocal refutation that never came . . . that money was the point when she lost faith.'

'Bloody expensive cello lessons.'

'Indeed. And the figure would never have been so perfect.'

Montgomery halted smoothly as a traffic light turned against them. 'It's perfect for something else, though,' he went on. 'Blackmail.'

14

'How long have I known Leo? Let me see . . . it must be fourteen years . . .' Eileen Brocklebank was professional enough not to express her surprise at the question, but Montgomery saw a fleeting shadow of perturbation pass over her wholesome features. They sat with Sergeant Bird in the stuffy relatives' waiting-room, while beyond the door the thump and rattle of hospital life carried on apace.

'He's a good man,' she continued. 'He always does more than just the minimum necessary for his patients. They love him – and so do his junior staff. Too many of his peers display the most nauseating charm to patients while humiliating young doctors and nurses at every opportunity. Leo isn't one of those. He remembers what it's like to be an inexperienced junior, the piggy-in-the-middle, and he's always supportive, always fair.'

'He does a bit of private practice, I believe,' said Montgomery.

'Most of them do. There's a special wing for private patients here in the hospital: Jordan House.'

'Doesn't that conflict with his, er, liberal image?'

'Not at all. After all, what does "liberal" mean? Tolerant, open-minded, unbiased . . . Leo believes in free choices. We were discussing this just recently: we both agreed that if a small businessman, for instance, wants to spend his money on health insurance rather than, say, satellite television, so that if he ever needs an operation he can choose the time to avoid wrecking his business, he should be allowed to do so.

'Ideally, no one would need to make such provision, but the demands on the NHS are so enormous, universal choice for "cold" surgery will never be a reality. For emergencies, of course, the Health Service is the nonpareil.

'So, yes, Leo does private practice, but he never lets it impinge on his NHS work. Unlike some other consultants I could mention, if one of his patients needs a catheter at nine o'clock at night, Leo will come in himself and perform the procedure, not ask the sister in Jordan House to call some already overburdened NHS junior . . .'

From outside in the corridor, they heard Janet Harper's voice: 'Peter, Mr Fenwick is back from his X-ray now. Shall I prepare a trolley for the liver biopsy?'

Peter Verity, perhaps. Montgomery remembered Sister Brocklebank's appraisal of that young man. 'Would you say Leo is attractive to the opposite sex?' he asked.

She smiled. 'We're all pretty fond of him here, if that's what you mean, the younger nurses in particular. He's considerate, as I implied before, and I think the African trip invested him with an air of glamour. On top of that, he looks so distinguished.'

'Sister . . . I'm sorry to ask this, but do you think there is any possibility that he might have been conducting an affair with Loretta Dawes? Have you seen any behaviour which might support that hypothesis?'

She was stunned. 'Leo and Loretta? No – I can't say I have. I've always had the impression that he's devoted to Cynthia. Despite the difficulties.'

'Difficulties?'

'Her hearing. You know? Yes . . . She simply won't wear a hearing-aid, and won't warn people about her problem, but she gets upset if Leo does. I'm sorry . . . I'm telling tales out of school here. Suffice it to say, he wouldn't do anything to hurt Cynthia.'

Like admitting to an affair? wondered Montgomery. Had Loretta threatened to tell?

Sister Brocklebank was looking at him anxiously. 'Really, I can't imagine Leo being mixed up in the recent tragedy. He's a genuinely kind man.' A memory sparked in her eyes. 'Let me tell you what he did one Christmas. The patients here on Ward 7 were all geared up to receive the usual pallid slices of "plastic" turkey from the canteen when Leo wheeled in a genuine bird,

149

beautifully roasted and decorated with stuffing balls, chestnuts, holly and all kinds of things. He'd bought it himself and persuaded the kitchen staff to cook it . . .

'He was wearing his green theatre clothes, and brandishing a huge serrated knife. Before he started to carve, he held up an X-ray and pretended to study it: the film proved to be from the bird itself! The patients were delighted. I know that nowadays, when every penny is accounted for, such a scenario would be impossible, but it didn't seem a waste of money at the time. It gave enormous pleasure to those patients: one elderly man died just two days later, but I saw him laugh on Christmas Day, and forget for a while that he was in hospital . . .'

'Breathe out . . . right out. Now – hold it!'

Deftly Peter thrust the biopsy needle through the intercostal space into the liver, his fingers maintaining a constant suction on the syringe. He then withdrew it. The patient, a sallow-looking man of fifty, made no murmur of complaint; the area had been well infiltrated with local anaesthetic.

'Well done. You can breathe again now.' Peter released the core of tissue carefully into the specimen pot Janet Harper was holding, while Alison pressed on the wound with a swab. Across the bed, two student nurses were watching wide-eyed. 'I'd like you to stay in bed for the rest of the day, Mr Fenwick,' he went on. 'The nurses will be checking your pulse and blood pressure, just to make sure everything's all right. You might feel a bit of discomfort in your tummy or the tip of your shoulder when the anaesthetic wears off. We'll give you some tablets if necessary . . .'

They wheeled the trolley up the ward to the clinical room, where ablutions were performed and labels written. 'Half-hourly obs for the first two hours,' he said to Janet. 'Then hourly if all is well . . . What complications are we watching out for?' he asked the student nurses.

'Bleeding,' said one.

'That's right. Intraperitoneal haemorrhage. Luckily it's rare – happens in about 0.2 per cent of these biopsies. Biliary periton-

itis is even rarer, but you must always be alert to the possibility
. . .' As he gave them an impromptu teaching session, he saw
Alison in the background, removing debris from the trolley
with ever slower movements. Only once did she look in his
direction, bitter pride vitrifying her face.

Suddenly a door opposite opened. Sister Brocklebank
emerged with two men, one tallish, with an athlete's figure,
carved cheekbones and frosty eyes, the other a few years older,
stouter, reminiscent of a Norfolk farmer. Montgomery and Bird
. . . Peter's own eyes flicked back towards Alison, who was
now reaching into a low cupboard, and he made up his mind:
he would speak to Montgomery.

'Excuse me just a moment,' he said to the two student nurses.
'I have to catch someone before they leave the ward. Think
about why we do a coagulation screen before a liver biopsy,
and we'll discuss that next – if Staff doesn't mind.'

'Go ahead,' said Janet. 'We can all learn.'

He rocketed along the corridor, and caught up with the
detectives just as Montgomery had his hand on the outer swing
doors.

'Inspector . . .'

Montgomery smiled at him. 'Peter.'

'I must speak to you, today, if possible. I've found out
something rather unfortunate, and I think you should know.'

'Are you free at lunchtime?'

'Someone can hold my bleep.'

'Right, then . . . what about The Mint, at one o'clock?' The
Mint, a bar in the basement of the imposing Albany Hotel, was
just down the hill from the Victoria.

'I'll be there,' said Peter.

Montgomery pushed the tall glass across the table to Peter. The
light was dim, their corner isolated. 'One bitter lemon, with
ice,' he said.

'Thanks. I'm afraid it suits my mood. I don't like doing what
I'm about to do.'

'Is it Alison?'

151

'Yes. John told me today about that note . . .' He fingered the condensation on the glass. 'Has Alison mentioned Leo Masters to you in a discreditable context?'

'No – but we know she's hiding something.'

Peter sighed. 'It'll have to be me who blabs, then . . . A week ago, Alison suggested to John and myself that the barbiturates may have been intended for her. While John was present, she justified this on the grounds that she'd left her barely touched plate unattended on a window-sill, and then Loretta had eaten from it. She also hinted that she knew a dark secret about someone in the hospital, but she refused to enlarge on this. When John had left, though, she became a little more specific: she alleged that a consultant had been prescribing medicines for private patients on NHS forms. Alison told me she'd challenged him personally, but been reassured that all was in order.'

Peter took a sip of his drink, and made a sheepish grimace. 'At the time, I must confess I didn't find her story very convincing . . . I thought she was either trying to make herself important, or she'd actually gone a bit loopy; she was in a *mea culpa* frame of mind, even claiming that Loretta had come back from the dead to be avenged. But when I asked a friend of mine who had done a secretarial locum for Leo if she knew anything about it, to my astonishment, she did.'

'Is this Sonia Ball?' asked Montgomery.

'You've got a good memory, Inspector. Yes . . . Sonia told me that Alison had appeared in her office in the private wing and asked to see Leo. She heard a good deal of what they said: apparently it all stemmed from a patient actually praising Leo for waiving half his personal fees when she'd seen him privately then run into financial difficulties; he'd also given her an NHS prescription to save her money. Leo told Alison he'd done that while the patient was transferring to the NHS for her future care, and there would be no more such grey areas.'

Peter raised unhappy eyes to Montgomery's. 'Before I say any more, I want to make something clear. Leo Masters used to be my boss. I admire him tremendously for his skill, his fairness, his personality. I know of no one else in the Victoria who has put more time and money into causes which directly benefit the hospital. If he's committed a minor misdemeanour, it would be a travesty if he loses his career as a result of it. The patients would lose out most of all. The trouble is, there's a precedent: an ENT consultant called O'Reilly was sacked two years ago for doing the same thing. The complexion of his case was quite different, but management at the Victoria aren't known for their powers of discrimination. The General Medical Council, too, can be very tough . . .'

'You're telling me there's a lot at stake,' said Montgomery.

'Yes. And I know what you're thinking: that note fits in. But you must listen to the rest – all of it – before you jump to any conclusions . . .

'Alison's implied supposition was that she'd scratched the surface of something very damaging to Leo, and that he'd tried to silence her at the party, but poisoned Loretta by mistake . . .' Peter drank some more lemon juice. 'Loretta herself knew, though. Alison admitted she'd told her. And Loretta may well have fallen out with Paula over the issue. She had very rigid views over matters like that . . .' He leaned forward. 'What I'm trying to say is: several people may have known. It wasn't just a cosy little secret between Loretta and Alison. I don't believe for one moment that Leo is capable of harming another human being, especially to protect himself, but might it be possible that someone decided to protect *Leo*?'

Montgomery sat in his parked Sierra with Sergeant Bird.

'Well, Verity was speaking the truth, at any rate,' said his companion. 'Pretty little thing, that Sonia.'

'Yes. Give me your ideas, Will. All our suspects seem to be falling over themselves to leap into the frame.'

'I don't know about "ideas", sir, but we can appraise this latest evidence. It's either relevant or it isn't. If it's relevant, then we have a choice between Leo Masters taking care of potential squealers, whatever people think of his character – and I'm not impressed with the "Loretta-by-mistake" angle – or someone else is doing it on his behalf. If he's our man, then that five hundred pounds may tie in nicely. Perhaps Loretta was blackmailing him on this issue alone, and the baby is incidental.'

'And the note to Alison?'

'Just ensuring she keeps her mouth shut.'

'Mm . . . We know Masters and Loretta spoke together at the party, but we've only his word for the content of the conversation. What next, Will?'

'The protectors. Not only Paula may have known, but Cynthia too.'

'That blasted yellow dress!'

'Yes. If the fraud evidence isn't relevant, we come against those three again, but for a different reason: the pregnancy.'

'From what we've heard, though, Loretta would be too busy hating Leo for abusing the NHS to get physically involved with him.'

'Tsk, sir. All the best romances start with conflict before the protagonists rush towards a heady affair. Who knows? Perhaps she tackled Leo about it herself, and one thing led to another. But the intrigue turned sour, and she demanded money . . . Even if Leo proves not to be the father of the child, Cynthia or Paula may have *thought* he was.

'But coming back to today's evidence, sir: I separate "relevant" from "true". We can't ignore the possibility that Alison has been raking up this story for reasons of her own . . .'

Paula stubbed out her cigarette and motioned the two detectives to take a seat at the edge of her bed before perching herself on the desk, her stockinged feet planted on the room's only chair. A gleaming band of sunshine burnished the bowl of oranges on the shelf behind her: this room felt much lighter and more open than Alison's, despite the similarity in size.

'I don't understand why Laurel's dress is so important to you,' she said to Montgomery. 'I borrowed it for the Radiology party, and I returned it to Auntie Cynth on Monday this week.'

Well phrased, thought Montgomery. She hadn't lied yet. 'You gave your aunt the impression that you'd worn the dress yourself,' he said.

'That's right.'

'But you hadn't, had you?'

Her expression of irritated boredom was belied by a glow of heightened colour. 'What makes you say that?'

'The garment was seen and identified at Robin Winterley's party. Whoever was wearing it had a totally different physique from yours . . . Would you like to comment, Paula?'

She was silent for several seconds, her body taut as a stick.

'Did you pass it on to someone else – or did you never borrow it in the first place?'

She gave a resigned shrug. 'I lent it to Beatrice Cunningham, a speech therapist who didn't have her own outfit. It was never right for me; I really shouldn't have borrowed it, but once I had done, I didn't want Auntie Cynth to know I hadn't worn it, so I implied that I had . . . What's the big deal? Aren't you meant to be investigating what happened to Loretta?'

'We are,' said Montgomery.

She looked at him, startled, and reached for another cigarette. 'You don't mind, do you?'

'It's your room . . . Now, could you tell us where we can contact Beatrice?'

'I'm afraid she's on holiday in Canada. She went last weekend.'

More details to check. 'All right. What costume did you wear?'

'Oh, I just cobbled a few things together and went as a man.'

'Can you be more precise? Were you a cavalier, for instance?'

Her dark eyes became even blacker.

'Perhaps you can show us the clothes you used?'

A few minutes later they had a good grasp of Paula's appearance on the fateful Friday night. Montgomery was uneasy; the colours of the costume were suspiciously similar to those worn by the as yet unidentified cavalier at Winterley's party. Could this young girl *really* be implicated in murder? She was the one member of his list of suspects who had never paid a previous visit to the Winterley flat, yet the problem was not insuperable: if she had arrived while most people were concentrating on the speeches, she could have found the capsules, slipped into the utility cupboard to prepare a lethal mixture,

155

then handed Loretta an innocent-looking glass in the dimly lit mêlée of the living-room . . .

But why? Why should Paula go to those lengths? Was it to protect a much-loved aunt from the terror of desertion? Or her uncle from a vengeful lover? Or could she have been protecting Leo from the threatened disclosure of his misplaced generosity? Whichever scenario might be correct, the response seemed extreme. There had to be an extra reason, something affecting Paula more directly . . .

Generosity. Montgomery had been struck by the recurrence of this attribute when witnesses had outlined for him the salient features of Leo's character . . . Perhaps there *had* been an extra reason: if Janet Harper was right, and Mr Thompkins was in trouble with his haulage business, perhaps Leo had been helping out the family financially, enough to enable them to hang on in their house with their favourite antiques until better times came along. Cynthia would have resented this – so he didn't tell her . . .

One other possibility remained.

'Paula,' he asked quietly, 'did *you* go to Robin Winterley's party?'

'You've asked me that before; I've told you I didn't.'

'I know what you said, but you may not have thought the truth was important on that occasion. You might not have wanted to be involved in all the questioning – perhaps so you wouldn't have to speak out against someone you care for . . .'

Paula's hand trembled, and ash fell from the cigarette on to the desk. Montgomery sensed that she was making a super-human effort not to thrust the filter between her lips and inhale. 'That's nonsense,' she said. 'I wasn't there.'

Beside Montgomery Sergeant Bird stirred, and the bed creaked ominously. 'Are you close to your aunt?' he asked in his deep voice.

'Of course.'

'Very fond of her?'

'Yes . . .'

He nodded.

15

'Sounds as if Paula may have made up the Beatrice tale to let her aunt off the hook,' commented Brian Jackson the next day when Montgomery had delivered a personal update to his team of detectives.

'It should be simple enough to check,' said Montgomery. 'The girls may have been masked, but they must have spoken to people they knew at the Radiology party, not to mention Winterley's flat. Ask Donald Duck and the French maid: we've got their names. But first, tell me why you and Graham are looking so smug. I presume the medical rotas have provided some interesting information?'

'They have that, sir.' Jackson rustled open a sheet of paper. 'The chart we've obtained from the switchboard staff shows a direct correlation between the dates Loretta annotated with a T in her diary and the dates when Leo Masters's surgical team was on take for the hospital. Now, apart from "take" nights, consultants don't have specific on-call duties: they provide a kind of last-resort continuous cover. The work-horses are the house officers, with second-on cover from various other grades of junior staff. Are you with me? Well – we looked to see if Loretta's asterisks fitted in with any of their rotas – and they corresponded exactly with Robin Winterley's nights for second on call!' He gave a knowing leer. 'So it's Winterley who's been giving it to her!'

'Playing away,' murmured Montgomery automatically.

'Same deed, whatever you care to call it.' Jackson was triumphant. 'And he's blood group A, you'll remember.'

'Did anyone else's on-call correlate?' asked Sergeant Bird.

'Only patchily. Peter Verity works for Kevin Cox, so his nights didn't often coincide. Neither did Barry Pritchard's.'

Montgomery was silent, considering the news. In many ways it was no surprise: Susan Pritchard had appraised him of Winterley's previous record of infidelities. Yet what did it mean?

Had Robin Winterley murdered Loretta in his own flat, with his own wife's capsules? Poor Frances; as if she hadn't borne enough burdens already. 'Did the switchboard staff tell you about any rumours concerning Winterley or Loretta?' he asked. Switchboard operators in busy general hospitals were notorious gatherers and purveyors of gossip. 'Did Winterley ever answer his bleep from the Nurses' Home?'

A thin layer of jauntiness fell from Jackson. 'I'm afraid they clammed up,' he said.

Montgomery sighed; he knew that Jackson's official manner could sometimes be as emollient as a Brillo pad.

'They're very loyal,' added Smythe. 'We didn't want to push too hard.'

'Fair enough. I might try my luck with the night staff . . . what we have is highly suggestive, but we need a touch of direct evidence to clinch it. For today's purposes, though, let us assume that Winterley *is* the father of the child. Does that make him the murderer? He certainly had every opportunity to prepare and administer the drug. But what about the threatening letter to Alison? How does that fit in? We'd be wise not to ignore our alternative suspects completely. In fact, this might be a good time to re-evaluate them.

'Take Leo Masters: he's not the baby's father, but Loretta probably knew about his fraudulent dealings with private patients. He'd been to Willow Court before, and he spoke with Loretta on the night of the party. Apropos Alison and the letter, he was aware of her knowledge because she had challenged him in person.

'Then there's Cynthia Masters. She may or may not have known about the fraud, but she admitted to Will and myself that she had suspected Leo of an affair with someone. If Paula is to be believed, then the masked woman in the lemon taffeta dress wasn't Cynthia – but Paula might just be protecting her aunt. As for Paula's own position, it seems more than likely that Loretta picked a quarrel with her over Leo's behaviour. If Leo was helping to cushion the Thompkins family financially during their period of business difficulties, his exposure could have had serious consequences for them. Paula might have been present at the Winterley party as a cavalier, giving her a late but adequate opportunity to silence Loretta. Then she may have thought that a threatening letter would be enough to keep Alison quiet . . .

'Who else have we got? Barry Pritchard could possibly be the "B" who sent the romantic card to Loretta, but there's no other evidence to link him with the case. Frances Winterley can't be ruled out in view of the latest findings, but both she and Susan Pritchard only emerged from the kitchen around the time of the speeches, and neither of them was seen anywhere near Loretta during the final half-hour before she hid herself away in the small bedroom. I can't fit any of these three in with the Alison note, either . . . So that's our main group of suspects.'

'Are we sure the note's genuine?' broke in Smythe.

'No, we're not.' Montgomery flicked an enquiring glance towards Allen, who gave a discreet shrug. His search for vandalized pages of *The Times* had been fruitless.

'Then shouldn't we be considering Alison as another possible? All right, she's religious and shy, but think what horrors have been perpetrated in the name of religion over the centuries! And she wasn't too shy to go and beard Leo Masters, a consultant surgeon no less, about his accounting irregularities.'

'Supposing she doctored Loretta's food herself. Let's face it, she had the best opportunity of all! Perhaps she only wanted Loretta sleepy for some obscure reason, and then it all went wrong . . . So she's stricken with guilt, and looking for exoneration, and hears voices or whatever – a kind of Banquo's ghost . . . sir?'

Montgomery was staring at him rigidly. 'Go on, Graham,' he said after a moment.

'Well, then she wonders who else will remember how good her opportunity was, so she pre-empts suspicion by hinting that *she* may have been the intended victim. She spins an old tale about Masters to Peter Verity with a show of reluctance, knowing that he's likely to tell us – then fakes an anonymous letter for good measure. What do you think?'

'Nothing is proven against Winterley yet,' said Montgomery. 'It's as good a scenario as any.'

*

159

Later, in his own office, Montgomery opened one of Loretta's diaries again, turning the pages slowly with his strong, lean fingers until he came to the entry he sought. Summer, two years earlier: Loretta had spent a year as a student nurse and was at that point in the throes of her brief affair with Peter Verity. 'Just mates, really,' Peter had said; 'amicable separation'.

Yet here in front of him were their two names in block capitals, LORETTA DAWES above, PETER VERITY beneath, and all the letters common to both names had been crossed out and printed again at the side: RETTE. By parameters which were mysterious to him, this had merited a circled score of five; as if in conclusion she had then penned LORETTA VERITY. The games of a young girl in love . . .

William Bird approached on the other side of the glass door; Montgomery lifted a hand and caught his attention. 'What do you make of this?' he asked when the sergeant had settled in the proffered chair. 'Your knowledge of the obscure is sounder than mine.'

'It's onomancy,' said William Bird without hesitation.

Montgomery's eyebrows shot ceilingwards.

'No, sir, not that. Onomancy is a form of divination using the letters of a name. In this example, Loretta was looking for compatibility with Peter, shared personality traits. She crossed off each letter common to both their names, and merited a point every time. That score of five is quite good. One point implies a couple have virtually nothing in common, seven or more points means they're ideally matched. She must have reckoned five was encouraging enough to start thinking of wedding bells.'

Hard-bitten Loretta Dawes . . . 'Sounds about as useful as horoscopes or daisy petals,' said Montgomery.

'You have no romance, sir. We used to take it seriously at my school. There was a girl I hankered after, who attended the grammar next door to mine. Her name was Lucy Guest. I did this test with the letters and scored all of *one*. Minimal congruity. The very next day, the class bully announced that he was going out with her. I wasn't bothered – I'd already been warned!'

Montgomery snorted. 'You accuse *me* of having no romance?'

'Ah, sir . . . surely the better part of valour is pragmatism.'

160

'Verity gave Loretta a gold ankle chain,' mused Montgomery, looking back at the diary. 'Presumably her choice. She was wearing it when she died . . .' He sighed. 'I need to trust Verity, Will. We've got to have a bit more evidence before we can confront Robin Winterley over Loretta, and I think the night switchboard operator may be the key. If he's as loyal as the day staff, however, I'm not going to get very far without some sort of cover. And that's where Verity comes in.'

'But,' said Sergeant Bird.

'Exactly. But. Loretta wore his trinket the night she died. Was that an expression of the fact that she'd moved on and could wear it without pain? Or did it signify a renewed bond between the two of them? We know his blood group is O positive, and the baby can't be his, but mightn't she have pretended to him that it was? Especially if the real father didn't want to know . . . Alison's wild tale may have suited him nicely: what if *Verity* sent her that note? And there's one more thing – he didn't want any resuscitation efforts to be made on Loretta.'

William Bird's plump face was thoughtful. 'He's a medic. He could see she was dead.'

'So is Robin Winterley, but he wanted to try.'

'That could have been an act on Winterley's part.'

Their eyes met across the desk.

'Do what you have to, sir,' said William Bird.

Montgomery picked up the telephone.

Joe Cochrane, sixty-three, sedentary and emphysematous, represented the night-time eyes and ears of the Victoria Hospital and all its outposts. His world was a chair and a huge semicircular console where red lights winked at him and buzzers sounded; co-ordination and communication were his *raison d'être*, and his friendly tones were often the first sound a hapless hospital junior heard after being jolted from the velvet depths of slumber by the strident demands of the bleep.

On this Thursday night, the usual trickle of resident doctors and pharmacists had passed through his smoky den, relieving his boredom and theirs, sharing a cup of strong tea, sometimes even bringing him a present of whisky or cake. It was now eleven fifteen, and calls appertaining to the late evening drug round had virtually petered out.

With a clatter and the most nominal of knocks, the outer door flew open and a dark-haired young man bounded into the room. Joe recognized the puppy-dog energy and high spirits immediately: it was Peter Verity. Flushed and grinning, his guest strode forward and placed a tall brown paper bag in front of the console. 'Hi, Joe,' he said. 'Something to while away the nocturnal hours.' He leaned over and added in a whisper, 'Jameson's.'

Ah! Irish whiskey, triple-distilled. No gut-rot firewater from Peter. 'Champion,' he said appreciatively. 'Stay and share it . . . Who's your friend?' A taller, older man stood in the background; he had cool blue eyes, hollowed cheeks and a face which would look broody in repose.

'Oh – this is Richard. We meet at Westwood. Richard – meet Joe, the heart of the hospital, the benign spider with a web of a thousand phone lines . . .'

'Steady on, young feller. Nine hundred and ninety, perhaps . . .' He cackled. 'You two been playing tonight?'

'Not each other,' said Peter, 'but I *destroyed* Timothy Pickles – remember that schoolboy upstart I told you about? Well, honour is satisfied.'

'Stay and celebrate,' invited Joe, padding off to his kitchenette for glasses while a red light winked forlornly on the switchboard. He poured three hefty slugs then answered the call. 'A young lady,' he said to Peter. 'She's asking if I know where you are.'

Peter frowned. 'Did she give a name?'

'Hang on . . .' Joe addressed the caller in his usual calm, disarming way: 'He's not on call tonight, my dear, but I think I might be able to find him. Who is it calling, please? Ros . . . Right. Just a minute . . .'

He turned back to Peter, who looked first trapped, then resigned in rapid succession. 'Want to take it here?'

'I suppose so. I think I may have blundered, Joe . . . Hello? Pete Verity speaking . . . er, no. No. Really? I'm sorry – we said Friday. Yes, definitely . . . Where are you now? I'll come over.

162

Stay there.' He replaced the telephone and made a face at them. 'Girlfriend trouble,' he said. 'A misunderstanding. She's at the porter's lodge right now; I'll just pop over there and smooth ruffled feathers.'

The man Richard made as if to leave as well, but company was golden to Joe. 'Stay here where it's warm,' he insisted. 'That young whippersnapper won't be long, I'll warrant. Heh! He's a one, all right. Here, pull up a chair . . .' He answered another call, then began to reminisce about the hospital's previous switchboard room deep underground, suffocatingly hot near all those utility pipes, accessed by dark tunnels. From there he adroitly swung his monologue ever backwards in time, from his discharge from the army on medical grounds, via the privations of services life, to his real subject of interest, the Korean War. Richard was gratifyingly receptive to these memoirs; he listened solemnly, nodding occasionally, sparing with his promptings.

Eventually, his narrative thread broken by another call to the switchboard, Joe remembered the absent Peter. 'She'll be giving him a right wigging!' he wheezed, with a knowing chuckle. 'None of them can pin him down. Nor some of them other young medics . . . We see it all, right here. It's not only the bachelors, either. You'd be amazed where some of the *married* men answer from . . .'

Richard smiled and sipped his whiskey. 'I know,' he said idly. 'I had a bet on with a mate of Peter's about Robin and one of the nurses – a fiver.'

Joe snickered again. 'Robin Winterley? Consider yourself a winner, lad. He's been answering from the Nurses' Home for these last four months.'

Richard gazed at the console, impressed. 'You can tell that? I thought the girls didn't have phones in each room.'

'No, but there's one for each corridor, and *that's* where the light used to glow . . .' He jabbed a nicotine-stained finger towards the console. 'Extension 1279.'

The man on the Casualty trolley winced as Robin crisply prodded the tight red swelling in his groin.

'Cough,' instructed the surgeon, his finger still on the lump. The patient weakly complied. 'And again.'

'The abdomen's tender and the bowel sounds accentuated,' proffered the houseman from the other side of the trolley.

Robin felt, and listened. 'X-rays?' he asked.

'I've just rung the department.'

'Right. Do the bloods, start antibiotics and send him to the ward with the films. I'm going to Theatre myself, so I'll arrange that end.'

The patient stared up at him with frightened eyes. 'Do I have to have an operation?' he croaked.

Robin glanced his way. 'You certainly do. This hernia's strangulated – that means the blood supply is now blocked. There's probably some bowel trapped in there, as well. If we don't deal with it soon, there'll be gangrene.' The bleep in his pocket commenced a series of high-pitched signals. 'Explain to him,' he enjoined the houseman, and swung out of the curtained cubicle to find a telephone.

The caller proved to be Inspector Montgomery. 'We need to see you,' he said. 'Today, if possible.'

Friday lunchtime, and already three emergency cases destined for Theatre. 'That's out of the question,' Robin answered abruptly. 'We're on take, and run off our feet.'

'Would tomorrow morning be convenient?'

'After a night of admissions we do a ward round, Saturday or no Saturday. If you really must, why not come to the flat in the afternoon?'

There was a pause. 'In view of the matter to be discussed, we feel that you may prefer it if Mrs Winterley wasn't present . . .'

Something squeezed Robin's chest, stilling his heart and lungs; the rebound a few second later was thunderous, a jungle pulse beating in his ears. He licked arid lips.

'I'll come to you,' he said.

16

'I felt it was time we talked about your affair with Loretta,' said Montgomery to the man sitting across the Interview Room table.

'My *what*?' Robin Winterley gave a harsh, incredulous laugh.

'Your affair with Nurse Dawes. For the last two weeks we've been trying to solve a murder mystery, and have received varying degrees of co-operation from the witnesses concerned. Varying degrees of mendacity, too . . . for reasons large and small, people have lied to us about their actions. I'd like to hear your reasons, Mr Winterley.'

'I've told you, my relationship with Nurse Dawes was purely professional. You speak of "co-operation" – why do you think I'm here on what's left of my weekend off? I've come to assist you in any way I can – but that doesn't mean conniving at fairy stories and implicating myself in things just to make your life easier!'

'We're unlikely to accuse you of that.' Montgomery was suave. 'Would you say you were at least a friend of Loretta's?'

'Yes.'

'And you'd like her killer brought to justice?'

A pause. 'Of course.'

'Then you'll hardly be pleased to hear that we've wasted days trying to identify the father of her child when he could simply have told us . . . Why didn't you?'

Winterley flushed angrily. 'There you go again! If all you can do is make unfounded assumptions, then I'm walking out of here.'

'Mr Winterley . . .' Montgomery was scarcely aware of Sergeant Bird sitting behind him, scribbling verbatim notes. He was too busy trying to calculate which key would fit this particular lock and release a confession. 'I assure you we have evidence. I understand your reticence, but let me tell you, we don't necessarily link the murder with Loretta's pregnancy. There could be other reasons. We need to clear away all these peripheral mysteries which are obscuring the truth . . . I believe you can help us.'

'You sound almost sincere,' marvelled the surgeon. 'Do they send you lot to RADA for a couple of terms before they let you loose on the public?'

Montgomery said nothing.

'Anyway, what do you mean, you have "evidence"? Since Loretta and I weren't having an affair, you must be mistaken – or you've fabricated something.'

'That's not the way we work.'

'Tell me, then,' he challenged. 'What is this marvellous, cast-iron "evidence"?'

Montgomery shrugged. 'There's your blood group for a start: it's consistent with the group we expect from the father of the baby.'

Winterley paled for an instant. 'I haven't been asked for any sample . . .' he began. 'You can't have – no, wait. The Blood Transfusion Service? But I haven't given blood for months . . .' Slowly his face cleared. 'The group, you said. That's all you've got, isn't it? Well, I know my group. It's group A: the same as two in five of the population.' He began to laugh derisively. 'Evidence!'

'As you point out, we haven't had a specific sample from you,' said Montgomery. 'But it may come to that if we can't solve this problem by simpler means. We'd ask for more *co-operation* from the gentlemen who knew Loretta . . . I'm sure your colleagues would comply. I wonder, though – would you?'

'If you've said all you have to say, I'd like to leave now.'

'Don't do that. You've only just arrived. We were talking about evidence . . . Let's discuss Loretta's diary.' Montgomery was addressing the ceiling, the walls, anywhere but Winterley, but he still sensed the sudden tautness in the man sitting opposite. Perhaps Winterley feared that Loretta had written all about him. 'The entries are most illuminating.'

'I'm afraid you've fallen into the oldest trap in the book, Inspector,' said Robin. 'Nurses traditionally hanker after doctors, and young women traditionally commit their fantasies to diaries. If Loretta wrote anything about me, I can assure you it was just wishful thinking on her part.'

'She didn't, actually. She just made a note of your on-call nights.'

Robin looked uncertain.

'Were you having an affair with Alison, Mr Winterley?'

'What? That little dumpling? Certainly not. I hardly know her.'

'Mm. What about Fiona McCrea? Do you know her?'

'Never heard of her. Who is she?'

'A second-year nurse who works on the radiotherapy ward.'

'Sorry . . . *should* I know the name?'

'These two girls live in the Nurses' Home,' said Montgomery conversationally. 'Not in the most salubrious part, I'm afraid. Their rooms are in the north wing; they open from a rather dismal, poorly lit cul-de-sac corridor. You know the type – high ceilings, green linoleum, plain walls with that vaguely stained look of age . . . Their only mod con is a telephone; in truth, one would hardly call it modern. It's one of those clumpy black Bakelite ones. Extension 1279. They can make internal calls on it, although the pay phone for outside calls is in the main foyer . . .'

Now he watched Winterley, with a deliberate, unwavering gaze, as if his blue eyes and the surgeon's brown ones were joined by invisible rods of steel. 'There are only three rooms in that cul-de-sac,' he said. 'Fiona lives in number 22, Alison in number 23. Since you weren't carrying on with either of them, it seems fair to conclude that you emerged from number 24 on the several instances you answered your bleep from that extension . . . Loretta's room.'

Winterley's mouth fell open. 'I – I said we were friends,' he gulped. 'There *were* one or two occasions when she asked me back for a cup of tea between emergency theatre sessions. It was a break just to get away from the hospital . . .'

'I see. Does this include the calls at three and four in the morning?'

Still Montgomery stared, and suddenly Robin Winterley sagged. 'All right,' he said. 'All right . . . let me think for a minute.' He lifted his head; they saw that the sardonic hostility had been replaced by something like anguish. 'I loved Loretta,' he whispered. 'I was going to marry her.'

'We thought it probable that Loretta was planning a future

167

with you,' said Montgomery lightly, giving the surgeon time to compose himself. He held out a hand towards William Bird, who passed him a brown envelope. 'This came for Loretta yesterday morning; the Nurses' Home have been saving all her post for us. It's an application form for a staff nurse job in Gosport – that's in Hampshire, isn't it? Just a few miles along the coast from Southampton . . .'

Robin nodded. 'I was looking for a house to the east of the city, so we could both travel to work easily. Loretta was very keen on her career; she didn't consider the baby an impediment. We'd agreed that we'd hire a nanny . . .' He exhaled briefly, a puff of frustration. 'This all sounds so dispassionate, doesn't it? But it's vital that you understand. How can I explain? Loretta was everything I'd never met before in a woman. She was beautiful, exciting and independent – she knew where she was going and didn't need to cling to a man to get there . . .

'The baby wasn't an accident: she got herself pregnant deliberately. I couldn't be angry with her, though; in fact, I found myself liking the idea, which is odd, really, because if it had been Fran . . . Anyway, I knew Loretta would keep the baby with or without my help. It wasn't moral blackmail; she said quite openly that she wanted something to remember me by, and if I turned my back on her, then that was that, but the baby would stay.'

A calculated gamble, thought Montgomery. It was consistent with the character study he had made of Loretta. But if things had gone wrong, the prize would have been squalor and Social Security hand-outs, not a rich, respected husband and a house by the sea. Had Winterley truly been so naïve?

Robin was now in full cathartic flow. 'I'd planned to tell Fran just after the party, but events made it impossible. She doesn't know anything about this – nobody does, not even Loretta's friends. For God's sake, don't tell her. It doesn't matter now.'

'I'm afraid I can't agree with you there,' said Montgomery quietly. 'This is a murder enquiry. A young girl is dead, and we still don't know why. We've only your word that you cared for her and intended to marry her.'

'Christ! Do you think *I* killed her? You're mad. I wouldn't have hurt Loretta for anything. I loved her!'

'Very well . . . but if you didn't kill her, someone else did, and we need you to help us find this person. Had you any rivals? Were there any threats from a previous boyfriend?'

Robin smiled tiredly. 'There wasn't anyone else. At least, no one who mattered. She was going out in a platonic way with a dental technician called Gordon Mudge, but he was just a cover, to stop all those butch medical students and junior doctors from pestering her. They never used to leave her alone . . . with her looks, that kind of attention was inevitable.'

What about the rules for old friends? wondered Montgomery. He was sure that Robin was unaware of the real nature of Loretta's relationship with Peter Verity. 'Let me ask you about the night of your party,' he said. 'Loretta was observed speaking to you in the room where the dancing was, before the speeches. What did she say?'

'Oh, she was piqued because I wasn't paying more attention to her. She wanted us to be seen together, I suppose in preparation for people finding out the truth. I felt she wanted them to look back and recall one perfect image of us as a couple . . . so she asked me for a dance, but I refused. I told her to be patient until I'd found the right opportunity to speak to Fran.'

'What was Loretta's mood when she left you?'

'You might describe it as peevish – put out.'

'Not tearful or depressed?'

'No; nothing like that.'

'Thank you. Let's move on to your wife. What were your plans for Frances?'

Winterley's flashily handsome face betrayed no vestige of embarrassment. 'I hoped she would apply for one of the vacant secretarial posts at the hospital,' he answered. 'She's a very competent typist and computer operator. I was going to buy her a small flat here in Nottingham . . . in fact, I still intend to. Our marriage has been a sham for years. Nothing changes that. I shall go to Southampton alone.'

'Do you really think she can have no inkling of your feelings, Mr Winterley?'

Robin gave an unpleasant little laugh. 'Oh, Fran is the perfect martyred wife. She may have suspected various things over the years, but she's never rocked the boat. Perhaps something in her psyche thrives on masochism. I do know she loves me. If I asked her to crawl to the North Pole and back she'd probaby do it, and be grateful that I waited for her. But I don't want that kind of devotion. I grew to realize that I needed someone with an independent spirit.'

Montgomery squirmed inwardly, but before he could pose another question, Sergeant Bird's deep voice sounded behind him. 'Mr Winterley, if you don't love your wife, why have you remained married to her for so long?'

Winterley cocked his head, considering, then shrugged. 'I suppose I didn't want the unpleasantness of a divorce. We drifted apart very gradually. Fran seemed happy enough cooking for me and keeping the flat clean – and she's an excellent hostess for dinner parties and the like. There was no real reason for drastic change before Loretta.'

Montgomery could stomach no more. He stood up, and brushed a faint crease from his trouser leg. 'Well, that's all clear,' he said. 'I don't think we need any more just now. You're staying in Nottingham for the next week or so, aren't you?'

'Ten days.' The arrogance began to recede again from Winterley's face. 'Inspector . . . I'm sorry I wasn't completely frank with you earlier on. I was afraid – afraid of being mixed up in a murder case, of perhaps being suspected myself. I appreciate now that my attitude was foolish. You must find the person who killed Loretta. It was a savage act. She was only twenty-two; she didn't deserve to die. If I can help you, I will.'

Now he sounded like Peter Verity, reflected Montgomery. 'We'll certainly be in touch if we need you for further enquiries,' he said.

The surgeon rose to his feet, but hovered near the desk, pacing the floor and clearing his throat. 'The baby,' he burst out at last. 'Do you know – what it was?'

Montgomery regarded him coolly. 'I believe it was a boy.'

*

170

Alison leaned over the tiny wash-basin at the back of the sluice room and rinsed her face with cold water, time and again. All day a dull, relentless headache had been pounding behind her eyes, and now it was getting worse. Her shift had another two hours to run: she would have to ask Sister for some tablets.

A low hum of conversation from the ward next door was audible where she stood. The Saturday visitors had poured in half an hour before with their flowers, gifts and fixed bright smiles; now each bed was under siege until four o'clock. The nurses on duty were keeping a low profile, either sitting in the office or clustered around the teapot in the kitchen, enjoying a gossip with the cleaners.

Slowly, Alison smoothed back damp strands of hair and repinned her cap. She didn't want to join the others, but neither did she want to be alone. Morbid thoughts had found her easy prey since Loretta's death, sapping with parasitic tentacles all that was positive and forward-thinking. She felt crushed beneath the guilt and sense of isolation . . . and full of trepidation for the moment when the police solved the case . . .

'Are you all right in here?' Sister Brocklebank suddenly appeared in the doorway, a mug in her left hand. Alison quickly averted her face; the pain throbbed in a sickening crescendo.

'Alison?'

'I've, er, got a slight headache,' she mumbled. 'Could I possibly have something from the trolley?'

With three brisk steps Eileen Brocklebank traversed the sluice room and peered into Alison's face. 'You look terrible,' she said frankly. 'Is it one of your migraines?'

'I don't think so . . . I didn't see any flashing lights, and the pain's not one-sided this time . . . I'm sure it'll pass.'

Shaking her head, Sister Brocklebank lowered her on to a chair and left the room, to return with a glass of water and two white tablets. 'Drink,' she commanded. 'Now,' she went on as Alison drank, 'I want you to go back to the Nurses' Home and lie down. We're not busy this afternoon. Sleep if you can. It'll do you good.'

Her token murmur of protest ignored, Alison found herself kindly but firmly seized by the shoulders and propelled off the ward.

171

Sleep? She dreaded it. Whenever sleep finally came, her waking shadows coalesced into cryptic images where well-known places and objects were mere façades, shells concealing nameless horrors. She would see a corridor, dark and distorted, which turned through a right angle to become darker still. Then there would be a door. A solid, oaken door with dull brass numerals . . . She couldn't quite read them – and yet she *knew* that behind the door lay something monstrous . . .

Damp air cooled her cheeks as she stepped outside the main hospital, and a tree nodded its branches in the sluggish breeze. Alison weakly chided herself for the growing feeling of apprehension which was lodged beneath her diaphragm. On Monday her situation would be much improved: she would be allowed to move into room 39, a spacious, first-floor room with a view of the castle.

With leaden limbs, she entered the Nurses' Home, glanced apprehensively towards the pigeon-holes then continued into the heart of the building. It was very quiet; when she reached the north wing the silence was almost absolute. Through the fire door to the right-angled corridor . . . She paused outside Fiona's room. There was no creak of furniture, or rustle of paper; Fiona was almost certainly away for the weekend.

Down to the other end, where the black telephone crouched in the gloom like some devil's familiar. Don't ring, she willed it soundlessly. Not now. It had never rung for her, though calls had occasionally come through for Fiona or for Loretta. And late at night, after the muffled high-pitched chirrups of his bleep had filtered through the wall, she had heard a man use that telephone.

As she reached for her key, there was a furtive noise nearby. Alison started back from the door, and stood rigidly. Loretta? Don't be silly . . . Loretta was dead, cold and still beautiful in some mortuary fridge. She believed that now. But the noise had come from one of these two rooms . . .

Alison's lips began to whisper a familiar refrain as she thrust the key in the lock of room 23: 'The Lord is my shepherd . . . He leadeth me in the paths of righteousness . . . I shall fear no evil . . . I shall fear no evil . . . no evil . . .'

The lock clicked, and the door swung open. There was an

atmosphere of expectancy inside the room, but all her comfortable, well-loved possessions looked the same. She crept forward, uncertain now, ready to relax and call herself a fool – and then she saw it. It lay on the coverlet of her bed, and it was dead. A white rat.

Alison gasped, and halted. Too late, she saw the lazy stirring of the orange curtains, and the narrow gap where the sash window had been opened . . . Too late, she began to turn away. Abruptly a strong hand came from nowhere to clamp her mouth in a vice-like grip; there was no time even to scream.

17

Montgomery had wanted to see the site for himself. Now he stood in the tangled shrubbery, carefully avoiding the thin gravel path where the scenes-of-crime sergeant was at work, and contemplated the blind frosted window in the wall above Alison's splintered sash.

'It's unlikely that we'll find witnesses,' said William Bird. 'At weekends, any staff not on duty try to get away from the hospital. At the very least, they spend their Saturdays in town. That window up there is a linen room, and the one next to it is stacked with old furniture. The frosted ones are bathrooms. I've been inside one of them; you'd have to lean right out in a very deliberate manner in order to observe anyone on the path beneath.'

'What did you find inside?' asked Montgomery, as he watched a man with a fine hair brush dusting powder on to the window-frame.

'There was an indentation on the counterpane, consistent with a size nine shoe, plus a few scattered pieces of gravel on the bed and carpet, including the area behind the door. The gravel matches that of the path. We also found two short whitish hairs on the coverlet, which have gone off for analysis. They appeared to be from some sort of small rodent.'

'So . . . size nine footprints inside and out. From which

direction does the SOCO think he came: from the right, where the main hospital is, or from the other side?'

'He both came and went from the right, sir.'

'Ah – so that indentation over there has no relevance.' Montgomery pointed beneath the window to the left of Alison's; a toe-shaped impression was just discernible in the gravel.

'We didn't notice that, sir,' Sergeant Bird admitted immediately. 'We were concentrating on Alison's room. Perhaps it was left by a gardener.'

'A gardener?' Montgomery indicated the mossy trees and snarl of unpruned shrubs with a sweeping gesture of his hand. 'In the absence of a gardener, who else would use this path? It goes nowhere . . . it provides the longest and least scenic route to circumnavigate this side of the Nurses' Home. Even in daylight it's gloomy . . . Let's have a closer look.' Keeping his own feet in the virgin border, he approached the area of interest: his gaze travelled slowly from the toe-print up to the sill, along to each corner and back again, then to the lower sash window with its peeling white-painted frame and grimy oblong panes of glass.

Suddenly he sucked in his breath. 'Look, Will.'

In the lower frame, almost hidden by a flake of paint, was a small round hole.

'Another break-in?' The sergeant was incredulous.

'Money on it,' said Montgomery. 'And that's Loretta's room.'

'Tell me what's been going on,' demanded Brian Jackson at the station the next day.

'Alison was attacked on Saturday afternoon,' said William Bird succinctly. 'She should have been on ward duty until four thirty, but she had a severe headache and the sister told her to go early. When she got to her room about a quarter to three, she saw something resembling a dead rat on her bed; she then noticed that the window, which she was obsessive about closing whenever the room was unoccupied, was slightly open. Someone seized her from behind at that point, putting a hand across her mouth before she could cry out. They wrestled, but he was strong, and within a few seconds he had bundled her into the wardrobe and locked the door. He escaped by the window, taking the rat, or whatever it was, with him. She remembers an odd chemical smell, which may have come from the rat.'

'Was the assailant definitely a man?'

'Yes. Alison is certain. He was tall, and she felt the muscles of his forearm.'

'Did she glimpse him in a mirror?'

'Unfortunately not. She has a tiny wall mirror opposite the desk, but they were never in line with it. There *is* a long mirror inside the wardrobe door, but the door would have had to have been fully open to have reflected her attacker. That didn't happen.'

'What about scratches?'

William Bird smiled, grimly amused. 'You evidently haven't seen Alison's nails,' he answered, 'or should I say lack of them? She did try to kick him, but without much success. Curiously, he said nothing at all during their scuffle: no "shut up and you won't get hurt", or whatever. That would seem to imply that Alison would have recognized his voice . . .

'Anyway, within seconds she found herself shut in one of those heavy, old-fashioned oak wardrobes, with the key turned on the outside. Nobody heard her muffled shouts and bangs; eventually her efforts with the door toppled the whole wardrobe over, so she was well and truly trapped. Even that crash went unnoticed, because that wing of the Nurses' Home was deserted. She might have stayed there until Fiona returned last night, except for the anonymous phone call.'

'Phone call?'

'Yes. Someone rang the hospital switchboard from a telephone box just after nine o'clock, asking to be put through to the night porter of the Nurses' Home. The caller was a man with a gruff voice – disguised, I imagine – and he told the porter a girl was trapped in room 23 and needed help. He hung up before any questions could be asked. The porter got into Alison's room using his master key.'

'So Alison was telling the truth after all!'

'It would appear so. I still don't know what conclusions should be drawn from these events, though. The way I see it, there are three possible interpretations. One: he thinks Alison knows something to his detriment, and he's trying to frighten her off, while stopping short of actual harm. He was probably going to leave an unpleasant note with that rat, but she returned unexpectedly and he only just had time to hide behind the door . . .'

'If you're right about the motive,' interrupted Jackson, 'then he's a bungler, because all he's done is drive her straight into the arms of the police.'

'Hence hypothesis number two. This whole business with Alison could be a blind, an attempt to make us focus on her, even believe that she was the intended victim. That would suggest that he had a clear motive for murdering Loretta, and needs to deflect attention away from that motive. The same goes for opportunity.

'The third possibility is that Alison really *has* been the target all along. But why didn't he kill her when he had the chance? Perhaps he thought it was unsafe just then, for some reason . . .' A thought struck him, vague but alluring. 'Or perhaps he was in the middle of some *chain of preparation*, and killing Alison this time was premature . . .' He frowned as he grappled with the new idea.

'What does the boss think?' asked Jackson.

Montgomery materialized behind him. 'The boss has some shadowy ideas, but too little as yet to substantiate them.' He sat down with his officers. 'Whatever else Robin Winterley may have done, he wasn't the person who attacked Alison. He was with us on Saturday afternoon: *we* were his alibi.'

'You don't like him very much, do you?' observed Sergeant Bird, who shared the sentiment.

'It's not our job to like or dislike – but we're not robots either.'

A sceptical look passed over Jackson's face as he regarded Montgomery.

'Where's Smythe, by the way?' went on the inspector. 'Ah – the College of Adult Education. Well, while we're waiting for him to return, I'd like us to consider the matter of "Banquo's ghost".'

'Banquo's ghost?' echoed Jackson.

'That's what Graham called it when we were discussing

Alison's apparent delusions. Loretta's reincarnation, the product of a fevered brain . . . Yesterday we found that not only had Alison's window been forced, but Loretta's, too, by a different method. Someone with size nine feet assaulted Alison, but an individual with size seven feet had been into Loretta's room sometime during the previous two weeks. It's my contention that the sounds Alison heard on the Monday after the murder arose from an intruder ransacking number 24. I surmise he was looking for documents, but he may not have found just what he was after.'

'Could it have been a woman?' asked Jackson.

'That's possible, but the shoe was a male size seven trainer. Now, I've been thinking . . . We can make exhaustive enquiries as to where all the various suspects were that night, or we can try to obtain a result more speedily, by actually asking them for a handwriting sample . . .'

Jackson shook his head uncomprehendingly. 'There's plenty of handwriting in the doctors' notes,' he said.

'No – we actually want to *avoid* subtlety on this occasion,' explained Montgomery. 'We tell them that we have accumulated a stack of cards and notes belonging to Loretta, and some may be relevant to the case, so we want to exclude the innocent ones by the quickest possible means. Say that we're asking for handwriting samples from all her friends and acquaintances. Sound semi-detached about it, if you like. Groan about your boss and his stupid ideas. Then – this is the hard part – casually let drop the fact that the collection is currently somewhere on hospital premises.'

Jackson's eyes had begun to gleam. 'I see,' he said. 'A trap!' His expression sobered. 'Our man won't fall for that, surely.'

'He will if he's desperate enough. You think of a place for the documents that sounds plausible – then you and Graham can organize some surveillance.'

'Even if it doesn't work,' observed William Bird, 'we'll end up with useful samples of writing to compare with the envelope of the anonymous letter.'

'True,' agreed Montgomery. 'Here comes Robert,' he added.

Detective Sergeant Allen threaded his way between the desks

and joined them in the corner. 'Graham's on his way,' he said. 'I've just seen him in the car-park. But guess what I learned this morning!' He was unusually animated, his Scottish burr suddenly promiment.

'Tell us.'

'I've been speaking with Andrew Halpern, the lad who went to the party in the guise of Donald Duck. He's a colleague of Paula's. He says he spent a few minutes with her at the Radiology party, and she was dressed as a cavalier. He saw her again later on at Robin Winterley's – he's positive.'

'Did you ask him about the Hanoverian costume?'

'Yes. He noticed it at both parties, but couldn't be sure who was wearing it.'

'Paula . . .' Moodily Montgomery tapped his fingers on the desk. 'I *knew* she'd lied to us. But why? What does she know – or think she knows?'

'Or what has she done?' murmured William Bird.

They fell to a discussion of Alison again, filling in details for Robert Allen's benefit. 'Where's the poor lass now?' he asked.

Sergeant Bird consulted his watch. 'At this precise moment, on the ward, but if you mean residentially speaking, rest assured. She's been given a new room on the first floor of the Nurses' Home, about as far away from the north wing as you can get. The domestic supervisor, Miss Grogan, managed to expedite the transfer at long last.'

'So Alison's safe, then.'

'For now, yes. She's promised to keep a low profile socially, and stay close to people she trusts. Ironically, I think her best defence is her complete ignorance of the attacker's identity. *She*'ll act naturally, and *he*'ll feel safe. Ah – hello, Graham.' He held out a chair for the young detective constable. 'We're talking about Alison Blake . . .'

'Thanks . . .' Smythe's poetic face was flushed, his brown eyes gleaming. He turned to Montgomery. 'Sir – I must tell you. You know I've just been to the college in Sheriff's Crescent? Well, I asked them about their lip-reading classes. There *is* a session on Friday nights, between eight and ten, just as Cynthia Masters said. But they insisted she's never been to that one . . .

'The class she attends is on Wednesday mornings!'

18

John Dyson glanced up at the sky as he left the main hospital building. It was uniformly leaden, dull as an unscrubbed saucepan, but no clouds had formed to herald a downpour. On the whole, John decided he was glad. While a good shower would relieve the oppressiveness which had hung over Nottingham all weekend, he was looking forward to an evening in his garden. A typical Monday at the Victoria – post-mortems, the lunchtime clinico-pathological conference, then an afternoon crouched over histology slides – had left him eager to grapple with his unruly compost heap, and tear out the weeds threatening to overrun his vegetable patch.

As he approached his car, he saw Alison and another nurse angling across the courtyard; they halted in the middle, exchanged a few words and separated. To his dismay, Alison turned to walk in his direction.

He could have leapt into the car, revved smartly and driven away, feigning oblivion. There would have been time. But John Dyson's conscience was too well developed for that: he saw her taut pale face and dragging step, and knew he had a further role to play.

'Hello, there,' he said in a tone of professional warmth.

'Hello, Dr Dyson.'

Now she was three feet away, the details of her appearance were brutally clear. John was shocked; she seemed to have lost a stone in weight since he had last studied her with any attention. Her face was white and pinched, the eyes deeply shadowed, the mouth a thin tight line. Incongruously, he could see at that moment that she had the makings of a pretty girl without the layer of blurring fat.

'John,' he corrected her with a smile. 'How are you?'

She gave an answering smile of her own, a faint twitch of the lips. 'Something's happened since we last met,' she said. 'I've been asked not to talk about it until the police have made some checks, but – I would tell you if I could. I'm so grateful to you for listening to me before. I didn't know what to do, but now the police are involved, I feel better. I like Sergeant Bird, and I trust him. They have tangible evidence now; I can sense that they're confident they'll find out who has been doing all these terrible things.' Her gaze fell. 'You might not believe this, but I wasn't sure I wanted them to succeed at first . . . I think it was because that would make it all *real*, rather than a bad dream. I was afraid, too, of facing the hard probability that someone we know is responsible. But now I've found out what he's capable of, I want to co-operate. He's got to be stopped.'

It was a long speech for Alison. She seemed to realize this, and covered her mouth with a protective hand. The fingernails were cruelly short.

For a few seconds, John thought of his beckoning blackcurrant bushes, the moist, sticky earth around his leeks, the evening scent of mint . . . then he thrust them firmly out of mind. A more important priority stood before him. 'I agree,' he said. 'But let's not talk about that just now. I've had a hard day, and I bet you have, too. Could I possibly ask you a favour?'

'Me? Yes . . . of course you can.'

'I've been wondering for ages about Flora, that restaurant on the Mansfield Road. They changed their management a few months ago, and people say the food is first rate now. I know it's Monday, but – would you be interested in giving Flora a try with me tonight?'

'Oh!' Alison was totally confused. As the ever-ready hot pink tide surged up her cheeks, she looked wildly around as if for inspiration. 'I – I'm sorry; I can't afford it,' she said at last. 'But thank you for the offer . . .'

John shook his head gently. 'My offer, my treat,' he said. 'No strings, I promise. I'd really like your company . . . won't you come?'

'I – I . . . are you *sure*?'

He laughed. 'I take it that means yes. Let's say eight o'clock, then. Wait for me in the foyer of the Nurses' Home.' With a small wave of the hand he turned to unlock the car; the sight of her incredulous joy was almost too much to bear.

Within the Nurses' Home, twenty yards from the foyer, Detective Constable Graham Smythe crouched behind the door of a narrow kitchenette. He was far from comfortable. Not only was his body twisted, but peering through a one-inch crack with his right eye meant squeezing the other eye tightly shut; the muscles on the left side of his face were becoming very tired.

Behind him, Brian Jackson did an impatient shuffle-step. The light from a tiny window high in the rear wall had faded away since they had first come; he could no longer read the disreputable newspaper he had brought along for entertainment. Smythe wasn't sorry; the rustling had affected his concentration, and might have reached the ears of their quarry. Besides, if he had to suffer, why shouldn't Brian?

'What's the time?' yawned Jackson. 'I can't see anything in this flaming twilight!'

Smythe checked his watch in the bar of light from the corridor. 'Eight thirty,' he whispered.

'God! How long do we have to wait?'

'As long as it takes, I suppose. Shh . . .' He drew back into the room as a dark-haired nurse walked smartly past the door. The squeak of her soles on the polished linoleum grew fainter; a door banged; silence descended.

Ten minutes later, Smythe's eye could take no more. 'Brian, it must be your turn by now,' he hissed. 'I feel like Long John Silver. I shall end up with a permanent squint.'

'That's because you're doing it all wrong. Keep your left eye open as well: it won't see very much, and gradually your brain will suppress the image from that side. At least, that's the theory . . .'

Smythe made one half-hearted attempt, but the double image was too confusing. He gave a quiet huff of displeasure.

'Honestly!' Jackson had no intention of taking his turn at the crack. He lounged in the background, visualizing beer. 'Have

181

you no savvy at all? If that doesn't work, try covering the left eye with your hand.'

Bliss! As Smythe resumed the contorted posture necessary to avoid the crowding wall cupboards high on the right, his moist brown orb scanned the five-foot area of corridor with new determination.

From the foyer to the right they heard the thud of the main door. Confident footsteps came nearer, turned the corner into their stretch of corridor, then became delicate, secretive. A white coat drifted into view as a man paused diagonally opposite the kitchenette and placed tentative fingers on the brass door handle of the General Office. Smythe wildly signalled Jackson to silence, but the gesture was superfluous; both detectives were already holding their breath.

As he rotated the handle, the white-coated figure gave a cautious sustained push against the door. To his apparent surprise, it opened. He stood on the threshold of the room, glanced to right and left, then flitted inside, closing the door softly behind him.

The detectives let out their breath, and Jackson rubbed his palms together in glee.

'How long do we give him?' whispered Smythe.

'Let's see . . . we described the box quite fulsomely this afternoon. He only has to look along the shelves and he'll spot it. Then he's got to put it on the desk and start sifting through the contents. I'd say . . .' He looked at his watch and counted an eternally long thirty seconds. '. . . *now!*'

They crept across the corridor to the inset wooden door, waited further seconds while Smythe gripped and turned the smooth brass handle, then flung it open.

Barry Pritchard gasped with shock. He stood by the sturdy mahogany desk, a clutch of letters in one hand, the box and the rest of the correspondence scattered across the desk's polished surface. As the two detectives strode into the room, he actually backed away from them, his mouth opening and closing like a fish straining for air.

'Dr Pritchard, how nice to see you again so soon,' said Jackson hammily. 'Would you mind telling us what you're doing here?'

No answer came; Pritchard was incapable of speech.

'I suppose you thought it was a real piece of luck, the door being unlocked like that,' Jackson went on. 'Unfortunately, that's the last piece of luck you're going to get. If you're after a card with flowers and water and a somewhat revealing message, it's currently residing in the files of our handwriting expert.'

'I – I don't know what you mean.' Pritchard paled, swayed, clutched the desk and finally slumped into a chair. 'I came to meet someone tonight. I was passing the office here, and I suddenly remembered what you'd said today, about a box of Loretta's things. I – I was curious. I wanted to see who her – friends had been. So I tried the door. Not very laudable behaviour, I know, but – surely not criminal!' His hands began to shake; his teeth rattled together.

'Whom have you come to visit?' asked Smythe.

'Er, Alison. Alison Blake.'

'I'm afraid it's not your night. I saw her going out half an hour ago.' Smythe wasn't entirely certain, but he had noticed a dumpy girl answering Alison's description trotting towards the foyer earlier on, her face a radiant mask of pleasurable anticipation. If it *was* Alison, she had clearly recovered well from her ordeal.

'Besides,' said Jackson breezily, 'we don't believe you. Shall we chat about the matter here, or would you like to accompany us to the station?'

For the first time in weeks, Alison felt relaxed. The restaurant had soft classical music and an intimate atmosphere, marred only by sporadic strident comments from a grotesquely made-up woman at an adjoining table. Fresh carnations in a thin crystal vase graced her own table; on the pale pink linen cover cutlery sparkled in the light from a single candle.

John was good company. By tacit consent they had avoided talk of hospital colleagues, and kept instead to light neutral topics such as the forthcoming ballet at the Theatre Royal, the Pan-European choice of food in the restaurant, and the resemblance of their waiter to the actor Tom Conti. Alison hoped that some conversational trigger would enable her to discover facets of John's personal life, but she was too inhibited to take the initiative herself. Perhaps during the course of the evening . . .

'Melon, madam.' A dish was placed on the table before her. 'Whitebait for sir.'

This was Alison's first encounter with whitebait; she stared at the little fish in consternation. 'John!' she whispered when the waiter had gone. 'You can't eat those. They've left the heads on!'

Calmly he selected a fish, speared it with his fork, examined it critically for a few moments then popped it into his mouth. 'Delicious!' he exclaimed, then relented, lips curving upwards as he chewed. 'Don't worry,' he reassured her. 'This is quite normal. Whitebait are such small fish, the chefs simply roll them in flour and paprika, say, and fry them as they are. Very tasty.'

'But the *eyes*! They're watching you as you eat.'

'Doesn't bother me. I'm not sure how I'd take to that Cornish dish, though, star-gazy pie, where mackerel heads poke up through the pastry and gaze at you mournfully.'

Alison wondered if she was being teased. There were so many things she didn't know, customs and modes of behaviour other people took for granted. A sheltered upbringing was one thing, incarceration was quite another. All she could be sure of in a restaurant was to eat using cutlery from the outside in, and to keep her elbows off the table. VAT and gratuities were complex problems which John would deal with, as Loretta had done before him.

'You're sure you won't have wine?' asked John. 'This is a really crisp Chablis.'

'No, thank you . . . Perrier is fine.'

'I've never seen you drink alcohol. You're not a Methodist, are you?'

She smiled. 'No. Church of England. We do drink wine at Holy Communion, unlike the Methodists – I think they use Ribena. But I don't really like the taste of alcohol: that's why I leave it alone.' As she spoke, Alison knew she was guilty of voicing a half-truth. Dimly she remembered her father shouting, his beery breath, her own beating heart as she hid in the pantry. He would cry out that charity began at home, and if his wife was at all interested in keeping her husband, she should drop the Bible classes and the do-gooding for the whole community and spend some time where she was really needed – with her own family. Then later, when he'd left them for good, how quiet the house had been! Mother had shed no tears, but had clutched her Bible to her chest like a talisman, and said, 'God comes first, Alison. Always remember that. Live your life for God.' And in Alison's mind, the incidents from that period of her childhood had slowly simmered together, coalescing years later into a final impression that alcohol was somehow ungodly.

'I've seen what alcohol can do to people,' she added, and here she was on more certain ground. She thought of Cynthia Masters slurring her words, spilling her wine . . . the embarrassment of the other dinner guests, the amazed disgust of her husband. And then there were the parties. Everyone was *expected* to 'be merry', to 'have a good time', but Alison had seen only heightened aggression and licentiousness, her colleagues turning into loud-mouthed, lolling strangers before her eyes . . . red sweaty faces, bodies Araldited together . . . the smeared lip gloss of Loretta as she hung in Peter's arms . . . no! Mustn't think about that. The ward, then. A yellow-faced man of thirty-six with a huge cirrhotic liver, vomiting blood from his oesophageal varices, and dying . . .

Stop it, she told herself. Put those things to the back of your mind . . . 'Do you lie in at the hospital?' she asked John brusquely.

He gave an easy smile. 'No. As Peter will tell you, pathologists are a canny lot. We don't do a barbarous number of nights on duty like the surgeons, so we're non-resident. I have a cottage in Southwell.'

'Oh! How lovely. It must be near the Minster.'

'True enough. No house in Southwell is exactly far from it.'

'Have you got a garden?'

'A long narrow one. I tend to choose the kind of flowers and shrubs that give maximum colour for minimum effect – my innate streak of laziness manifesting itself. I've got a lilac bush at the front, some lupins, carnations and phlox. What else? Ah, yes – roses. I don't know their names: they were established when I bought the cottage. At the back there's a Forsythia and a strip of lawn, then down at the bottom there's a herb patch, two rows of leeks and some old blackcurrant bushes. I keep meaning to dig another herb patch nearer to the house, so I don't have to cross soggy grass whenever I want a sprig of parsley.'

Alison was entranced. 'I'm glad you have flowers to come home to,' she said, 'especially with your job. Sometimes it gets so claustrophobic in the hospital that you just long to be in a garden, somewhere quiet, where the flowers aren't wilting in tall ugly vases but are growing free. You feel a sense of – renewal, God's promise fulfilled, a feeling that whatever silly things Man does, Nature will carry on, and everything will be all right in the end.'

John was thoughtful for a moment, his eyes reflecting some sad distant memory. 'I know someone else who used to say that,' he murmured, before visibly shrugging away the retrospection. 'Tell you what, young Alison, I've got no hotline to Him Up There, but if you have, perhaps you'll ask Him to re-route his ant columns to my bonfire-mad neighbour's house, and allow me a year without a wasps' nest while He's at it.'

She chuckled, a timid little sound. 'I was envying you just now,' she said. 'Perhaps the grass is always greener.'

'Enjoy your years free of a mortgage,' he urged her. 'You'll never be so foot-loose again this side of old age! Travel, see things, do things . . .' Their main courses arrived as he pursued his theme, describing to Alison holidays he had enjoyed as a student: backpacking in the Himalayas, exploring India on a bicycle.

'. . . And look at me now, a staid old property-owner,' he concluded as Alison laid down her knife and fork. 'Middle-class respectability in . . .'

A short, high-pitched shriek overlay his next words. At the adjoining table, the garishly made-up female they had noticed earlier was flapping her hands at the startled waiter. 'I don't want *sugar*,' she hissed. 'I call it *White Death*. Take it away!'

John leaned forward confidentially as Alison stifled an embarrassed giggle. 'She wasn't too bothered about the "white death" in her gâteau a few minutes ago,' he whispered.

Alison froze. A sudden memory had rippled across her mind, leaving total blankness in its wake. The restaurant seemed unreal. Somewhere beyond the stifling blanket was a thought – sharp, mocking . . . molecules . . . a chemical? It remained elusive.

John was still speaking, his eyes scanning the nearby sweet trolley. 'It's not very adventurous, but I rather fancy the gâteau myself. There's Tia Maria and fresh cream in it . . . what about you, Alison? Have you any thoughts?'

She dragged her consciousness towards the question, wading through varnish, getting no nearer. In another few seconds he would notice that something was wrong.

'I believe they've got some nice sorbets round the back,' he continued. 'Barry Pritchard recommended the grapefruit one. Would you prefer one of those?'

Her senses tilted and slid. The thing she couldn't remember was important – terribly important. Reflections from the guttering candlelight danced from John's wineglass; Alison focused all her beleaguered powers of concentration on the kaleidoscope of images. 'May I try the wine first, please?' she articulated thickly. 'I've changed my mind.'

'Certainly.' He gave a friendly smile. 'I'm afraid they've pinched your glass, though. Have a sip out of mine.'

He held the wineglass towards her, exposing two inches of white shirt cuff and the tendons of his wrist. A faint but pungent smell rose to tantalize her nostrils, and Alison recoiled.

'It's not that bad, is it? I thought the Chablis had quite a nice bouquet.' He sounded puzzled, then started to laugh with a note of relief in his voice. 'Oh, I know what's wrong. That wretched formalin from the Path lab. We use it to preserve the specimens. Sorry, Alison. Even when I've washed my hands and hair, it still seems to cling. You wouldn't think I wore gloves, would you?'

Alison was dumb. A giant hand was squeezing her throat, and she knew she was staring at him, appalled. That smell – formalin. Here in the restaurant, in his car . . . in her room. Now he was returning her scrutiny, his eyes deep and watchful in the flickering light. Abruptly they widened. With a twist of terror in her gut, Alison could see that he knew.

*

The television programme was holding Leo's full attention. A young woman with a shawl and her swarthy-faced lover were earnestly conversing on a wind-swept cliff-edge while gouts of sea-spray flew into the air behind them. Try as she might, Cynthia could not follow the gripping drama. The volume was already uncomfortably loud for Leo, but she was missing most of the dialogue. She sat marking time, beside her husband and yet isolated from him, unable to share a simple experience.

The girl began to run, abetted by a swell of orchestral music, then a strange jarring monotone overlay the soundtrack.

'Damn,' said Leo. 'Someone's at the front door.'

'I'll go,' offered Cynthia at once, sliding off the sofa. 'If it's Mrs Pocock I might be able to head her off.' She entered the hall, closing the drawing-room door behind her, and crossed to the sturdy front door. Through its whorled glass panes she could see two dark figures, one of them tall, silhouetted by the security light outside. Cricket club money, she thought. Or the Mellors returning the hedge trimmer. Or even the vicar and his wife seeking pledges of support for the Autumn Fête . . .

She pulled open the door, and gave a small gasp.

'Mrs Masters,' began Montgomery politely.

19

Alison stood up abruptly. Her mouth was bone-dry, and her gaze remained locked with John Dyson's like that of a mongoose with a cobra. 'Excuse me,' she managed to whisper, 'I shan't be long.' The door of the restaurant was barely ten feet away, but any attempt to leave that way was clearly doomed. She swung round and skirted the other tables until she reached a baize door at the back, discreetly marked 'Ladies'. It opened with a creak.

Inside, a stout woman was powdering her face. She peered closely at her reflection in the gilt-edged mirror, then took out a coral lipstick and smeared a further layer across lips which were already sufficiently startling. Belatedly, as she applied liberal

188

bursts of perfume to her neck, she became aware of Alison's presence. 'There you are, dear,' she said, waving a plump hand at the mirror and wash-basin, as if they were a personal gift.

'Thank you.' Alison's voice was a thread, but the woman perceived nothing amiss and swept out in her cloud of fragrance. The door creaked again, then closed with a dull thud. Muffled sounds from the kitchens were just audible. Alison leaned against the washstand, trying to make some sense out of the maelstrom in her head. A warning surge of nausea swilled and receded, leaving her forehead damp and deadly cold.

There wasn't time to work it all out. Instinct screamed at her for the seconds she had already lost. Only one thing mattered – escape. She glanced over her shoulder, then walked into the single toilet cubicle and locked the door behind her. To the right of the cistern was a small frosted window festooned with cobwebs. Awkwardly she climbed on to the lavatory seat, laid her handbag on top of the cistern, and began to grapple with the window's rusty catch. After considerable grating protest the metal bar began to rise, allowing her to apply pressure to the window itself. Slowly, reluctantly, the frame swung outwards, but the widest gap she could create was twelve inches.

'Too fat, too fat,' Alison scolded herself. Surely she would get stuck – and which way was she to slide through? There was no window-sill to speak of, and no support within the cramped cubicle which would enable her to twist her body round: she would have to go head first.

Praying now, starkly aware of the seconds ticking away, Alison thrust her head and shoulders through the gap and launched herself out into darkness. Something hard and smooth broke her fall: it toppled with a clatter and Alison found herself sprawled among the kitchen waste in a narrow back courtyard, bruised and shaken. As she crawled to her feet and stumbled down an alleyway leading from the yard, she realized that her bag was still on the cistern. Well, that was just unfortunate. She began to run, but almost immediately barked her shin against a crate of bottles lying on its side in the shadows. Her cry of pain was lost in the outraged howl from a cat she had disturbed.

Alison emerged in a side street of terraced houses, her

189

stomach muscles cramping tight. The street-lamps were lit. Twenty years away to the left, traffic was flashing past on the Mansfield Road, which would lead her straight to the centre of town. To the right were small, unfamiliar streets where she might get lost, or be trapped in some cul-de-sac.

What was John Dyson doing? Was he still waiting at the table, or had he already left the restaurant? Alison cast a final, fleeting glance at the sinister back streets and turned resolutely towards the main road. She walked briskly for a few paces then broke into a trot, uncomfortably aware of the noise her heels were making. The shoes, her only elegant pair, could hardly have been less suitable for running. On the corner she paused, looking first behind her, then up the road to the spot where the restaurant's windows spilled a cosy orange glow on to the pavement. At that precise moment the door opened, and John Dyson's tall silhouette stood limned against the background light. Unerringly he turned in her direction.

Panic spurted in her chest, and Alison began to run, clattering down the pavement, weaving past occasional pedestrians, dodging a car as it swung into a side street.

'Alison!' he shouted. 'Wait!'

There was more, but she barely heard him, so complete was her mindless horror. On she ran, heart pounding, ankles in imminent danger of twisting. The concrete bulk of the rear of the Victoria Shopping Centre loomed ahead on the left, but clearer still was the mental picture of John Dyson's athletic body loping easily, unstrained, just waiting for the most propitious moment to reach out and seize her by the neck.

Already her breath was coming and going in audible sobs. Her throat burned, her calves ached and a tight, inexorable band seemed to be crushing her ribs. The road junction with Upper Parliament Street was flying towards her. Without pausing for the traffic lights, she lurched across; the sound of squealing brakes and angrily tooting horns followed her into the relative quiet of Clumber Street, a pedestrian walkway lined with shops. She staggered along, whooping for breath, until she emerged in a street which led past the majestic Council House to the Market Square at the heart of the town. Here, she risked a glance over her shoulder. Clumber Street brooded emptily. John Dyson was nowhere to be seen.

Perversely, his disappearance was almost as alarming as the sight of his figure in the distance. Was he lurking in a shop doorway, playing cat and mouse, waiting for her to tire? He knew she was heading for the hospital; plenty of people would be around in the centre of town, but the steep streets near the Victoria were quiet and dark. No, she decided. It was much more likely that he had been held up by the traffic. She had a few seconds of grace, but no more. Wildly, Alison looked around for somewhere to hide.

Two telephone boxes stood directly in front of her. A scruffy young man leaned casually in one of them, his silent mouthings visible through the glass. The other one was empty. For a brief moment, Alison stretched out a longing hand towards the door, then her heated imagination took over. The film was very short – her fingers grasping the receiver, the young man sauntering away, a shadowy figure outside her own telephone box, the door opening slowly, deliberately . . . his knowing smile, lupine now. The ending was hackneyed, just a telephone receiver hanging from its cord, accompanied by the flat monotony of the dialling tone.

Terror returned in a rush. To the right was King Street, leading back up the hill to Upper Parliament Street. Diagonally to the left, on the other side of the road, stretched the gardens, fountains and concrete strolling areas of the Market Square, known affectionately to the local people as 'Slab Square'. That pleasant open space would afford her no concealment, but the colonnaded frontage of the Council House, which dominated the square, contained a series of deeply shadowed archways where she might crouch.

Alison's physical condition was the deciding factor. The unaccustomed exercise had left her with leaden legs which trembled with fatigue. She would barely be able to crawl up King Street. Once again, she broke into a shambling trot, and a few seconds later stood in front of the Council House. The entrance was guarded by a pair of stone lions couchant impass-ively facing each other across a twenty-five yard gap. Behind the creatures rose the broad stone steps which led to the archways.

A muffled giggle reached her ears. In the gloom, she could just discern a young couple sitting on the top step, cuddling. Immediately she abandoned the idea of hiding in the dim recesses, and staggered over to the second lion, where she gratefully lowered herself down on to the hard, cold floor and waited, hidden by the base of the statue.

The square was relatively quiet, as most revellers were still inside the pubs and restaurants. Raucous laughter from a distant wine lodge was muted by its passage through the night air, accentuating her feeling of loneliness and isolation. A girl in a headscarf stood by one of the fountains, waiting to meet somebody.

Alison curled up, like a terrapin withdrawing into its shell, careless of how ridiculous she would appear to anyone approaching from behind. Her heart was thudding heavily, a rhythmic percussive pulse which threatened to burst through her ears and skull; she bit viciously into the back of her wrist to suppress the rasping sound of her breathing.

'Damn, damn . . . damn.'

The muttered voice was John Dyson's. He was standing on the other side of the lion, a bare six feet away. Alison held her breath. For dragging seconds he stood there, scanning the square, then with a deep sigh he turned away and walked noiselessly back towards the other lion. As she risked a peep, he began to jog over the pelican crossing, his limbs graceful despite the sober suit, and disappeared into King Street.

It was five minutes later, when Alison was wavering up Friar Lane's substantial gradient, that she realized she had just passed a whole row of taxis. Her rigid conditioning had governed the action – no money, no taxi. Alison had not even been aware of this piece of subconscious reasoning. Perhaps it didn't matter. She was now within striking distance of the hospital, and safety. She would go straight on to one of the wards and ring the police.

A gang of youths shifted menacingly in front of her as she turned towards the subway which would take her beneath Maid Marian Way, a busy thoroughfare. Any other time, Alison would have been daunted, but tonight they seemed hopelessly callow. 'Good evening,' she said, walking briskly past, and their mouths hung open. She pattered down the steps, made a brief detour round a shuttered sweet kiosk, and hauled herself doggedly up to street level again. The pain in her ribs was becoming intolerable. Alison slackened her pace for a few yards, then looked across the road and immediately regretted it. A tall, bearded man was just shouldering his way past the gang of youngsters; from his build and gait, there was little doubt as to his identity.

The hospital was near, but not near enough. How stupid she had been! Not only could she have taken a taxi, but she could have gone into any restaurant or pub in the centre of town and asked for their telephone. It all seemed so obvious now, as obvious as the ultimate price for her folly which was surely less than a minute away. Unless . . .

There was one last chance. The Albany, a large, modern hotel, among the best in Nottingham, was a mere street away. Alison had often seen the doorman escorting various well-heeled guests to their Mercedes and Rolls Royces during her off-duty window-shopping trips. If only she could manage to get there . . .

Left, right, left, right, she forced her flagging limbs onward relentlessly. The upper storeys of the Albany towered above her. A vision of the foyer, with its lights and glass doors, appeared ahead, jolting and jerking as she staggered the last few yards up the hill. Her mouth and throat were on fire. There was no air; she would faint . . .

She pawed at the door, and a smart young woman came to open it, an expression of startled enquiry on her face.

'Telephone,' gasped Alison.

'I couldn't help it,' sobbed Barry Pritchard. 'She was so beautiful, so *celestial* . . . I felt valued again, instead of a worthless liability who got under everyone's feet at home . . .' He sniffed, and fumbled in his white coat pocket for a handkerchief. He dabbed his eyes and blew his nose.

'They didn't seem to want me at all once Christine was born, and home from the hospital. Sue's mum came to stay, and her sister was always popping in . . . whenever I tried to help, they told me I was doing it wrong. They didn't give me time to *learn*, they just did it themselves. I – I felt like a stranger in the flat. An unwelcome one.

'Sue was coping fine. She'd always wanted to be a mother. But . . . but . . . everything was geared to the baby. Every facet of life. Week after week, month after month . . . I told myself that that was as it should be, but . . .' His voice shook. 'I – I began to dread coming home. She always wore stained, shapeless tracksuits, and the place was chaotic, and smelt of milk, and vomit, and nappies . . .'

He swallowed. 'Loretta was like a liberation. I couldn't believe a woman of her calibre could possibly be interested in me. But she was, and for a short while I thought I was in heaven. She promised total discretion, and never went back on her word. But then – she told me it was over. She didn't want to break up my family.

'It was hard, but I knew she was right. And once away from her – her charisma, her magnetism – I was horrified by what I'd done. You can't imagine how horrified. I thought of my marriage vows, and Sue's innocent trust in me, and little Christine . . . God!'

He clasped his hands together and thrust them towards Jackson and Smythe in vehement appeal. 'Don't tell Sue, I beg you. I'll admit everything I've done, make statements, whatever you want. But don't involve my wife. Please. It would break her heart.'

'Well, Dr Dyson?' Montgomery addressed the bearded man sitting across the desk in the Interview Room.'

'Well, what?'

'Are you ready to co-operate yet? Will you tell us why you've been terrorising Alison Blake for the past week? We'll find out sooner or later – you know that. Surely sooner is preferable for all concerned.'

Dyson looked sick, his face drawn and defeated. 'I have nothing to say,' he murmured for the eighth time.

'Do you deny that you broke into Alison's room on Saturday afternoon, struggled with her and shut her in the wardrobe?'

'Nothing to say,' repeated the pathologist.

'Well, the forensic evidence will soon be saying it for you. This morning we found gravel in the ridges of your canvas shoes which exactly matches that of the shrubbery path. The footprints also match. In the pocket of your navy yachting jacket was a collection of short white hairs consistent with the animal hairs we found on Alison's coverlet. They are currently undergoing more specific examination, including being matched against the white rats used for experimental purposes at the university – in particular, the Pathology Department. We have other evidence in the pipeline, but I won't trouble you with it at this stage. Would you like to comment?'

There was no reply. Montgomery waited, then continued: 'Why did you take Alison out to dinner last night?'

'I felt sorry for her,' said Dyson after a pause. 'The poor kid was having such a bad time. I thought a meal out would take her mind off things.'

'So you weren't intending that she should meet with an "accident" – fall in front of a car, or something?'

'Of course not! What a vile idea.'

'In that case,' said Montgomery patiently, 'can you explain to someone simple-minded like myself why you should go out of your way to frighten the girl witless with anonymous letters and dead rats, then invite her for a cosy dinner *à deux* to help her to forget these traumas? It doesn't make much sense – does it?'

Dyson forbore to answer.

'All right,' said Montgomery. 'Let's leave Alison for now. Let's consider Loretta Dawes, the girl who actually died. She was Robin Winterley's mistress, and was pregnant with his child . . . You don't look surprised, Dr Dyson. So Winterley was potentially embroiled in a nasty scandal. Was he going to stand by her? He claims he was, but we've no evidence to sustain the assertion. He'd abandoned his previous conquests readily enough . . .

'Suddenly, Loretta is dead – in Winterley's flat, with his own wife's capsules, circumstances guaranteed to draw official attention to Winterley. Who benefits, I wonder, from his being the chief suspect?'

'Are you asking me?'

'Yes.'

'I – I don't quite follow the question.'

'It's straightforward enough. If Robin is clapped away on a murder charge, who benefits? His wife?'

'No. Fran loves him.'

'Did someone else want that Southampton job really badly?'

'Not to my knowledge. No one from Nottingham.'

'Did anyone have a grudge against him – apart from you?'

'Apart from me?' echoed Dyson faintly.

'Well, obviously. Who had the blazing row with Winterley? Who has been after his wife for years? . . . But you knew there wasn't enough proof to clinch it, didn't you. So you sent Alison a note and positively *encouraged* her to involve us. The rat episode went wrong because of her unexpected return, but doubtless you'd intended to leave another unpleasant little missive. And sooner or later, you'd have implicated Robin. Some paper that he'd just handled, perhaps. Or an envelope. You'd have found a way – wouldn't you?'

Stark fear swelled in Dyson's eyes before he averted his gaze and lifted a shielding hand from his face. 'No comment,' he whispered.

Hours later, Sergeant Bird emerged from the Interview Room and ascended the stairs to the CID floor.

'He's not going to crack,' he told Montgomery. 'Not today, at any rate. I was very soft and persuasive, but all to no avail.'

Montgomery nodded, unsurprised. 'Then we'll have to do this the other way round,' he said.

20

Flat 5, Willow Court, was different this time. The triumphant floral creation had gone; only a few desiccated survivors remained, clustered in a slender bud vase on the serpentine-fronted table. That wasn't the only change, though. As Montgomery and his sergeant approached the living-room, preceded by a grim-faced Robin Winterley, they could feel the unease of the flat's four occupants all around them, as thick as a bygone Sheffield smog.

'We're in here,' said Winterley, his tones clipped and hostile. Perhaps he feared he was about to be pilloried in front of his friends. 'You implied John Dyson would be joining us, as well. I rang him earlier, but the Department said he'd called in sick today.'

'We can start without him,' said Montgomery. 'Thank you for agreeing to see us at such short notice. Sergeant Bird and I want to recapitulate some details from the night of the party here: who was where, who drank what, etc. We have suspicions about the identity of the murderer, but we need to confirm that there was indeed an opportunity to administer the poison to Loretta.'

No one was bold or unwise enough to ask about the subject of his suspicions. The two women, Frances Winterley and Sue Pritchard, edged close together for moral support, their hips almost touching; Barry Pritchard, like Robin, stood isolated, arms hugging his chest, the horror of prospective exposure stamped across his face.

'I'm not sure we can enlarge on what we've already told you,' ventured Sue at last.

'You'd be surprised what people remember with the right prompting,' said Montgomery. 'Now, you spent the Friday afternoon in this flat, preparing for the party – is that correct?'

'Yes,' said Robin. 'Saturday would have been better, of course, but Leo had fixed a visit to his son's school on that date,

197

and the following weekend was no good for a lot of people. Barry and I took some time off work to sort out the music and drinks.'

'Did you begin your own drinking before the party started?'

'Yes. By five-ish we'd broken the back of the work, so Barry and I had a Holsten apiece and we opened a bottle of wine for Fran and Sue. It was Italian white: Soave.'

'Did you drink lager for the rest of the evening?'

'Barry did, I think. Yes. I moved on to whisky and ginger.'

'And you two ladies?'

'After a couple of white wines I drank orange juice,' supplied Fran.

Sue looked shamefaced. 'I drank Soave throughout,' she confessed. 'I was making the most of a night out.'

'It's not as bad as it sounds,' put in Barry supportively. 'Sue and I went back to the flat at six fifteen to shower and change. It wasn't non-stop boozing from five.'

Montgomery gave a faint smile. 'When did you return?' he asked.

'About twenty past seven. People started arriving from half-past.'

'John Dyson and Peter Verity came at eight, I believe. Can someone remind me where Dr Dyson established himself, please?'

'He sat in the kitchen while we served the food,' said Fran. At Montgomery's behest they all trooped across the hall, and she described with the aid of dumb show the arrangements for cooking the risotto and transferring it to plates, the position of the salad bowls, the stool where John Dyson had taken root.

'So you had your back to Dr Dyson for much of the time,' Montgomery pointed out to Sue Pritchard. 'And Mrs Winterley was standing at right angles to him as she served the risotto and passed the plates down the breakfast bar?'

Both the women nodded slowly, concern in their eyes.

'What was he drinking?'

'Beer; the same as Peter.'

'Mm. When Loretta and Alison arrived, were they given anything at all to drink in the kitchen?'

'No.' Barry Pritchard swallowed. 'Peter escorted them through to the bar, and I poured wine for Loretta.'

'Can you show me the glasses which were used?'

Barry looked helplessly at Fran.

'Most of them were hired,' she said. 'We initially wondered about buying those cheap plastic cups, but decided against it. The party was meant to be special. We felt that decent wine deserved decent glasses.'

'What size were they?'

'Ordinary wineglass size – like this.' Fran bent down to a low cupboard and produced a stemmed glass with a faint grey tint. 'We kept the odd ones for ourselves.'

'Thank you.' Montgomery turned to the others again. 'We know from Loretta's blood alcohol that she had more than one glass of wine or spirits. Did any of you actually notice her receive a top-up or a second drink?'

'I saw her pouring herself a glass of wine and knocking it back just after she'd spoken to Leo,' said Robin in cautious tones. 'The bar had become a free-for-all by then.'

'When did John Dyson join the main party in the living-room?'

No one seemed to want to answer. 'Fifteen minutes or so after Loretta and Alison,' said Sue eventually, with a shrug.

'Did you see him at any point with a wineglass in his hand?'

Fran Winterley's blue eyes darkened. 'Sue and I were in the kitchen until the speeches,' she said. 'We can't help you there.'

'Mr Winterley? Dr Pritchard?'

'I have no idea,' said Robin coldly, 'and I think perhaps you should be addressing these questions to John Dyson himself – when he comes. You *are* expecting him, aren't you? That isn't just some little fabrication of yours, to try to get us to make incriminating statements when he isn't here to answer back? If it is, I'm having no part in it.'

'I thought we all wanted to find the truth of the matter,' said Montgomery gently. 'You seemed to indicate that when we last met.'

'Yes, the truth! But I'm not framing an innocent man. We may have had our differences, John Dyson and I, but I know he isn't capable of murder.'

'I wonder if we ever know what people are really capable of.' Montgomery slowly turned to the doorway and looked full into Frances Winterley's white face. Horror and despair were etched there, as if someone had taken a Stanley knife to her beauty.

Barry Pritchard was speaking in a low, halting voice. 'Is he really in trouble, Inspector? Serious trouble?'

'I'm afraid so. Dr Dyson is in custody. I'm sorry it was necessary to mislead you earlier on.'

'But – why?' Sue Pritchard's simple question was pierced with shock and disbelief. Fran remained silent.

'We are satisfied as to the motive. Unfortunately for him, Dr Dyson put a lot of concrete evidence into our hands when he attempted to mislead our enquiry. Enough for a charge.'

'No.' Fran spoke in a tired, slurred whisper. 'No, you're wrong. Totally wrong.'

Montgomery gave a little nod to Sergeant Bird, who went to stand beside her. Her slender legs seemed to be on the point of giving way, and she gripped the door-jamb with nerveless fingers.

'Would you like to talk to us, Mrs Winterley?' asked Montgomery softly.

'Yes. But not here. Anywhere else.'

'Of course. Why not collect some things? Sue will help you.'

'What's happening?' Robin's loud, overbearing voice broke into the subdued atmosphere and shattered it. 'Fran – do you know something about all this? Have you been holding things back?' He strode across the room and stopped a yard in front of her, but for once she didn't flinch.

'Yes, Robin, I have. It was me. I killed that girl.'

Astonishment, then fury, flooded his face. His hands clenched into rock-like fists, and the muscles of his neck stood out in corded relief. Sergeant Bird braced himself to check the onslaught, but it didn't come. As the two detectives walked down the corridor on either side of Frances Winterley, an anguished howl reverberated through the flat behind them.

'You bitch! You bloody, bloody bitch!'

*

200

'You ask me why, Inspector?'

The room was very quiet and cool. The walls were plain, devoid of distracting pictures. Behind Montgomery stood the solid pillar of Sergeant Bird, with Smythe, their amanuensis, at his side. Across the desk sat a grave-looking man whom Frances Winterley barely acknowledged: her story was for Montgomery alone.

'I can tell you . . .' she went on. 'Robin and I married eight years ago. At the beginning everything was marvellous, and I can say with truth that we were both in love. I knew that a doctor's wife never has an easy time, but I was quite prepared to tolerate his heavy work commitments; I made a conscious effort not to nag, or be an extra burden. We're all human, though, and there must have been times when he could see that I felt neglected and unhappy.

'His first affair occurred when we'd been married for two years – perhaps I should say the first affair I found out about. "Friends" in the Surgical Office thought it their duty to tell me, and I was devastated. I challenged Robin and we had a row, but he was defensive, not apologetic at all; I ended up with all the guilt. He'd been working hard for exams at the time, and I'd been feeling resentful because I hardly saw him. He used the flat like a hotel. It seemed very unfair that he should spend what little leisure time he had with someone else. But after the row, I tried to see his point of view: the strain of work, the ready availability of a sympathetic nurse. Yes, this one was a nurse, too . . . I decided it was an isolated lapse.' Fran's marble features softened into a wistful look.

'You must think I'm such a fool. The pattern was set for the next six years, the only difference being that he was more discreet. I found out from subtle clues, rather than from the mouths of so-called well-wishers. I continued to challenge him, trying to bring a breath of honesty into our lives. Then one day, he turned round and said, "If you don't like it, you know what you can do." I was terrified. I loved him so much. I couldn't imagine being without him.

'It was sharing, or nothing. Once again I made excuses for him – he seemed to need these affairs; flattery made him come

201

alive. Please understand, there was nothing wrong with the physical side of our marriage, but I supposed it lacked the excitement of illicit meetings. Somehow, I hoped he would grow out of this phase, especially when he started rising in the hospital hierarchy. I took comfort from the fact that he had never actually threatened to leave me – he didn't *live* with these other girls.

'We papered over the cracks, and carried on as before, and then – then James was conceived. He was an accident, but oh! how I wanted him. Robin had made it very clear that I wasn't to have any children until he was "established", as he called it. He meant being a consultant. I thought that was an excessive time to wait. Anyway, we went on holiday to Austria one autumn – five years ago – and I left my pills behind. I knew he'd be angry if I told him, so I trusted to luck. I'd read that people on the contraceptive pill tended not to ovulate for some time after stopping . . . that wasn't true for me.

'Robin was furious. His rage seemed disproportionate. Perhaps he felt that I'd deliberately flouted his wishes. He ignored the pregnancy completely, as if it didn't exist, and while that obviously upset me, I told myself that once the baby was born, he'd be bound to love it. I would make sure that Robin had plenty of attention.'

A sheen of tears rose suddenly to cover her eyes, diluting their intense blue as if an artist had splashed water across his newly painted sky. The small muscles around her mouth jerked and quivered, but her voice when it came again was calm and flat. 'You've heard about James? Yes. He died the day he was born. He was too little, you see; his lungs weren't ready to cope. Robin – wouldn't talk about him at all. It wasn't grief; I think subconsciously he was almost glad, and felt guilty because of it. That sounds terrible, I know, but he really wasn't ready for a child. He was like a child himself.

'Within three months my best friend, Jackie, died of leukaemia. She was John Dyson's wife. He'd been very kind to me when I was in need, so I tried to help him, too. It was a dreadful time for us both, and I must admit that I was taking a lot of pills from the doctor. I couldn't seem to get over it – first James, then Jackie. They called it post-natal depression. Whatever it was, I made a big mistake in giving up my job. I did freelance typing at home, but that wasn't the same. More time to brood, you could say.'

Fran grimaced, and gave a little shake of her head as if to shrug off the picture of despair conveyed by her words. For a moment, she looked confused as the thread of her narrative slipped away, then appeared to collect herself.

'Pills. Capsules . . . You'll want to know about those, I should imagine. Everything I said before was true. I did hoard them, because nothing seemed worthwhile, and I actually felt better knowing that – if ever the day came, I had the means . . .'

Her voice trailed off altogether, and Montgomery decided it was time to prompt. 'How did you know about Loretta, Mrs Winterley? Your husband thought it was a total secret.'

'Oh yes,' she agreed bitterly. 'As I said, Robin was more discreet after that first time. It wasn't for my sake: he knew his promotion prospects would be jeopardized if word of his affairs got around the hospital and reached Leo Masters' ears. So I was – protected.

'It's ironical, but Loretta told me herself. She suddenly rang me one day, to say it was her half-day and could we have lunch together? She suggested Flappers in Cross Street. I hardly knew her; at our dinner party she had been one of twelve. I accepted with all manner of suspicions flashing through my mind.

'As soon as I saw her, dressed up to the nines and casually smoking a long cigarette, I had the strong feeling that it was some sort of *act*. How can I explain? It was as if – she'd seen it in a film, or something, and had set up the whole arrangement because she thought it was the way she ought to behave in a given situation. I still didn't know what that situation was, but I could guess, and I didn't like it at all.

'She started almost confidentially, telling me she had a lover, someone who worked with Leo Masters. Then she named him as Robin. She said they were both very much in love, and were going to move south together as soon as possible. She was sure I appreciated that my marriage had been cracking up for some time, and she knew I'd be sensible, not like those wives who couldn't face reality and refused to let go . . . Robin hadn't got round to telling me yet, but she felt it wasn't fair on me to be making plans for Southampton when I wouldn't actually be moving there. She was quite matter-of-fact. I said very little, mainly because I hadn't worked out how to handle the interview. So she continued . . . She told me that she was pregnant and Robin was delighted. She couldn't hide her triumph at that point – it was bursting out of her; she was all aglow. That was when I decided that she must die.'

Montgomery froze at the icy tone which had crept into her last few words. For a moment he glimpsed a woman who in moments of crisis could act with implacable resolution, diamond-hard beneath her graceful exterior. It gave him an uncomfortable feeling. The silence stretched; he opened his mouth to ask another question, but she pre-empted him.

'You're wondering why I acted this time when I'd let all the others go.' She could read his thoughts. 'Well, I'll tell you. I believed her. I believed every word. Her little act, her presentation, that was nothing compared with the fact that I knew this was different, he really was going to leave me for this – this tramp, this jumped-up little whore who'd obviously set her sights on him from the beginning . . . No doubt you've heard what a good nurse she was. "Dedicated", that's the word people like to use, isn't it? She was dedicated, all right. They all are: dedicated to getting their hooks into the nearest doctor, and if he's married, all the better. My God, if only you knew what goes on in hospitals!'

'Why did you believe Loretta?' interjected Montgomery. 'She could have been spinning you a tale.'

Weariness stole over Fran Winterley's face, as if her reserves of emotional energy had finally drained away. 'No,' she answered bleakly, 'I knew. It made sense. Robin had been acting strangely for months: all the signs of a new affair coupled with an odd sort of consideration for me. That's what frightened me most. It wasn't in character. I felt that changes were coming – Loretta merely spelt them out. Please, have you any water?'

'Would you prefer tea?'

She shook her head. Sergeant Bird left the room and returned with a glass of water, apologizing for its quality. Slowly she drank, then pushed the glass away.

'Loretta,' murmured Montgomery.

'Loretta . . . yes. She told me her news, as I said, looking more exultant by the minute. I realized there was only one way to play it. I was meek and mild. I said I understood how difficult it must have been for her to tell me such things, and I appreciated her honesty. I confirmed that Robin and I had had problems for some time, and I had recognized that something like this was inevitable. I suggested that Robin was probably waiting for the right opportunity to tell me himself, and might be angry with her for jumping the gun, so it was best that we both kept quiet for a little while longer, and I would pretend to be surprised when he eventually spoke.

'She was completely fooled. So sure of herself, so confident. She actually thought that *she* was the one in the position of power. The idea of a party occurred to me then and there. I told her that we had been planning a farewell evening for all our friends, and I would be grateful if she could withhold her news until afterwards, when Robin was sure to tell me. She asked if nurses were invited, and offered not to turn up, but I said that would look odd and might give the game away. We parted very cordially.'

'Tell us about the party,' said Montgomery.

'Yes. That's probably the only bit you're interested in, isn't it?' She gave a tight smile. 'You know most of what happened. I read everything I could find about barbiturates from Robin's old pharmacology textbooks, then one morning I took the powder out of all the capsules – it's quite easy, you just twist the two halves. Most of it I kept in an egg-cup hidden in one of the kitchen cupboards, but I stirred a small portion into water as a test. At first I was puzzled because it didn't seem to dissolve properly, which wasn't what the books said about that particular barbiturate. Then later I realized that the capsules probably had a "filler" of starch, or something, which I could filter out through a muslin handkerchief.

'On the Friday evening, when Barry and Sue went back to their flat to get changed, I mixed the rest of the powder with a little water and filtered it into a wineglass. I kept the glass on the breakfast bar with me, alongside the herbs and spices, and got rid of my own drink. At that stage, I wasn't sure how or when I was going to use it, but I wanted it ready. Loretta was bound to come, and despite her promises to keep a low profile, I felt that she would be unable to resist flaunting her new possession at a big party. In the event, I gather Robin was quite irritated with her.

'When she'd arrived with Alison, my chance came much more quickly than I'd anticipated. I'd had vague notions of mixing the drug with a drink for her later on – then suddenly, there they were, talking with John Dyson by the door, and Sue had her back turned. I tipped it straight on to her meal. The opportunity was perfect, because Alison had asked for a small helping, so there was no possibility that the plates would be mixed up.

'Someone offered me a drink shortly afterwards; I asked for orange juice, which was being served in tall tumblers, to avoid having to hand over the wineglass for a top-up.'

'And the wineglass was washed up with the other dirty glasses,' finished Montgomery. 'Tell me, Mrs Winterley, how could you be sure of killing Loretta? She might easily have been found in a coma, and rushed to hospital.'

'I know. I couldn't be sure, of course, but I thought she'd gradually become drowsy and people would think she was drunk and pack her off home. She would have died in the night, in her own room. Robin wouldn't have been with her, so she'd probably have been alone. It was a painless way to go – a kind of euthanasia.'

Once again, a chill pierced Montgomery's professional armour. Something glacial seemed to emanate from the woman across the table, from the smooth skin pale as Arctic wastelands, the cerulean eyes. 'We are assuming that she did feel drowsy at the party, and took herself off to a quiet room to lie down,' he said. 'The effect of the alcohol almost certainly added to that of the drug, or she might still have survived . . . What did you expect people to think?'

'Oh – suicide,' she answered quickly. 'I was horrified to find a murder enquiry under way. I thought it would just seem like the old story – young nurse becomes pregnant, boyfriend doesn't want to know, panic, then overdose. My only worry up to that point had been whether anyone would trace the link with Robin and blame him for her suicide. But they'd been very careful. Loretta herself assured me that no one knew their secret.'

'What about the effect on Robin? Surely you knew he'd be devastated?'

'Yes – yes, I did. But I thought he'd get over it. Always, before, his attachments were like flares – the touchpaper lit, a sudden incandescence, and then nothing but burnt-out debris fluttering away on the breeze. I knew this was a special case, but I hoped that – once her influence was broken, he'd come back to me as he'd done before, time and time again. I was longing to comfort him. I loved him, so much . . . I still do!'

With shocking suddenness the ice core fractured and she began to cry: harsh, heaving sobs, desolate, inconsolable. Her body was racked with suffering, her hands convulsively gripping strands of hair as if they would drag them from her scalp. Sergeant Bird slid a box of tissues towards her while Montgomery eased himself out of the chair, suspended the recording and quietly left the room.

What a mess, he thought. What a tragic tangle. And it wouldn't be the last, either.

He stood in the corridor, planning to wait a few minutes before returning, but as he reflected upon the imponderables of human nature, Sergeant Bird emerged from the Interview Room behind him.

'She'd like another word with you, sir.'

'All right, Will. Thanks.' He re-entered the room and looked down at Fran Winterley's pale, tear-blotched face. 'Yes, Mrs Winterley?'

Her voice when it came was surprisingly even. Already she was clawing back the vestiges of her self-control; she would need them for the ordeal ahead. 'Inspector. I just wanted to say – I'm sorry for all the trouble I've caused you and your colleagues. Everything that's happened is my responsibility. You said you had some charges against John Dyson, but I presume that was just a bluff. He hasn't done anything at all. It was me. He's entirely innocent.'

Montgomery acknowledged her words neutrally. John Dyson was his next unpleasant task.

'We've just charged Frances Winterley with murder,' Montgomery told John Dyson.

'Oh, no.' The pathologist sagged in his chair, every limb manifesting his utter defeat.

'You knew, of course.'

John hesitated a moment, then slowly began to speak. 'Yes. Latterly, but not at first. No one knew what to think at the beginning, but later, the tenor of your questions to people . . . I had to face the fact that a murder investigation was going on.'

'What made you suspect Mrs Winterley?'

John gave a short, mirthless laugh. 'Pure chance, or was it mischance? At that damned party I spent my first hour after arriving in the kitchen, because I wanted to be near Fran. We chatted intermittently as she served food, and I was on the alert to be helpful – top up her drink, that sort of thing. Unlike Sue, though, she didn't seem to be drinking, even when she wasn't busy. The wineglass just stood there on the breakfast bar, alongside some packets of herbs. I remember it had an unusual, smoky colour.

'Loretta and Alison came in, and she served them both. Then Peter came back from the living-room to wangle himself a second helping, and he offered Fran a top-up. I was quite surprised to see that her glass was suddenly empty, because I'd never noticed her lift it to her mouth.

'The matter was curious, but I didn't dwell on it. In fact, I didn't give it another thought, even when people began to mutter about barbiturates. It was only when Alison started speculating one night as to how the poison could have been administered, and whether or not it was really meant for Loretta, that the incident came back to mind. We all knew about the pregnancy by then, and the "married man" story. While I wasn't certain that Robin was involved, I knew his past record, and his penchant for a quick fling with an available nurse . . . I remembered Fran and that wineglass, and the image just wouldn't go away.

208

'The next day I couldn't believe the suspicions I'd been harbouring, so I rang Fran for a friendly, supportive chat, fully expecting to kick myself for being ridiculous. She was very strange: brittle and hostile. It turned out that you'd left minutes before, and taken some sauce bottles with you, and she shouted at me that you obviously suspected her of murder. Then she tried to turn it into a joke, but that sounded hollow, a sham . . . I rang off quickly, but I felt really apprehensive, so I rang her again an hour later. If anything, that time was worse. Fran would hardly speak to me at all. I could tell she'd been crying, and there was a sense of overwhelming tension. Something was badly wrong.'

John paused, stared at his forearms as they rested on the table in front of him, then raised to Montgomery's face eyes heavy with a tortured appeal which was not for himself.

'I knew,' he said. 'I just knew. One other thing convinced me . . . I danced with Fran at the party. She didn't want to, at first: said something about Robin disapproving. I'd had a few beers by then, and I thought, to hell with Robin. So we danced, and – she was rigid, taut as a bow-string. I suppose it was nervous shock at what she'd done, but at the time I imagined she was upset because Robin was dancing very provocatively with one of the nurses.

'The rest you know. I'm not proud of it. I love Fran, and the knowledge that she'd been driven to those sort of lengths was terrible – indescribable. She was going to crack up, I could sense it – either give herself away or confess. Someone like Fran would be destroyed by prison. So I wondered how on earth I could help her . . . and the idea came. Funny, isn't it – it was Alison's own idea, and I made use of it. I didn't know then that Leo Masters would be implicated: Alison had been very vague in her assertions while I was around. All I could think of was providing you with a line of enquiry which would lead you away from Robin and Fran.'

'You did a cruel thing to Alison,' said Montgomery sternly. 'She could have suffered irreparable harm.'

Now John Dyson's eyes flashed. 'Do you think I don't know that?' he cried, with more spirit than he had shown for the previous twenty-four hours. 'Do you think I didn't stew over every alternative before deciding that was the only way? Alison's a nice kid. I know I can't make it up to her, but I'd like someone to tell her that I never felt any – personal antagonism towards her. I would have explained it myself, in the restaurant, but she ran away.'

'Actually, Alison understands everything,' said Montgomery. 'We had a long chat this afternoon, and she asked most earnestly if the charges against you could be dropped. I'm afraid we can't do that: it's not in our hands. Perhaps in some context other than a murder enquiry . . . but I'm sorry, all the information relating to this case has to go to the DPP.'

'Don't worry. I'm quite prepared for what's coming to me. Maybe I'll be struck off the Medical Register, but I was aware of that when I started. Alison – oh, hell!' He broke off and stared across the room, appalled. 'You said Alison understands everything. That means you knew as soon as you caught me why I sent that note. I led you straight to Fran!'

Montgomery took pity on him. 'No, that isn't strictly true. I'd considered Mrs Winterley as a likely suspect for quite some time, certainly following Robin Winterley's confession with respect to Loretta and the baby. There were just some practical difficulties to be overcome, opportunity in particular. We'd have got there without your interference, but admittedly more slowly.'

John Dyson seemed lost in thought. Eventually, he looked up at Montgomery and framed the question he had obviously been mulling over. 'Do you think there'll be – *mercy* for Fran, Inspector?'

Montgomery considered. 'Not in the way you're hoping, no. If she'd picked up a knife and stabbed Loretta in the middle of a furious argument, there would have been a "crime of passion" element to it. As it was, she poisoned her in cold blood. I suppose the defence might try for manslaughter on the grounds that she was after revenge but didn't mean to kill Loretta, just make her ill. But from what I've seen of Frances, she'll want the whole truth to be told. It'll be a substantial sentence.'

John's lips hardly moved, but Montgomery's finely tuned ear caught the whispered pledge:

'I'll wait for her . . . as long as it takes.'

21

'It still seems a very uncertain way of killing someone,' observed Carole Montgomery, turning her neat dark head towards her husband. Across the table, his face rosy with wine, their guest William Bird was enjoying his second helping of *tarte tatin*. Their evening was both a cosy dinner for three and a private inquest.

'Not necessarily,' said Montgomery. 'It's easy to fall into the trap of thinking that anyone remotely connected with hospitals can get their hands on dangerous drugs whenever they want to. That's simply not the case. There are strict safeguards, and the best poisons are kept locked up, either in the pharmacy or in cupboards on the wards. So Fran Winterley was thrown back on her own resources, with all the concomitant risks of becoming a suspect.'

'She volunteered that her barbiturates were missing, though.'

'Yes. That was clever, but really, she didn't have a lot of choice. Once rumours about the drug reached Robin's ears, he would have made an immediate association with her capsules. Amylobarbitone is only prescribed in a very limited way now, and the coincidence of that being the drug involved would have been just too great. Hence she appeared to "come clean".'

'But someone might have found the girl and revived her!'

'True. It was a gamble, but look what happened – it worked. Robin thought Loretta had left the party in a huff, and wasn't unduly bothered. Alison, poor child, was convinced that her friend was in a bedroom with Peter. Everyone else there had their own concerns. They were all adults: live and let live.'

'Except that she died . . .' Carole's voice held a kind of awe. 'I still don't understand,' she hurried on, 'how come no one saw the poison being given.'

Montgomery glanced towards the end of the table where coffee cups and mints were lying in readiness. 'A demonstration might be best,' he said, rising to his feet and positioning himself near the cups. 'Let's say you two represent three people: John Dyson, Alison, and Loretta herself, all casually conversing near the kitchen door. We can forget Sue Pritchard; her back was turned. Now suppose I'm Fran Winterley . . . I've served the risotto and I'm now tipping up a wineglass – this cup – with my left hand. Would you notice the movement?'

'No,' said Carole.

'Yes,' said Sergeant Bird at almost the same moment.

Montgomery grinned. 'Exactly. It would be risky, wouldn't it?' He picked up the pepper mill with his right hand. 'Now, let's do it again. This is the tabasco sauce bottle. Remember you're a few feet away, chatting. I'll briefly shake this bottle, and empty the wineglass at the same time. Would you notice?'

'No,' they both replied.

'It disguises the other movement completely,' commented Carole.

'That's right,' agreed Montgomery. 'There's a reason for her hands to be moving – it's expected. No doubt she'd have done it anyway, even if Loretta hadn't wanted the sauce, but the enterprise would have been more hazardous.'

'So you weren't far wrong, sir, when you took those bottles away,' said William Bird generously.

'I *was* wrong,' mused Montgomery, 'but it was enough to panic Fran Winterley into giving herself away to Dyson, and that precipitated her downfall.'

William Bird nodded. 'Like you, I'd wondered about Mrs Winterley,' he said, 'but Loretta's affair with Robin had seemed so hush-hush that I couldn't imagine how she'd have heard of it, alone in that flat, isolated from the hospital scene. And then she appeared to have had no opportunity to administer the poison. Like Mrs Pritchard, she was in the kitchen for half the evening. When John Dyson came to our attention, it crossed my mind that he might have made a mistake – tried to divert us because he *thought* Frances was to blame, when in reality it was Robin . . .

'But two incidents stood out against that theory. The first was Winterley's attempt to resuscitate Loretta.'

'We've discussed that. A guilty person would have simply checked to make sure she was already dead.'

212

'No, sir. Barbiturates are tricky things. I've been talking with a pathologist, and apparently someone who's overdosed on barbiturates can go into a coma resembling death: they're cold and lifeless, with no spontaneous respirations and sometimes even fixed, dilated pupils – and yet they can still be saved. It's a bit like people who've drowned: worth persisting with resus efforts. If Robin knew the cause of Loretta's collapse, he couldn't have risked trying to revive her – he might have succeeded! In the event, neither he nor Verity knew. And she probably *was* dead at that time.'

'I see . . . and your other point?'

'Earlier in the evening, Loretta strode up to Leo Masters and told him where he could shove his offer of a job reference – not quite the way he described their discourse to us. She then went to the bar table, poured herself some wine, and started pestering Robin for a dance. *He was heard telling her to watch her drinking.* Now, we know with hindsight that he had the baby's welfare in mind, but a murderer would hardly be so solicitous about his imminent victim's drinking habits. In fact, if Robin *had* been the killer, he would have known that the effects of alcohol and barbiturates are additive. Wine would have hastened Loretta's death.'

'But also possibly loosened her tongue first.'

'True enough. Either way it should have hinted to us that he was involved.'

Carole was thoughtful as she poured the coffee. 'It seems like a typical triangle,' she said, 'now that all the misleading factors have been stripped away. Husband, mistress, jealous wife . . . But the baby must have been the crux.'

'Most emphatically,' said Montgomery.

'I wonder,' she went on, 'was it all a calculation?'

'On Loretta's part?' Montgomery considered. 'It's true that she always wanted to better herself; her sisters have validated that. She fell very heavily for a handsome junior doctor, Peter Verity, but he was young, he didn't want ties and he didn't take the relationship seriously. Loretta found herself playing a distant second fiddle to his work and various masculine pursuits; when she joined the CAMRA club herself, that simply underlined his perception of her as a "mate" with whom he sometimes went to bed, rather than a potential wife. Within three months the affair had foundered.

'Loretta was bruised: this wasn't what she had expected. In a move to restore her confidence, she began an affair with Barry Pritchard, but scotched it as soon as her self-assurance was intact again. For the next year, she simply enjoyed life as an attractive young woman, engaging the attentions of a succession of beaux, many of them medical students.

'Her ambitions reasserted themselves when Robin Winterley fell into her net. Here was a bigger fish than Peter had ever been, and he seemed genuinely infatuated with her. It was heady stuff . . . I believe that Loretta did convince herself that she was in love with him. She was determined not to lose out this time. So she conceived his child . . .'

Yes, thought Montgomery, the baby at least was a calculation. But if Robin the philanderer had met his match in Loretta, Loretta had in turn succumbed to someone with an even greater capability for ruthlessness . . .

When had he first suspected Fran Winterley? It was difficult to be precise: inconclusive little pointers had niggled in his brain since the beginning. The party had been Fran's idea, the capsules were hers, she had wanted champagne cocktails – those piquant, bubbly drinks comprising a sugar cube covered with brandy, a few drops of Angostura bitters, and a generous top-up of champagne or sparkling wine . . . drinks where sediment was acceptable: partially dissolved sugar cube if you were lucky, amylobarbitone excipient if you were not. But Robin had said no, and Fran had been forced to find another way.

Only when Cynthia Masters had tearfully confessed her true Friday evening destination had Montgomery been sure about Frances. Cynthia had driven into town to meet a representative from Alcoholics Anonymous, and had waited outside Willow Court *en route* in case Leo emerged with Loretta Dawes. Why Loretta, though? The button had been as anonymous as the five hundred pounds. Because, Cynthia had gone on to say, she had seen Loretta in an alcove of Flappers, telling an invisible friend all about her new lover, and mentioning Leo Masters as she did so.

Montgomery had understood it all then. The circle was

complete. Why should Loretta need to go out to lunch to impart the information to someone? Her nursing friends lived in the same building as she did, her family were in Mansfield. Why 'dress up to the nines'? Because she wanted to impress the individual concerned, to flaunt her power, even while persuading herself that her motives were altruistic. It was totally consistent with Loretta's character for that person to be Frances Winterley.

So Frances had known all along . . . Even as Montgomery reflected on this, he acknowledged the subliminal clues which had also shaped his final impression. Frances had a dry wit, but hers was not the cheerful, open personality of a Sue Pritchard. No: Fran was an ice-woman, blue in her eyes, her clothes, even the choice of carpet for her study. How could he ever have imagined that radiant sunshine flower arrangement had been given life by *her* pale hands . . . ?

For an innocent remark of Smythe's had triggered a memory: Frances Winterley, standing tall and gaunt by those same flowers in the hallway of her flat, lamenting that 'someone died here. Right here, in our home.' And Montgomery had been once again a schoolboy, gazing up in awe at a mesmeric actress on a Stratford stage, at an infamous woman who had just received news of the bloody murder of her guest. 'What,' she had gasped, 'and in our house!' Black and scarlet, not blue and white. But one in soul, and likewise doomed to torment.

Lady Macbeth.

'We haven't talked this over. We haven't solved anything.' Leo Masters's voice was ragged with despair. 'Cynthia, my love – we must!'

'It's too late,' she answered. 'I've let you down. I've been living a lie for the past two years.'

'The alcohol? Phoo! You aren't from a family of hardened drinkers. You're not genetically or environmentally predisposed. It was a symptom of your unhappiness, and I was too busy planning bloody hospital fund-raising ideas to notice. What did the girl from AA actually say to you?'

'You want to know?'

'Of course I do. Please tell me.'

'Well . . . We met informally, just the two of us. I told her what I'd been doing, how ashamed I felt, how frightened that I would lose control. She listened carefully, then said from what she'd heard I wasn't an alcoholic as such. I felt so relieved! We agreed that . . . that I had some psychological dependency on drink, but she suggested various coping strategies, including methods which had worked for her own problem. She said I was welcome to meet her again, or come along to one of their open meetings, but she didn't think I'd need to.'

'And?'

'I don't think I do. At least, not just now . . .'

'You won't need to, Cynthia. We'll crack this together. You won't be on your own.' His voice fell, and he looked at her sadly. 'Has it been so bad?' he whispered. 'I really thought you were adapting to – the deafness in your own way. I didn't want to push you, challenge you with situations that would only cause anxiety. You had to find your own level.'

She gave a rueful smile. 'I've cursed and I've cried,' she admitted. 'I've been bitter and I've been scared. But it wasn't fair to push the burden on to you. What happened was an act of God, a test that – that I failed.'

'No, you didn't. You had no support. You didn't complain because . . .' Unspoken words hovered between them. Because it was his enterprise which had brought her such disaster. Because by appearing to cope she saved him from intolerable guilt. 'I'm sorry,' he said. 'I'm so sorry, Cynthia.'

'Not your fault,' she murmured, but she was comforted all the same. 'Sorry' had broad shoulders: it could express regret, it could imply responsibility. Let the recipient choose as their need dictated, and be at peace.

Leo came closer. 'We mustn't give up,' he said. 'Things are changing all the time in the field of hearing enhancement. There are new ideas, new technologies. We can explore them all – if you're willing.'

'But I can't wear a hearing-aid: remember, I tried several at the beginning. The sound is all strange and distorted, and sometimes there are whistles . . .'

'It takes time to find the right aid, get used to it and accept its limitations. Perhaps you weren't quite ready then? I think we should try again.'

She knew he was right. Disbelief at the diagnosis had given way to denial and searing resentment. She would manage without these stigmatizing devices, whatever the experts said . . . So she had given them no chance. Instead, she had resorted to bluff, tendering large notes in shops rather than ask for a price, telling friends that she had a persistent head cold, loudly joining in when others laughed at dinner parties. Only gradually had she realized that she was making a fool of herself. People knew; they had merely played along out of kindness. The insight had heralded her descent into apathy and depression.

'If you succeed with a hearing-aid,' went on Leo, 'we can buy one of those loop systems for the television; it would cut out the background noise for you and allow us to enjoy programmes together. What do you think?'

It was an enticing prospect. She badly wanted to share leisure time with Leo again, to be a part of family banter and contribute to discussions. 'I'm ready now,' she said. 'I'll do my best to co-operate. People at the lip-reading class tell me that combining speech-reading with the use of an aid can be very effective.'

'You're half-way there,' he enthused. 'You turned the psychological corner without my help.'

Suddenly Cynthia felt the need for total honesty. 'I had no choice,' she said. 'I was losing you. You were keeping secrets from me, you were either absent or irritable . . . I was afraid.'

Leo met her gaze and swallowed. 'I had some anxieties at the hospital,' he said. 'I didn't want to involve you. Maybe that was a bad decision, but I meant it for the best.'

'Tell me now.'

As he explained about the prescription misjudgements and his fear of an investigation, Cynthia's concern for him gave her the courage to ask again about the five-hundred-pound debits.

'You won't like the answer,' he warned. 'But since we're clearing the air . . . I've been loaning the money to Bill and Sarah. The haulage business has been in trouble, and their house is on the line, but if they can just hang on a little longer things look set to pick up.' He held up his hand, palm towards her. 'I know what you're going to say. They've lived ostentatiously, there's plenty they could sell. But Sarah's my sister, and they *have* done their best to economize, and for the sake of a smallish sum we were able to help them out when they needed it . . .'

'You're right,' said Cynthia stonily. 'I'm not thrilled. Not so much at what you've done, but the fact that it should have been a joint decision. If we can't communicate on financial issues, what chance have we?' Even as she admonished him, she felt a vast sense of relief. It wasn't blackmail money, or maintenance money, or gifts to some young nurse. She believed his story; it was typical of Leo.

'Things will be different from now on,' he promised. 'With common goals and goodwill, we can restore the partnership we once had. I want it – do you?'

She hugged him. 'Oh, yes.'

'Okay, so I didn't tell the truth. Does it matter?' Paula's dark eyes were haughty with challenge, but Montgomery sensed the apprehension behind her confident façade.

'You lied,' he said. 'And, yes, it does matter. There's already one person in trouble for attempting to mislead our enquiry. We didn't need another.'

'But you've got the murderer now.'

'No thanks to you. I'd like an explanation, Paula. You attended Robin Winterley's party late on, dressed as a cavalier. Why did you deny being there?'

She perceived his determination, and shrank away a little. 'I – I didn't want to implicate Uncle Leo.'

'In what context – his prescription irregularities?'

Her pupils flared. 'You know?'

'Yes. We wondered if that was the basis for the quarrel between Loretta and yourself.'

'She gave that impression.'

'You don't sound very sure.'

'I wasn't. It seemed an extreme reaction to something which didn't concern her anyway. She said she hadn't realized that Leo attended private patients . . . I couldn't believe that Loretta would cut me dead over a matter you could describe as ideological. Uncle Leo was always so generous to his patients, and *never* skimped on his work for the NHS . . .' Paula hesitated, then sighed. 'I thought there must be more to her attitude than met the eye . . .

'Around that time I saw Uncle Leo in odd circumstances. I was walking through The Park on my way to visit a friend who lives there . . . it was a Saturday morning, bright and sunny. I saw Uncle Leo's Volvo parked up a side street in the shade of a tree. He was sitting inside, leaning towards the passenger seat, kissing someone. I had no idea who this person was, but it obviously wasn't Auntie Cynth. He wouldn't be parked there with *her* . . . I was desperately keen not to be spotted, so I dashed across the road and round the corner without another glance.

'When Loretta died and the "married man" rumours began, it abruptly occurred to me that she might have been Leo's secret lover. Maybe she had broken off our friendship so I wouldn't find out . . . The idea did make sense. If I'm honest, Loretta was always an ambitious man-eater, and my uncle has undeniable charisma. I knew he'd been having a bad patch with Auntie Cynth . . . I wondered if perhaps Loretta had been making some silly gesture with sleeping tablets at Robin Winterley's flat, and miscalculated . . . that seemed even more likely when I heard about the baby.

'I was never in any doubt that Uncle Leo was innocent of murder. He's a good man, with enormous respect for human life. But if I'd admitted being present at the party, you might have asked me all sorts of awkward questions, with ramifications capable of wrecking his career and destroying Auntie Cynth's peace of mind. So I thought if I denied being there, you wouldn't be interested in me: I even tried to keep out of your way by bombing off to my parents' home at every spare moment . . .'

'The truth is always best,' said Montgomery soberly. 'Your deception only served to focus attention on your uncle and aunt.'

Paula was crestfallen. 'I'm sorry,' she said. 'I've been very stupid. Is Uncle Leo still in trouble?'

'We've been investigating a murder,' said Montgomery with caution. 'No one has asked us to look into anything else.' He was greatly startled to feel the sudden imprint of two warm lips against his cheek.

'We can't meet again like this,' said Leo to his companion. 'I do hope you understand.' Bird-song rang out lustily from the tree branches above the Volvo, but the leaves were beginning to shrivel.

'Of course I do.' Eileen Brocklebank turned her head and smiled at him. 'I'm glad things are getting better for you now. I like to think I helped just a mite.'

He covered her hand with his own. 'You kept me sane,' he said. 'You're a good friend; nothing will change that.'

She flushed: from gratification, he knew, not from offence. For they *had* hovered on the brink of a new level of intimacy, but both had recognized the danger and retreated, not without some regret.

'How is Cynthia now?' she asked.

Leo shook his head in amused wonder. 'A changed woman. She's so active these days . . . She goes to yoga lessons, she's started a home tailoring business making nightdresses and wedding gowns, and she's applied to teach adult literacy. That's all on top of her work in the Oxfam shop.'

'Adult literacy teaching sounds an excellent idea. Would it be one to one?'

'I believe so.'

'Well, I take my hat off to her. She's channelling her energies into areas where her hearing problems won't matter. It sounds very positive, Leo.'

'Like Cynthia herself,' he chuckled. 'She's become . . . not aggressive, exactly, but – assertive. That's the word. For instance, she told me on Thursday that she'd never been comfortable with our domestic help: said the woman was nosy, insolent and not even particularly competent. She wanted to give her notice. I asked if she'd prefer me to do it, but she said no, she wanted to handle the matter herself. Astonishing. *And* she told me the loyalty bonus I suggested was too generous . . .

By the way, Eileen, I've just remembered something. I don't suppose you lost a brass button a few weeks ago? One we couldn't identify turned up in the car; we've still got it.'

'I did indeed. It's from my favourite suit. That's wonderful – I thought it had gone for good.'

'I'll bring it in on Monday. Cynthia will be glad that the owner has been found.' He reflected, with mild irony, that his wife would be particularly pleased that the aforesaid owner had turned out to be Sister Brocklebank.

Peter Verity walked slowly across the broad expanse of grass, uncomfortable in his dark suit. In the distance shimmered the ornate Elizabethan splendour of Wollaton Hall, while to his right an inquisitive fallow deer watched him from the adjoining parkland.

Suddenly, there was Sonia, her cream dress rippling against her knees, her blonde curls bouncing. Her face, however, expressed uncertainty; she came close, but didn't touch him.

'How was it?' she asked.

Peter gave a helpless shrug. Loretta's funeral had been traumatic, as with that of any other young person, but the family had wanted him to be there, and he had appreciated the opportunity to say his own personal goodbye. Now he felt as if one phase of his life had been buried with Loretta: a necessary phase of fickleness and brief, intense experiences, of sampling and rejecting, of short-term aims. For the first time, he found himself craving stability.

He recalled how, back at the house after the interment, Cheryl and Chloe had prised him away from Alison and Paula, and led him into the bleak little garden. There, with swollen eyelids blinking, they had confided to him that Loretta had been buried wearing the gold ankle chain. 'Because it was really you that she loved,' they explained. Poor Loretta . . . ready for her own stability too soon. Perhaps they had only missed commitment to each other by a couple of years – or perhaps such a union would never have worked.

'I'm glad it's over,' he answered.

Together they made a leisurely ascent towards the formal

gardens which surrounded the Hall, Sonia wisely abstaining from her usual chatter. Peter stopped. 'Sonia, would you do me a favour?'

'Of course.'

'Word process a CV for me?'

'Oh . . .' A cloud blotted out the weak sunshine above. 'Have you seen a new job advertised?' She knew his current contract had only months left to run.

'No, but one's coming up soon: a registrar rotation.'

'I see.' Absently she chewed her lip. 'Just what you need to progress . . . Is it far from here?' She had seen a recent advertisement for a London hospital post.

'I'm sure we could manage to stay in touch if I got the job.'

'Oh . . .' In Sonia's experience, commuter relationships always foundered eventually. 'Tell me how far.'

'At a rough guess, I'd say four miles.' He smiled at her dawning comprehension. 'Nottingham District Hospital.'

The cloud moved on; the sun began to shine more strongly than ever.